CW01640563

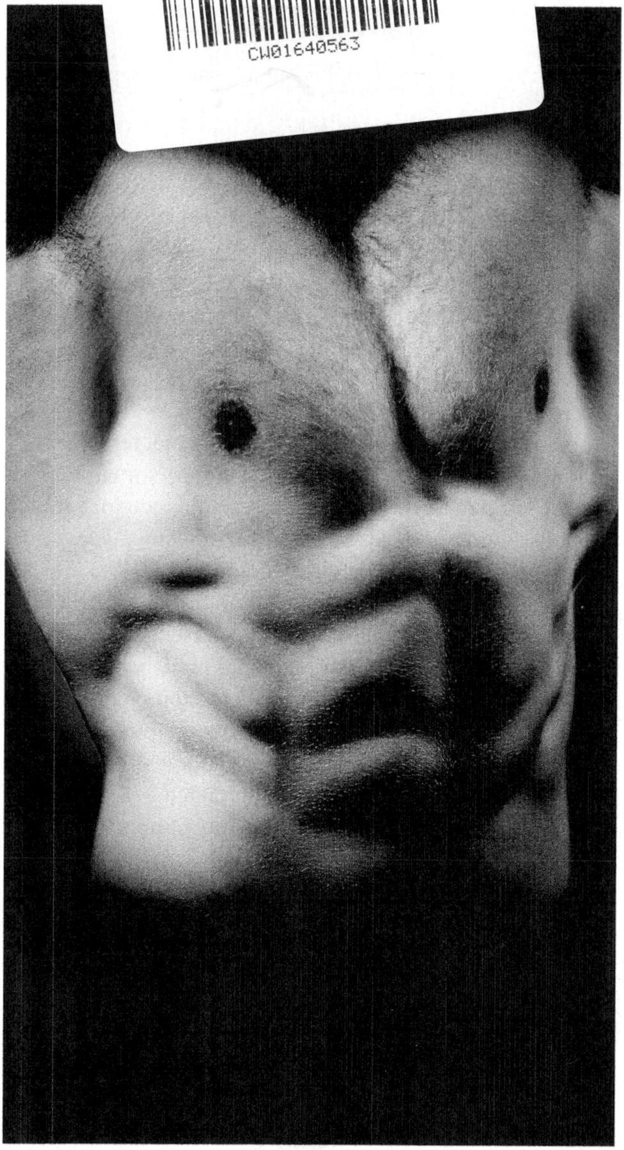

Copyright © 2023 Alanea Alder

All rights reserved. No part of this publication may be reproduced, distributed, or transmitted in any form or by any means, including photocopying, recording, or other electronic or mechanical methods, without the prior written permission of the publisher, except in the case of brief quotations embodied in critical reviews and certain other noncommercial uses permitted by copyright law. For permission requests, write to the publisher, addressed "Attention: Permissions Coordinator," at the address below.

PUBLISHER'S NOTE
This is a work of fiction. Any names, characters, places and incidents are the product of the author's imagination or are used fictitiously, and any resemblance to actual persons, living or dead, business establishments, events or locales is entirely coincidental.
The scanning, uploading, and distribution of this book via the Internet or via any other means without the permission of the publisher is illegal and punishable by law. Please purchase only authorized electronic editions, and do not participate in or encourage piracy of copyrighted materials. Your support of the author's rights is appreciated.
www.sacredforestpublishing.com
P.O.Box 280
Moyock, NC, 27958
Digital ISBN- 978-1-941315-25-5
Print ISBN- 978-1-941315-26-2
Sacred Forest Publishing

MY SOLACE

BEWITCHED AND BEWILDERED

ALANEA ALDER

Dedication

~*Omnia Vincit Amor*- Love Conquers All~

It's been a long time coming.
The story continues…

PROLOGUE

ORON LAY IN BED GASPING as he stared up at the ceiling. His mate was a walking, talking disaster. She was like Gavriel's mate, except it wasn't fate causing mishaps and mayhem around her, she did it to herself, but in the most adorable, curious ways possible.

His dream had been a sequence of reactions and events caused by his innocent mate. When all was said and done, her place of employment had caught fire.

He scrubbed his hands over his face. Mother would know of a way to keep her safe from herself. He took a deep breath, of course mother would know what to do. You didn't live for over ten-thousand years as a queen and not learn these things.

As soon as he could, he would slip away and visit the city of his birth. He just prayed that his hapless mate didn't accidentally set off a nuclear weapon between now and then.

CHAPTER ONE

ORON LOOKED AROUND LEVEL SIX at the reception that was in full swing celebrating Warrick Fortier's mating to young Avery Therian. Having only arrived yesterday with Amelia and Darian to escort the menace to Éire Danu, he was desperately trying to keep everyone's names straight, but he knew it was a lost cause. He had no sooner stepped through the portal and Meryn began rattling off names, most of which either got confused and mangled together in his mind or had evaporated completely.

The only ones he had no problem remembering were Nigel and Neil Morninglory because Meryn was right, they did look like young Keelans.

Darian walked over to stand beside him. "Have you ever seen so many vampires smiling this much?" he asked.

Oron shook his head. "Never, and in Noctem Falls at that. But, from the stories I've heard since arriving, the city has had more than their fair share of grief, you can see that they've bonded and grown stronger." All around them vampires and wolf-shifters laughed and toasted each other, teasing the couple mercilessly. Their Noctem Falls unit brothers kept snatching Avery away from Warrick causing the warrior to hiss at his fellow men at arms.

"Almost feels like Lycaonia… almost," Darian said, grinning.

Oron chuckled. They both had a soft spot for their adopted city. "So, how long do you think Menace will be in Éire Danu before she's arrested?"

Darian smiled wide. "As if our queen would ever imprison her favorite human."

Oron noticed that his brother only referred to their mother by their familial relationship while they were safe within the borders of the fae city. He personally agreed with the decision, one never knew who was listening, and neither of them would allow their enemies to hurt their mother and queen.

"I'm more worried about Portia throwing Meryn into a bespelled closet to keep the queen's schedule running smoothly," Darian admitted.

Oron winced, his brother was right. Portia Kilardin was an absolute genius when it came to keeping the palace running, but she had no patience for anything she deemed a disturbance to her detailed itinerary. Growing up, she taught both of them etiquette and deportment so they wouldn't be an embarrassment to the queen. Cord ruled the kitchen and domestic issues, Allia managed the queen's day, but Portia kept the entire palace running.

He sighed. "She isn't mean, but she will absolutely hate Meryn for doing what she does best, bucking the system."

"I do, do that pretty well, huh?" a voice said from behind them.

Both he and his brother turned and smiled at Meryn. "Yes, you do," Oron agreed.

"So, this chick is like a super squire?" Meryn asked.

He exchanged looks with Darian who shrugged. He looked down at the menace. "She isn't a squire, she's not really an advisor either."

"How about an 'estate manager'?" Ryuu suggested.

Oron nodded slowly. "I think that's as close as we'll get to a description. Portia manages everything to do with the royal palace itself. The staff, events, invitations from other noble and founding families, birthing presents, celebrations, communications from the queen, the list goes on."

"So, I should just stay out of her way?"

Darian exhaled. "Absolutely. You'll more than likely be staying in the royal quarters and that's more Cord's domain, he'll love you," Darian ruffled her hair.

She knocked his hand away. "Stop that!" She straightened. "If Cord is the food source, then I'll stay glued to him."

Oron laughed out loud. "Gods is he ever going to love you, that man lives to cook."

Meryn's eyes rounded. "More than Sebastian?"

"Did someone say my name?" the Rioux squire asked, walking over.

Meryn pointed to them. "They said that the queen's squire lives to cook and that he'll love me. I was wondering if he's a better cook than you because you totally kick-ass."

Sebastian cheeks tinted. "It is such a pleasure to cook for young appetites, you made every day a joy." He leaned down and kissed her forehead. She scrunched up her nose at him and he laughed. "As for Cord Danual, he, like Ryuu, is somewhat of a legend amongst squires. He has held his position as the queen's squire for as long as anyone can remember. I honestly believe he has forgotten more recipes than I have ever learned," he admitted.

Meryn licked her lips. "Super fae squire food."

Ryuu sighed. "While I am ecstatic that you are eating more, the drastic return to your tapeworm like existence is worrisome."

"It's the cinnamon, the baby loves it, so I am putting that shit on everything." Meryn rubbed her rounded belly.

"Cinnamon?" Oron asked.

Meryn nodded. "Yup, evidently my kiddo really likes fae cinnamon. I promised Sebastian I'd find some more for him and send it back. I think I decimated his stash and it's tough to get too," she said, looking guilty.

Sebastian frowned. "Do not worry yourself over such a trivial thing. I would give every speck of fae cinnamon in this city to ensure that you and your little one stayed healthy."

"*Denka,* I will see to it personally once we arrive in Éire Danu that a shipment of fae cinnamon is sent here, will that make you feel better?"

Sebastian went to protest, but Ryuu held up his hand.

Meryn nodded. "Yes, please. That way he can keep making Magic Pudding."

"And I will ensure that you receive your Magic Pudding no matter what," Sebastian promised getting misty-eyed.

Meryn blinked furiously. "Stop that! I don't want to think about tomorrow," she grumbled, rubbing her eyes with her arm. Ryuu wrapped a supporting arm around his charge's shoulders.

Oron watched as one of the most influential squires in their world swallowed hard and put on a bright expression. Sebastian cleared his throat. "Of course, it is not as if we will never see one another again. Magnus is negotiating for another portal from the queen, I will just remind him that visiting Lycaonia may be in his best interests."

"That would be so amazing!" a young voicc exclaimed.

"Avery!" Meryn practically jumped the newly mated shifter.

Oron looked over to Darian who looked just as shocked as he felt. They had never really seen Meryn be so exuberant with her affection.

"*Denka* has made some very dear friends while here, I believe that this is the first time she will ever have to say goodbye," Ryuu explained.

"Meryn, thank you so much for being here. I couldn't have had the ceremony without you,

you're like my best friend," Avery ran his cheek over Meryn's wild curls.

Meryn stood back sniffling. "Well duh, I had to be here. And you better call me later and tell me all about the butt sex."

Darian choked on the champagne he had just sipped. "I'm sorry, what?"

Avery blushed a deep red. "Only if you add me to the judges' panel you have for the warriors," he countered.

"Deal!"

"Whatever is the matter, darling?" Amelia asked, rushing over to rub Darian's back.

Darian pointed to Meryn then to Avery, then let his hand drop. "Nothing, just Meryn being Meryn."

Amelia brightened. "Did I hear correctly; Avery is now one of our judges?"

Oron stared at his baby sister. He knew Amelia heard the other part as well, but she was more worried about their warrior watching. He looked at his brother who was now scowling at his mate.

Meryn grinned evilly. "We picked up a few more judges here in Noctem Falls. I feel like we're being very inclusive."

Amelia clapped her hands together happily. "I wonder how many we can get in Éire Danu."

Darian huffed. "The ladies of Éire Danu are refined and above such things."

Oron clinked his champagne glass with his brother's as they drank together in solidarity.

Meryn gave him a sly look and held up her phone. "Then why do I have an application from the queen herself to join my Facebook cult?"

Both he and his brother gasped in union, causing them to inhale their champagne.

Amelia eyed her mate. "You kinda deserve that for being uppity."

Oron's eyes watered. "It burns," complained. "Bubbles, burn!"

Meryn giggled. "I should put that on a tee shirt."

Avery held up a fist and Meryn bumped it.

Sebastian was fighting to keep a straight face as he handed them glasses of water. "This may help."

Oron grabbed at the glass and chugged the water. Breathing hard, he looked at his commander's tiny mate. "You truly cause chaos wherever you go."

Meryn shrugged. "Hey, what can I say, I'm playing to my strengths."

Amelia frowned. "She does not cause chaos, she is amazing."

Oron backtracked. "I meant that in a good way," he said quickly.

Amelia's face cleared and she smiled again. "Oh, that's okay then."

Behind her big-sister cousin's back, Meryn stuck her tongue out at him. With no other avenue of recourse available to him, he stuck his out in retaliation.

"Meryn!"

Everyone turned to see the red-headed twins come running up to them with a smaller vampire in tow.

Meryn eyed the twins. "Why are you yelling my name like ferals are chasing you?"

One of the twins grinned. "Neil and I just heard, Prince Magnus has accepted the Wolf-town pack as citizens of the city, they're going to be living here permanently now!"

"Whoa, that's pretty huge. What about the kids, don't they need air?"

Nigel frowned. "Meryn there's air here; other-wise we'd all be dead."

Avery giggled as Meryn gave them a flat expression. "You know what I mean, don't they need to be outside? Like sun and wind in their fur yadda, yadda."

Nigel nodded. "Oh yeah, that. Evidently, Queen Aleksandra has granted Prince Magnus additional portals. They are building a new council estate on this huge piece of land one of the vampires donated, it's something crazy like five thousand acres that butts up against the national preserve. There's plenty of land for the pups to run and the wolves' enforcers will act as security for the new estate."

"And they're expanding the current property where the council estate is in Albuquerque. The wolves will be opening up businesses there since it's in the heart of the city," Neil continued.

Pip waved his hands back and forth. "That is not even the best part! Prince Magnus has personally purchased the properties on either side of the existing building and will be funding a new private clinic for paranormals in the area. He wants to turn Noctem Falls into a center of healing for paranormals everywhere, including the first ever paranormal neonatal intensive care unit," he exclaimed, practically vibrating where he stood.

Meryn blinked. "That is freaking amazing."

"And all thanks to you my dear," Prince Magnus said, walking up to them.

"Me?" Meryn asked, looking confused.

"Her?" He and Darian asked together.

"Why did you say it like that?" Aiden demanded, walking up from behind Magnus to pull Meryn into his arms. Oron simply raised a brow. Aiden rolled his eyes.

Beth chuckled as she and Gavriel walked over with the rest of the Alpha and Eta Unit's members and mates. "Be honest Commander, they have just cause for the question," she teased. Aiden simply huffed in reply.

Magnus took Meryn's hand. "Yes, most of what was accomplished was inspired by this little one. She not only saved so many here, but she has taught us all to think beyond ourselves." He smiled down at her gently. "She will forever be remembered as one of this city's saviors."

"She has heralded a new Golden Era for Noctem Falls!" a voice yelled above the crowd.

Magnus released Meryn's hand. "Speaking of golden." Magnus met Meryn's eyes. "I meant to give this to you earlier." He pulled a gold card out of his pocket and handed it to the now confused looking Meryn. "This is similar to the card that Elder Vi'Ilsimir gave you. With it, you can reach out to me at any time, however, the back is different."

Meryn flipped it over, when she did Aiden inhaled sharply. Oron caught a glimpse of the engraved filigree and felt his own breath catch. The ornate design acted as proof that Meryn not only had the full support of Magnus Rioux as an Elder, but also the entire city of Noctem Falls. It effectively assured that Meryn could ask for practically anything and she would receive it, no questions asked.

Meryn pointed to the card. "What are these squiggles? They look different than the fae squiggles Darian showed me."

Behind Magnus Beth covered her face with her palm. "Squiggles? Really Meryn?"

"What! They look like squiggles," Meryn protested.

Kendrick inched closer, his eyes locked on the card. "That is our ancient language Meryn, it states that the bearer of this card is to be treated as a Royal and be given whatever they desire."

Meryn's eyes narrowed shrewdly. "So, like unlimited meat kebobs?"

Around them, silence fell. Oron felt as though with that one statement Meryn had somehow managed to lift the darkness that was closing in on them and lighten his heart.

"I just can't!" Beth exploded, throwing her hands in the air.

Beside her Gavriel had covered his face as he laughed silently, tears streaming down his face.

"Be quiet, Beth!" Meryn retorted from her

mate's arms. "You're staying here while stuff settles down so you can eat meat kebobs and Sebastian's Magic Pudding whenever you want!"

Her reply unfroze the crowd around them as one fit of laughter erupted after another.

Magnus was still chuckling as he wiped his eyes. "We will be sending shipments of your meat kebobs and pudding to Éire Danu, so you can use that card for something bigger."

Meryn shrugged. "Okay, I guess, it's not like you wouldn't give me what I want anyway, you said so, Sebastian heard you."

Sebastian nodded. "Yes, darling, but that card ensures that others know how important you are to us. If anyone dares to hurt or insult you, they will have the entire City of the Night to face." Behind them the crowd roared their agreement.

Meryn looked up at her mate. "I have Aiden, that's kinda the same thing."

Aiden stared down at her. "Why do you say these things when I can't get you alone?" he demanded, nuzzling her neck.

She grinned impishly. "Because it makes the time you finally get me alone, that much better."

He harrumphed. "Every time."

Meryn stuck the card in her pocket. "I guess it's time for presents. Nigel and Neil, if you would please?"

The twins raced off to one side and came back, dragging Warrick and a carrying wrapped box. They pushed the enormous warrior over to stand next to his new mate.

Nigel handed the box to Avery then stepped back with Neil and Pip to stand beside Meryn.

Avery stared down at the box.

"Well, don't just look at it, open it!" Meryn prompted.

Avery looked up at Warrick then tore into the box. When the lid opened and he moved aside the tissue paper his breath caught. Tears began to stream down his cheeks. Oron thought Avery was being emotional until he saw that Warrick wore a matching expression, his tears running unabashedly down his face. With trembling hands, Avery lifted a statue that seemed to glow from within.

"Oh my," Beth gasped.

Oron leaned in and was shocked at the detail captured in the delicate figurine. It looked like it was about to come to life at any moment.

"It was kinda my idea. I found that footage from when Warrick's douche cousin tried to attack you," Meryn explained.

"I found the stone; I knew it would be perfect for what we wanted to do. It is from Level Five too, so it seems fitting," Pip said, pointing to the brilliant colors of the opal-like stone.

"Nigel and I shaped it using our earth magic. If either you or Warrick touches the inscription it moves," Neil said, pointing to the small lettering at the base.

"And Felix helped us polish it, being so small, he was able to get into the delicate bits," Nigel added.

Avery gently touched the base, and the sculpture began to move. The figurine of Warrick dropped to his knees and took the likeness of Avery's hands in his own before kissing them. In response, Avery's figure brought their joined hands up before rubbing his cheek along Warrick's knuckles. After that, the figurine resumed its original position.

Warrick turned his head to one side and rested his cheek on top of Avery's blond curls, the giant unit warrior was absolutely undone. Around them, many of the men also looked moved to tears as the women wept openly.

Avery turned in Warrick's embrace. He very carefully passed the priceless sculpture to his mate before he turned and simply launched himself at his friends. He was sobbing and trying to thank them but was barely making any sense.

Meryn kept awkwardly patting him on the head while Nigel and Neil rubbed his back. Pip just wrapped his arms around all four of them and squeezed tight.

Oron stared, he had never seen such close bonds amongst different paranormals before, outside of his unit brothers.

"Do you doubt my earlier praise now?" Prince Magnus asked softly.

He shook his head. "I will never doubt Meryn again," he vowed quietly. Because as Warrick shared the marvel that was their gift with his fellow unit warriors, a human, a shifter, a sprite, two witches and a vampire gripped each other tightly as family.

CHAPTER TWO

ORON'S HEART BROKE AS HE took in the scene before him. After last night's display he knew exactly how hard this would be on both the menace and the adorable vampire.

He and those leaving for Éire Danu had made it as far as the Ledge before the small vampire began to have an epic meltdown. They quickly returned to the Grand Hall.

"I want to go!" Pip wailed, clinging to Meryn desperately.

Meryn kept swallowing hard as she tried to blink back tears. "Maybe we can open a portal right to the city?" She looked over to his brother hopefully.

Darian shook his head. "I could absolutely take Pip directly from the antechamber to Éire Danu, the only reason we were going via the Ledge was to show him the desert but…" he trailed off before turning to him.

Oron walked over and ruffled Pip's hair. "The fae city is all open-air kiddo."

Pip looked up at him with tear-streaked cheeks. "Why is it so open? What keeps the sky from falling down?" he asked pitifully, hiccuping between words.

Oron smiled down at him. "I'm afraid those questions are above my pay grade, but I can assure you, that in my thousands of years of living, I have never had the sky fall on me, not once."

Meryn nodded. "Me either, Pip."

Pip looked up at Meryn. "I cannot go, can I?"

Meryn frowned fiercely before turning to her mate. "Fix this!"

Aiden's eyebrows practically disappeared into his hairline. "Fix the sky?"

Sebastian wrapped an arm around Pip's shoulders. "You will be able to go, just not when Meryn leaves. Together you and I will work on getting you comfortable with being outside the city. Before you know it, you will be able to join Meryn and enjoy the hospitality of the fae," he said, in a reassuring, fatherly voice.

Magnus stepped up behind the young vampire and squeezed his shoulder. "I will help as well. This is not your fault Pip. The ones who raised you failed in their duties to acclimate you to the open sky at a young age, but rest assured, we will not fail you now."

Avery took Pip's hand. "We'll help too, won't we Warrick?"

Warrick smiled down at them. "Of course, we will."

Pip's lower lip was trembling as he stared at Meryn. "But she is my sister, she saved me. She covers me with blankets and feeds me."

Different emotions flew across Meryn's face. It was clear even to Oron that in the brief time she had been in Noctem Falls; she had miraculously opened her heart up to the three youngsters she claimed as brothers.

Meryn took a deep breath. "Here's what we're going to do. I'll head on to Éire Danu and set up our base, you know, somewhere we can game and watch TV. You work on being outside and when you're ready to join us, I'll have everything set up and I'll be able to show you around."

Pip sniffled. "Really?"

Meryn nodded. "Yup."

Oron watched as Nigel and Neil exchanged glances before turning to look at Kendrick who smiled and nodded at them. Neil stepped forward. "We'll stay with him Meryn. With everyone's help, he should be ready in no time at all."

Meryn looked relieved, though her eyes were sad. "That sounds like a plan. But, I'm going to miss you guys and probably be real bitchy and cranky, so y'all will have to hurry, okay?"

The boys converged on Meryn, wrapping her up in a group hug. Meryn disappeared under their youthful exuberance. Aiden reached in between the bodies and lifted out a giggling Meryn. "Come on, baby, time to go."

Aiden looked at the twins. "He's in your care," he said, pinning them with a stern expression.

Nigel huffed. "Of course, he's our brother too, you know."

Aiden reached out and bopped Nigel's head

around. "As Meryn is my mate, all three of you are my brothers. I don't want anything happening to any of you. So, keep the shenanigans to a minimum and hurry up and join us."

Nigel and Neil's eyes widened. "We never even thought of that," Neil whispered, before turning to his twin. "The Unit Commander is our brother now." Nigel grinned. "Does this mean we don't have to do drills anymore?"

Behind them, Colton laughed. "Sorry boys, but if I still have to do them despite pulling his hairy ass out of more than one scrape, you definitely still have to do them."

Aiden gave his best friend a flat look. "There better still be units in Lycaonia when I get home."

Colton shrugged. "No promises. Sascha let Emmy get herself into danger, I will need to impress upon him how upset I am about that."

Oron winced. Emmeline Albright was Colton's adorable younger cousin. She had wrapped Colton and Aiden around her finger the day she drew her first breath. The other Lycaonia unit warriors fell like dominoes when she started visiting during training. He truly felt sorry for Sascha, but not enough to intervene, he adored Emmy as well.

Aiden looked over to where Gavriel stood smirking next to Beth. "How long are you staying here again?"

Gavriel shrugged. "Just until things settle."

"Good luck with that," Vivi murmured under her breath. Etain turned away to hide his smile.

Magnus gave Aiden a cunning look. "I may take this opportunity to take a vacation, I have not had one in centuries."

Gavriel looked over at him startled. "What?"

Kari sighed. "Make it a short one, I still have not finished breaking you in."

Declan chuckled at Magnus' expression. Rex held up his fist and absently Declan bumped it. Rex grinned from ear to ear. "Told you I would get my fist bump before leaving the city."

Declan rolled his eyes at his brother, and Meryn gave Rex a thumbs up.

Gavriel stared at Magnus, eyes wide. "What?"

Beth patted him on the shoulder. "You'll be fine."

Adriel chuckled. "Better you than me." He pinned Micah with a fierce expression. "Do not embarrass us while you visit with your mate's family," he instructed.

"No promises," Micah grinned impishly, mimicking Colton. Serenity bumped hips with her mate playfully. "Be nice."

Both Adriel and Aiden exchanged commiserating pained expressions before Aiden turned to Gavriel. "Please return home quickly. Sascha may kill Colton before you get back. As he is my second in command to take over as Unit Commander, you are my second in command for the Alpha Unit, I kinda need both of you alive."

Rheia rolled her eyes. "I'll try to keep everyone from killing each other."

Aiden exhaled. "Thank you, Rheia."

Kendrick leaned over and kissed Meryn's

cheek. "Anne and I want to check on Keelan, but we'll follow soon."

Ellie stood beside Grant, balancing Benji on her hip. "It won't be the same without you all here."

"Ya got that right," Eva Mae agreed.

Meryn smiled evilly. "I know I'll be coming back a lot, I needs muh Magic Pudding and meat kebobs."

Aiden just stared down at her. "Really?"

She nodded. "You have no idea."

Oron looked around. "Are we ready then?"

Darian nodded and opened the portal to Lycaonia. Waving, Kendrick and Colton along with their mates stepped through.

"We will miss you little human!" a voice called out.

Oron turned and was shocked to see that almost the entire Grand Hall had filled while they were talking.

"Just going to leave without saying goodbye missy?" An older vampire asked.

Meryn grinned. "It's not goodbye. I'll see you again when I crave my meat kebobs."

The older vampire laughed. "Anytime, youngster!"

Everywhere Oron looked unit warriors were smiling, wolf-shifters were waving and the children were jumping up and down. Had the entire city turned out and snuck up here to see them off?

Darian closed the Lycaonia portal and glanced back at them.

Sebastian clapped his hands together. "Okay, time to depart. The quicker you get to Éire Danu, the quicker you can return for a visit."

Aiden winced. "I would like to go home at some point."

Meryn shrugged. "It's better to travel before Meryn two-point-oh gets here, then we can hibernate at home for a while."

Aiden smiled. "I like that idea."

Oron bowed to his brother and stood. "Any time you're ready."

Darian winked. "Many thanks," he replied grandiosely. He held up the hand bearing the ring their mother gave him, and a golden portal opened. "Ladies and gentleman, after you."

One by one, the departing members said good-bye and stepped through the portal. The last ones to leave were his brother, himself, Aiden, Meryn and Ryuu.

Meryn turned to Sebastian her eyes pleading. Sebastian placed his fist over his heart. "I swear to you that Pip will be safe and well looked after."

She nodded once before Aiden stepped through, followed by Meryn, then finally Ryuu.

Oron turned to his brother. "Let's head home."

Oron stretched and inhaled. The deep forest where they stood was completely different than the desert-city they just left. The air was rich with earthy smells and a light breeze danced through the trees.

Meryn looked around. "I expected more buildings."

Darian chuckled. "This isn't Éire Danu Meryn, this is the wooded area outside of Monroe, the closest human town to the established entry portal to Éire Danu."

"Why in the hell are we here? Are there ticks?" she demanded, looking at the underbrush.

Aiden scrubbed his hands over his face. "Liander, Rex, Jedrek and Catherine will head to the city. We'll be taking a slight detour to the Vanguard camp outside the town to verify their non-feral status so they can security check others. One of the problems with them signing up for your app, I discovered, is that the Vanguard squads in this area are pretty spread out, so without one being verified, it would be hard to get the ball rolling," he explained.

"Why didn't some of the fae unit warriors from Éire Danu verify them?" Meryn asked.

"They just got city-wide Wi-Fi by copying your setup from Noctem Falls, most of the fae warriors are still setting up their own profiles. Since we're here, it's easier for us to knock the local Vanguard out in one go," Aiden said, stretching his arms over his head.

Jedrek stepped forward. "I will do what I can to get our fair city ready for your arrival, but I have a feeling we will be woefully ill-prepared."

Catherine cuffed the back of her mate's head. "What he means to say, is that we will be hard pressed to adequately greet such an amazing person as yourself Meryn."

Rex grinned openly at his father's chagrin before turning to Aiden. "I'll let the other unit warriors know you're coming. I'm sure they will be excited to meet with you."

"I'd appreciate that," Aiden said, clasping forearms with the lion shifter.

Liander bowed. "Until we see you in the Land of Eternal Sun."

Oron inclined his head as the smaller group headed east.

Micah waltzed over and placed a hand on Meryn's head before whispering a spell. Once finished, he ruffled her short curls. "Serenity and I will be staying with you Dewdrop. To security check a squad you need at least four unit warriors, so this frees up Gavriel and Colton to do their other duties. That spell should keep the bugs off you until we reach the fae city."

Meryn sighed in relief. "Thanks, I'm not trying to get eaten out here."

Law looked around. "Our escort to the Vanguard camp should be here soon."

Amelia edged closer to Micah. "About that bug spell."

Micah spun and wrapped an arm around Amelia. "But of course, my Dewdrop's big-sister cousin. Bugs have no right to nibble on your delicate self." He whispered the spell and Amelia smiled. "Thank you."

Micah beamed before swaggering up to his own mate who was crouched down a branch in hand. "Do you need my help too, my one and only?"

She looked up from where she was examining a particular set of leaves. "Of course not Micah, you know I can do my own spells for that." She went back to looking at the vegetation.

Micah grabbed at his chest. "Shot down in the prime of my life!" he exclaimed.

Serenity didn't even turn back. "Micah, come here and look at this fern, I've never seen anything like it," she replied, ignoring his histrionics.

"Yes, dearest," Micah said sensibly, before dropping down next to his mate.

Darian was still scowling at the witch when he turned to Amelia. "I will get you a fae charm to repel insects when we reach Éire Danu."

Amelia giggled. "There's my frowny face," she teased.

Oron shook his head in wonder. Growing up, he had seen many mated pairs, but in all his years he had never seen couples so finely in tune with each another as his fellow unit warrior brothers and their mates. He thought back to his dreams and sighed; he could only pray he would meet his little disaster soon.

"I should send some of these to Laelia and Radclyffe so they can press them into our journals," Serenity said, standing with the ferns in hand. "We haven't had many opportunities to study the fauna on the east coast."

Micah turned to them. "Can we do this once we reach Éire Danu?"

Oron looked at them. "Quite easily, there's a

courier service dedicated to deliveries between the pillar cities."

Micah nuzzled his mate's neck. "Thinking about home?" Serenity nodded silently.

"I can open another portal now to Storm Keep if that is what you wish," Darian offered.

Serenity shook her head. "The Witches' Council stripped me of my position as Head of the Water Temple and banned me from Storm Keep," she whispered, almost as if speaking the very words caused her pain.

"Why on earth would they do that?" Oron demanded.

She met his eyes. "Because I disobeyed them and went to Noctem Falls to assist with the virus. Thank the gods they listened to Troy. He told them he would flat out quit if Laelia and Radclyffe weren't allowed to return. So, the council deemed that they were influenced by me to act and they were accepted back to their positions, with Troy being promoted to Temple Head," she chuckled. "And he is not happy about it one bit. I am getting emails from him daily, complaining about how hard it is to get anything done while hogtied by council rules and regulations. It would not surprise me in the least to hear one day that Troy has flooded the council chambers in a fit of frustration."

Oron groaned. "That's what the queen meant when she said Allia and Ailain were in a tizzy. Zach was on a rampage and they were scheming along with him. I kinda feel sorry for the Witches' Council, they set off the fae twins."

Serenity laughed. "I think it all worked out for the best. This way I can design and grow the healing center Magnus wants at Noctem Falls. Marjoram and I were drooling at the budget he gave us. But, as much as we want to race out and get everything we need; we are taking this slow and planning every step so it's done properly."

"Anything you do will be perfection," Micah assured her.

A familiar warrior jogged over to them from up the worn path. "Commander McKenzie, welcome to Monroe!"

Oron stepped forward. "Commander, this is Liam Donahue, wolf-shifter and longtime Vanguard squad member for Monroe."

Aiden clasped arms with the warrior. "Well met."

Liam stepped back. "Gods, you look like your father."

Aiden grinned. "So I have heard."

Liam pointed back up the trail. "Let me show you to the Vanguard compound."

"Compound?" Meryn asked.

Liam looked down at her. "Are you the Menace?"

She nodded. "I am."

"Just a word of warning, tales of your exploits have reached our remote and humble facility, you're kinda famous," Liam explained.

Meryn eyed him. "Like celebrity famous or serial killer famous?"

"Hmmm, maybe a celebrity falsely accused of being a serial killer famous."

Meryn brightened. "Awesome."

Aiden shook his head. "Baby, that's not awesome."

"So awesome," she repeated, following Liam.

Oron turned to Darian. "You heading to the palace?"

Darian glanced back at his mate and shook his head. "Amelia wants to arrive with Meryn to show our support."

"And you don't want to miss a second of the Meryn Show."

Darian gave a lazy shrug. "What can I say, it was boring at home without her." He wrapped an arm around Amelia as they followed their commander who was still arguing with his tiny mate.

Oron "Never a truer word was spoken."

Aiden disappeared for most of the afternoon meeting with different warriors and verifying them as they gave reports. This left Meryn in the kitchen with her cousin, squire and dedicated fans. Micah and Serenity watched on in amusement.

Once the verification process finished, Darian had decided to stay with Aiden as a member of the Alpha Unit while even more meetings continued, which meant Oron was guarding both his baby sister and the menace.

"Did you really blow up the Council Manor?" one warrior asked a rapt expression on his face.

"No!" Meryn exclaimed slamming her small hands on the counter. "When I find out who is spreading that rumor, I'm gonna kick them in the nuts!"

The guy laughed. "I see the violent tendencies weren't an exaggeration."

Amelia turned to the warrior as she was trying to calm Meryn down. "She really didn't. All she did was coat the entire square in flour glue. Oh! And she also took out a lot of ferals with a sniper rifle. If we're talking destruction, I'm the one who ripped up all the cobblestones in the square to halt the invading ferals so that the guys could kill them, though I accidentally incinerated them instead, with Kendrick's help of course." Amelia's adorable ramble to profess Meryn's innocence had them both looking like homicidal maniacs.

Micah nodded. "That's what I heard from most of the Alpha Unit warriors as well. Though Colton did admit, he still has nightmares about the time Meryn almost blew them both up with a hand grenade."

Serenity elbowed him in the ribs. "Not helping."

The guy closest to Meryn stared. "You almost blew up Colton Albright?"

Meryn sighed. "Yeah, sort of. But, he's being a big baby about the whole thing."

Oron leaned his chair back and watched the varying degrees of horror on the men's faces.

Liam turned to him. "I would say it's because they're human and half-human, but the humans in Monroe don't act like them."

"We've just been blessed by the gods," Oron said, smiling wide.

Amelia turned to him her eyes shining brightly. "Thank you."

And that right there was why he'd die protecting her, her joy always seemed to radiate about her in calming waves, despite the macabre way she had accidentally burned their enemies to death.

"You're easy to love baby sister."

Meryn poked her head around her cousin. "What about me?"

"Meryn, you're just as easy to love despite yourself, and I don't know who that surprises more, the people in your life, or you."

Ryuu nodded as he rubbed his chin. "That is a shockingly accurate statement."

Meryn looked thoughtful. "Thank you…I think."

"You're quite welcome, Menace."

The men laughed. "I see that rumor is true, they call you Menace and Amelia is the Little Terrorist."

Amelia sighed. "I will never get rid of that dratted nickname."

Oron heard the door to one of the meeting rooms open and more men filed into the large kitchen area.

Meryn turned to her mate. "Do you love me, despite me?"

Aiden got that deer in the headlights expression. "Uhh, I love you no matter what baby," he said hesitantly.

"Good, okay. I love you too." Meryn picked up the bag of Cheetos the guys had ridiculously presented to her, evidently having read it on Facebook that they were her favorite snacks.

Tension immediately eased around them. Aiden sighed a bit and sat down in the bar stool across from her.

"Well, well, well, what have we here?" A deep voice asked.

Oron recognized the warrior but couldn't place the name.

"Yum," Meryn sighed.

"Meryn!" Aiden growled.

"What? He's like seven feet of cocoa perfection. Shit, now I'm craving chocolate."

"What!" Aiden roared.

"Not like that, like maybe some Nutella. Yeah, Cheetos dipped in Nutella." She looked over at the built warrior and sighed. "Damn, dude."

Aiden stood and rotated her, chair and all, to face the opposite direction before sitting back down.

"You act like I won't get up and move my chair," Meryn threatened.

Everyone waited.

"I will later," Meryn huffed, sticking her nose in the air. Aiden gave a satisfied smirk. "Sure, baby."

Ryuu walked over to the pantry and rummaged around. "Is this what you are craving *denka*?" he asked, holding up a small jar.

"Yes! Ryuu you kick-ass."

Smiling, he placed the container next to her Cheetos bag.

The dark warrior walked over to stand next to Ryuu. “Gorgeous and kind, what’s your name sweetness?” he purred.

Meryn inhaled sharply and began to choke on her chocolate covered Cheeto. Ryuu was at her side in an instant rubbing her back as his hand glowing blue.

Ryuu lifted an ebony brow at the warrior. “Ryuu Sei, I am squire to Meryn McKenzie, pleased to meet you.”

“My name is Pierce Almarez; I’m enchanted to meet you as well. I think I’ll tag along with your group and visit Éire Danu; it’s been a few decades since I was there last and the company then was nowhere near as arousing.”

Meryn stood her eyes blazing. Without a word, she wrapped her arms around her squire’s waist placing her hands directly over his ass.

The men looked on in shock. Aiden’s mouth dropped open, he seemed unable to form words.

Ryuu looked down at his charge his mouth twitching furiously. “*Denka*, what on earth are you doing?”

“I know what he’s after, I learned all about this stuff in Noctem Falls, you gotta protect the butt,” she said, glaring at Pierce.

“Oh Meryn,” Amelia said, covering her face with her hands.

Pierce smiled down at small human defending her squire. “What exactly did you learn in Noctem Falls?” he asked, curiously.

"Never mind what she learned. Meryn move your hands!" Aiden tried pulling his mate away from the chuckling squire. "Dammit Ryuu, help me here!" Aiden growled.

Gently, Ryuu disentangled Meryn's hands. "You do not have to worry about me *denka*, I am more than capable of defending myself. I am aware of his intentions and they do not bother me. I am, however, quite moved by your concern, no one except for Kendrick has defended me in over five thousand years, you continue to surprise me at every turn." He leaned down and kissed her forehead. Unlike earlier with Sebastian, she didn't seem to mind when it came to her own squire.

She looked over at Pierce. "I learned all kinds of cool things in Noctem Falls and so did my best friend, Felix. He got real proficient with a sword and he doesn't hesitate in stabbing or chopping people to defend his family." Meryn glanced down at his crotch. "Feel me?"

Pierce winced. "That's just cold."

"You have been warned."

Oron watched as Felix crossed his tiny arms over his chest in an effort to look menacing, though he and Darian were probably the only ones who could see him.

Law wiped at his eyes from silent laughter. "She does this to me every damn time," he complained, barely able to breathe. Two of the other warriors around the room buried their faces in their hands to hide their own laughter.

Pierce looked over at Aiden. "Seriously though, what did she learn about butts in Noctem Falls?"

Law inhaled as he leaned back slightly and fell off his chair. To see a man that size laughing on the floor was all it took to set everyone off.

"Serenity, I don't think he's breathing," Micah commented, watching Law wrap his arms around his mid-section, making pained facial expressions.

"If he can laugh, he can breathe," she said, shaking her head at Meryn's shenanigans.

"See, I told you Izzy, this is a nice place." A warrior commented, coming up behind them from the direction of the front door.

"I don't know, it's mostly men and they look kinda drunk to me. Maybe this is like a bar or sex dungeon. Like a drunken, gay, sex dungeon," a piping female replied.

"Oh gods above, I can't breathe!" Law called from the floor. Oron shook his head at the man's plight.

Micah's eyes bugged out. "A drunken, gay, sex dungeon?"

Meryn nodded. "They're all a buncha mannequins."

"They like the rough stuff, huh?" the sweet voice asked.

"No! What?" Aiden looked from one female to the other then paused. "How did you know she meant masochist?"

"We were talking about sex dungeons, I kinda extrapolated that the misused random word that began with the letter 'm' was a term that more accurately fit the conversation. It wasn't that hard actually."

"She meant masochist?" Micah asked.

Serenity stood over Law now looking concerned. "Okay, my earlier assessment may have been off, I don't think he's getting any oxygen." She placed her hands on his chest and eased his laughter.

Law gasped for air. "Gods Meryn, you can't keep doing this to me!" he managed to croak out.

"So, not a sex dungeon?"

Chuckling Oron turned in his chair and suddenly he couldn't breathe for reasons of his own, the petite auburn-haired beauty who had understood nutty Meryn perfectly was his mate!

CHAPTER THREE

ISABELLE CAMPBELL TOOK IN THE scene before her. The men were laughing uncontrollably, except for the tall blond in front on her. He looked positively gobsmacked.

"Hello," she said, unsure of what to do. He *was* staring after all.

He rose from his chair and walked over to her. He cupped her face in his two large hands before using a thumb to wipe the soot from the top of her nose.

"You really did set that coffee shop on fire, didn't you?" he asked, a note of wonder in his voice.

She frowned up at him. "How on earth could you possibly know that? We just got here." She turned slightly to face Cameron. "Did you call ahead and tell everyone?"

Cameron looked as confused as she felt. "No Izzy, I swear I didn't."

"Gods above, she's your mate, isn't she?" The huge man asked before sitting down next to the smaller woman.

The man standing over her, nodded slowly.

"I've been dreaming of her." He grinned. "She always seemed to be in trouble."

Izzy brought her hands up to his wrists to remove his hands and stepped back. "It's not my fault, trouble just finds me," she protested.

The god-like man just raised an eyebrow. "So, you didn't try using the culinary torch to make s'mores?"

"Well…"

"And it produced enough smoke to set off the smoke alarms and sprinklers?"

"Actually…"

"Which then, in turn, caused a panic, resulting in said torch getting dropped and setting fire to the cabinetry?"

She sighed. "Yes."

"It's why we brought her here. She's our favorite little barista in town and the owner of the coffee shop was enraged. He fired her and kicked her out on the spot," Cameron explained.

The golden hottie turned to Cameron. "Kicked her out?"

"He was my landlord too, I rented one of the apartments over the shop." She pointed around the room. "I've known these guys for years. They come by the shop all the time. If they hadn't been there, I'd be on the streets. I should've taken them up on their offer last year to be their live-in barista," Izzy mumbled.

Cameron pointed to her three small boxes. "Thank the gods we were there, or I doubt he would have even let her get her stuff."

"You have my thanks," the gorgeous guy said to Cameron.

"Seriously?" she put her hands on her hips.

"What?" he asked.

"How about hmm… I don't know, like who the fuck are you? Why do you care what happened to my stuff and what in the hell is a mate?" she poked his chest with each word. Breathing hard, she looked up at him and was surprised by the fact she had actually backed him up a bit. Feeling fearless she gave him one last poke before glaring up at him.

"What was it you said to me? 'You mated into that craziness?'" Another blond to her right asked, laughing his head off.

The man before her flipped him off then smiled down at her. "I'm sorry for the poor introduction. My name is Oron Vi'Eirson. I care about your belongings because you are my mate. A mate is one half of a destined pair, Fate has determined that you would be the perfect partner for me, and I have to say, never in my thousands of years did I ever dream I would be blessed enough to deserve someone as special as you."

Izzy felt her brain trying to make sense of what he just said. She knew he was speaking English, but somehow what he was saying simply wasn't clicking.

"Mates? Wait… thousands of years?" Izzy reached around her blindly looking for a chair as her head began to swim.

"It's okay, just breathe," a soft voice said,

guiding her to a stool. "I know it's a lot to take in, but you're doing very well."

Izzy looked at the gorgeous woman helping her. "Your eyes are purple."

The woman paused, then smiled. "Yes, they are like my father's. My name is Serenity Meadowsweet." In a calm voice, she went around the room and introduced everyone. The one named Amelia set a glass of water down in front of her. "Thank you," she said, gripping the glass tight.

"You're very welcome. Izzy wasn't it?" Amelia asked.

She nodded absently. "Yes, Isabelle Campbell, but everyone calls me Izzy." Her eyes went back to Oron. "You're supposed to be like my soul mate?"

He nodded. "It's okay if you don't believe me right away, as long as you give us a chance to get to know one another."

She looked down into her water glass. "You won't stick around. No one does. I'm a mess."

The women around her began to laugh. Bristling, she glared at them. Amelia shook her head. "We're laughing because you're in excellent company." She pointed to the short-haired Meryn. "She covered our town square in glue, called one of our Elders a douchebag and likes to electrocute people." She pointed to her own chest. "I'm an empath and almost caused a major earthquake when I was two, I tore up the Lycaonia's town square's cobblestones and almost got stuck being a dog when I tried a shifting spell for the first time."

Meryn sighed. "You were so damn cute though."

Izzy felt herself beginning to relax. "That sounds nuts." She looked over to Serenity. "What about you?"

Serenity winked. "I disobeyed council dictates to go halfway across the country to help a city of vampires to fight a virus."

"Bad*ass*!" Izzy whispered. "Wait, Elders? Shifting? Vampires?"

Meryn exchanged looks with Amelia. "I'm really missing Kari right about now. She'd have an entire explanation whipped up in PowerPoint, in like three seconds flat."

Oron stepped forward and took the seat next to her. "How about this? Let's eat lunch. Over lunch we'll explain things as they come up in conversation until all your questions have been answered."

Izzy nodded slowly. "I think I can do that."

The other men vacated the kitchen, giving them some space. Amelia and Serenity helped Ryuu churn out some sandwiches as Oron started explaining what he called the 'basics' to her. Every once in a while, Micah, Serenity, Law or Darian would add things. Pierce helped Ryuu by passing him ingredients. Every time he got close to the gorgeous Japanese man; Meryn would practically growl. Izzy thought it was adorable how protective Meryn was of her friend.

Somewhere between her tuna fish sandwich and her ice cream sundae she was sure someone had slipped her the good drugs.

"So under normal circumstances y'all have ferals, but you just found out that there are like serial killer type ferals?" she asked, wishing she had more ice cream to process all of this.

Meryn nodded. "Yup, plus a lot of possible 'been going on for decades' type evil schemes in action."

She looked around the table feeling panicked. "I just make coffee, that's it. I'm not a witch or a shifter. Why me?"

Oron reached over and gently took her hand. He tugged on her fingers until she relaxed. She had been digging into her palm with her nails.

"Because I need you," he said simply. "Forget about the ferals and schemes. Don't worry about anything else, I'll keep you safe."

That was another thing she didn't understand. He was perfect. No one was this perfect and even if he were real and not part of a caffeine-induced dream, there's no way in hell she'd end up with someone like him.

"Are you sure?" she asked.

He lifted her hand to his lips and kissed it softly. "I have never been more sure of anything in my life. Your soul's light shines for me."

"Hold the fuck up, you make coffee. You're a barista, right?" Meryn asked, a devilish look in her eye.

"No Meryn, you're pregnant remember," Aiden said, shaking his head.

"Yeah, and? Meryn-two-point-oh loves coffee, I need Izzy in my life."

Izzy grinned at the small woman. "You are my people."

Meryn pointed at her. "See! She gets it!"

"I promised Rheia I'd look after you shorty, so don't OD on caffeine on my watch, okay?" Serenity pleaded.

Meryn rubbed her hands together. "We need supplies."

"I have a distributor account for most coffee wholesalers," Izzy volunteered.

Meryn turned in her chair to face her handsome friend. "Ryuu, please do that squire thing and get stuff for Éire Danu," she pleaded, her hands clasped in front of her chest.

Ryuu bowed. "Of course, *denka*. Lady Campbell, if you are comfortable with providing me with your log in information, I can arrange for supplies to be sent to our next destination."

Izzy nodded. "Sure, but I don't have much money on the card stored with the profile." She looked between him and Meryn. "Why did she ask you to get supplies? What's a squire thing?"

Ryuu gave an elegant half bow. "Squires in our world run the households of important families, leaving them free to assist in the leading of our many peoples. Unlike the human world, which denotes the position disdainfully, squires in our world are revered and respected." He handed her a piece of paper. "With your permission, I'll add our house account to the profile. I have a sneaking suspicion I will be ordering quite often in the future."

Izzy eyed the gleeful Meryn and the concerned

looking Aiden. "That's cool." She wrote down the sites and log in information on the piece of paper, then handed it back to Ryuu. She turned to Oron. "What now?"

"Now, I'd like to invite you to take a walk with me outside so we can get to know one another better," he offered.

Izzy turned to the other women and they nodded. Amelia took pity on her. "Oron is both noble and kind. You couldn't ask for a better man. He will not only keep you safe, but put your needs above his own. Take a leap of faith Izzy, I promise you, you won't regret it."

Izzy looked back to Oron to see the concern in his eyes. She squeezed his hand. "Okay, but only if we find some bug spray first. I fucking hate bugs."

Meryn shuddered. "Amen."

Oron pulled his hand from her grasp and looked over to Micah. "If you would?"

Micah stood and placed a hand on her shoulder. He said something she couldn't quite understand, then was done. "There, you should be safe now."

Izzy raised her arm to her nose. "I don't smell anything."

Micah grinned. "It's a spell, not a chemical."

"So, I'm like bug proof now?"

Everyone nodded.

"Okay, being bug proof may just make all this craziness worth it."

Oron gave her a sardonic look. "Is that the only thing?"

She smiled sweetly. "So far."

"Have fun," Amelia said happily.

Oron stood and held out his hand to her. "Shall we?"

"Yes, but remember, the short one needs me in her life," she said, pointing to Meryn. "And she likes to electrocute people," she warned.

Oron grinned. "Trust me, I know."

Hand in hand, he led her outside.

I really hope he isn't a psycho killer, he's hot, and it would be such a shame if Meryn had to kill him.

Oron didn't waste a single moment after they began walking to reclaim her hand. She had to admit, it felt nice. His hand was warm without being sweaty and he seemed to exude safety. Despite having only known him a couple hours, she felt completely at ease with him, as if she knew he'd do anything to keep her from harm.

"What did Ryuu mean when he said he'd arrange for supplies for our next destination?" she asked, after a few minutes.

"I wondered if you had caught that," Oron stopped and turned to stand in front of her. "Remember me telling you that Darian and I were fae?" She nodded. "Our next destination is Éire Danu, the Land of Eternal Sun and home to my people."

"Why do I think that it's not as simple as hopping in the car and heading down the road?" she asked.

He winced. "Because it's not. After the Great

War, our queen saw the devastation our people were experiencing by losing their human friends and neighbors. The people back then were as close to the earth as we are and they were like curious children to us, but so susceptible to age, death and disease. To keep her people's hearts from breaking, our queen moved the entire city of the fae into a different realm, a sort of pocket existence parallel to this one. It can only be reached via a portal, and a portal can only be opened by the fae."

Izzy began to get excited. "A new realm and a fae queen! How cool is that!" They began walking again, ambling along the path.

When they reached a small clearing with a downed tree Oron led her over to it. He removed his jacket creating a cushion for her and had her sit.

"Thank you," she said, before sitting down and getting comfortable.

He simply sat directly on the ground. Even with her sitting above him on the tree he was still taller than she was. She watched his face, he seemed to be struggling with something.

"What?" she asked.

He looked up, surprised. "What?"

"Either you're constipated or you're trying to figure out how to tell me something awful, I kinda hope it's neither."

He blinked, then began to grin wryly. "It's the latter I'm afraid. There are things I must tell you about me before we return to Éire Danu, people may treat you differently being my mate."

"Different as in bad?"

He nodded silently.

"Listen, I just burned down my apartment and place of employment this morning. I've kinda gotten thrown into the deep end of this paranormal pool, but as far as movie scenarios go this," she waved her hand around at the serene picture the clearing provided. "This isn't so bad. I mean so far no one has tried to rip out my throat and aliens aren't trying to kill me, so I think I can handle what you're about to lay on me."

When he blinked at her, she realized how her pep talk might have seemed odd. "I suck at this comforting thing, don't I?"

He shook his head. "Actually, what you said helps. Maybe I have to realize that what is happening now far eclipses what happened in the past."

Izzy grimaced. "When you say past, please mean a couple years ago. Because if it's something horrible and traumatic that happened recently, I'm going to feel like an asshole."

"It happened almost five thousand years ago."

"Huh? What did? Like the pyramids being built?"

He chuckled. "No." He took a deep breath. "My family murdered an entire fae house."

"Your whole family? Grandma too?"

"No, both sets of my grandparents were lost in the Great War, but yes, all of the males participated."

Izzy felt so far out of her depth she didn't even

know what to say. "I feel like saying 'I'm sorry' would sound trite."

"Trust me, I understand."

"So, did they get caught?"

"Yes, I overheard them planning. I was about to get help when my uncle caught me and threw me in the cellar. It took me all night to break the door down."

"Oh God! How old were you?"

"Ten."

"What happened to them?"

He drew in a shuddering breath. "By the time I reached the queen and she dispatched her royal guards to House Alina, it was too late, they were all dead."

"All of them?"

"All except one. Before going to the queen, I snuck into the Alina nursery to see if their youngest had survived. I found him alive and sleeping. I picked him up and ran as fast as I could." He covered his face with his hands. "I was so scared someone would find me before we got to safety. I wanted my father, but, then it hit me, I was running from my father, he was the monster I was terrified of."

She didn't know about the whole mate thing, but she couldn't hear his story and not comfort him. She scooted closer and wrapped her arms around his neck to hold him. "You saved the baby; I think that is pretty amazing."

He tilted his head, leaning into her embrace. "My parents didn't know I had been going over to House Alina to play with him. Back then there weren't many children in the city. He was one of the closest to me in age. I used to help his mother change him and feed him breakfast. I knew that had I been too late to save him, I would have let my father kill me."

"Don't say that. You were only a child yourself; how could you possibly be responsible for the actions of the adults who were supposed to be teaching and guiding you?"

He looked up at her. "I loved him so much that, had he been murdered by my family, I knew that I would follow him into death so he wouldn't be scared or alone. I promised him when he was born that I would take care of him and that we would be best friends and warriors someday. Dying wouldn't have been me not wanting to live, it would have been me trying to find him."

"Oh Oron," she squeezed his head tight in a fierce hug.

He laughed and pulled her down into his lap holding her close. "There much better."

She glared up at him. "You didn't like my hug?"

"You mean your headlock?"

"Whatever. So, what happened to the baby?" she was completely vested in the story now.

He leaned back. "The queen started looking for families to adopt him. There was a list a mile long of couples who wanted to add him to their family. I would sleep in the nursery every night and tell him all the wonderful things his new family would do for him. One day the queen asked me who I thought should receive the baby." He smiled softly. "I told her that he had to go to one of the few families that had a boy because he needed a brother to watch over him."

Izzy felt her heart melt into a puddle in her chest. "That is so sweet. So, who adopted him?"

He grinned down at her. "The queen. She looked at me and said it's a good thing I am adopting both of you, you can be his brother."

Izzy's hands flew to her mouth as tears filled her eyes. "You got to stay with him!"

He nodded. "The queen saw how much I cared for him and knew that no one would adopt me, so she decided the best course of action was to keep us together. She was the best mother two boys could ever dream of having."

"Why wouldn't anyone want you? You're a hero!"

He looked surprised. "You really believe that, don't you?"

"Duh!"

"You don't think that I carry tainted blood?" He pointed to his warm brown eyes. "Hardly any of the fae are born with dark eyes, rumors about me were swirling long before my family's treachery. I carry some serious marks against me. Are you that sure I am not a bad seed destined to be evil?"

She gave him a flat look before busting out laughing. "You? Evil?" she kept laughing.

"You seem so very sure I'm not."

"You may be a lot of things, but evil certainly isn't one of them. You are one thousand percent marshmallow fluff." Izzy knew without a shadow of a doubt that the man who held her so carefully could never be evil. The little boy who would go against his family to save a baby could never be tainted. Maybe Fate knew what they were doing after all because he was quickly becoming everything she had ever looked for in a husband.

"Fluff, huh?"

"Yup," she paused. "Wait, is that why people will treat me differently because they think you're evil?" He nodded. "I need Meryn to show me how she electrocutes people because the first asshole to talk bad about you, is going down."

He blinked down at her. "I understand Aiden a bit more now. From an outside perspective that must sound horribly violent, but as you are defending me, I think that has to be the sexiest thing I have ever heard."

"You think I'm sexy?"

"Absolutely."

"Is it just because we're mates? Have you been brainwashed to like me?"

He rubbed their noses together. "No, being mates is not like being brainwashed. It's more like feeling as if you're a complex jagged crystal. You go through life thinking that it's a smart way to be. You have sharp edges that help protect you, but it's a lonely existence. Then one day you find another crystal whose serrated edges align perfectly with yours. You experience this odd feeling of coming home, and you're fascinated to discover all the tiny ways you fit together."

Izzy felt tears fill her eyes. "We fit?"

He leaned down and pressed their foreheads together. "I think we're perfect for one another. You need a bit of stability and I need to be shaken up. I've lived my entire life trying to please everyone out of guilt. I think I've lost of bits of myself in the process."

"Maybe you didn't lose yourself, maybe Fate or whoever gave me your pieces for safe keeping."

"If I weren't already half in love with you, that alone would do it."

"How can you be half in love with me? We just met."

He sat back. "Yes, but I've been dreaming of you for weeks."

Izzy thought back to her recent dreams, how she hated waking because in her dreams she felt someone standing behind her, watching over her, and protecting her. "It was you!" she said excitedly, turning so that she now knelt between his legs. "I never saw your face, but I knew that no matter what was going on, you'd protect me."

Oron nodded. "I have a lifetime of experience looking after a little brother, I feel confident I can pull you out of your scrapes."

"Did you see the dream about the cracked car windshield?" He nodded. "The shaved dog?" He snorted then bobbed his head. "My attempt at creating a baking sheet sized cookie?" He frowned. "That was the first fire right."

She gave him a sour look. "My 'first' fire was when I was like three."

He paled. "Oh, gods."

She gave him an evil grin. "I can't wait to see this fae city. Will I get to meet the queen?"

"Of course, she is my mother."

"Wait, so she's a queen and your mom. Does that make you a prince?"

He gave her a roguish smile. "Does that make me more appealing?"

"I, no shit, get a prince. Like a fairytale prince!" she jumped to her feet and thrust her fist to the sky. "Take that Emily Jenkins you empty-headed rerun! Who's voted 'Most Likely to Die Alone' and 'Most Likely to Amount to Nothing' now!"

Oron stood and swung her around laughing. "You tell them, Izzy!" He set her on her feet. "Is there a class reunion we need to go to?"

Izzy knew right then and there she was falling hard and fast. "You'd do that for me?"

He spread his hands. "You're willing to electrocute people for me, it's the least I could do."

"You're kinda wonderful."

"As long as I'm wonderful to you, that's all that matters."

"There's someone I want to meet more than your queen mom."

He frowned. "Who could that possibly be?"

"I want to meet the baby you saved. The little boy who became your brother."

Oron's eyebrows shot up. "But you have."

"Huh? When?"

Oron jerked his thumb toward the path that they had followed. "Back at the house. You remember the other blond guy who was teasing me and I flipped him off?"

"No! Seriously?" Izzy had a burning desire to get to know Darian better and hear from him how Oron was growing up.

Oron groaned. "You can't believe anything he says."

"Uh, huh." She turned toward the house.

"No, really Izzy. He lies. He is a horrible liar."

She began marching up the path.

"And he exaggerates, even about the smallest of things."

"Right."

"Izzy…baby. Come on, let's go torture your old classmates instead," he suggested.

"Later. Right now, I want to get to know my sort of mate's brother."

Oron stayed at her side. "I felt like we were bonding, let's just stay here." He halted dead in his tracks. "What do you mean 'sort of' mate?"

She stopped and looked back at him. "We haven't even kissed yet. I don't think we can be called mates if we haven't even kissed."

Wrong. Thing. To. Say.

She watched his eyes darken before he closed the distance between them in a single step. "I can remedy that." He leaned down and captured her lips.

This was no hesitant kiss from a blind date gone awkwardly wrong, this had the intensity of a starving man devouring a banquet. He licked and teased her until she felt her knees give. He easily caught her and held her against him. When he finally pulled away, she found she had difficulty breathing.

"Mates?" he asked.

She nodded, still feeling befuddled. "Mates."

"Good," he stepped back and steadied her on her feet. He gave her an elegant low bow. "After you," he said, nodding toward the house.

"Right. House. Good. Houses have bedrooms," she murmured, still feeling off kilter. She heard a loud thump and cursing. Confused, she looked behind her. "Why are you on the ground?"

Oron simply shook his head and stood. "Never mind. Let's go." He took her hand and led her back up the trail.

CHAPTER FOUR

ORON SAT AT THE LARGE dinner table with his Vanguard brothers, his friends, family and mate. He didn't think life could get much better. He watched Darian's eyes shine as he regaled an enraptured Izzy with stories of the two of them growing up. Even Amelia and Meryn had gotten sucked into the storytelling.

"And then there was the time Oron used briar brambles to tie Molvan Vi'Lerido to a wall," Darian said, smiling wide.

Oron groaned. "Not that old tale."

Darian shook his finger at him. "It's only old once you've heard it few dozen times."

Cameron and Liam leaned forward. Liam grinning broadly. "Do tell. I've crossed paths with Molvan before, I'd love to hear this story."

Darian took a deep breath. "Let's see, this was back when I was six, no seven."

Oron shook his head. "You were five."

"Right. So, when I was five, I was innocently wandering around the city…"

"He had escaped his nanny," Oron interjected.

"As I was saying, I was meandering around

minding my own business when I came across Molvan teasing a tiny sprite. I was outraged, so I marched up to Molvan and demanded that he stop it at once."

"Cheeky little brat," Oron muttered.

Darian ignored him. "Molvan acted confused. He asked me what I was talking about."

"Why would he ask that?" Meryn wondered.

Darian turned to her. "You know how not all fae can see sprites?"

Meryn and Amelia nodded. Darian continued. "Well, there are caveats to that based on age. The older a fae becomes, the more likely they are to gain the ability to see sprites. Likewise, as a sprite gets older, they gain the ability to make themselves visible to everyone."

Izzy pointed to where Felix sat on Meryn's shoulder. "So, he's old?"

Everyone stared at Meryn, trying to figure out who Izzy was talking about.

Meryn's eyes widened. "You can see him?"

Izzy scooted closer to him. "Am I not supposed to?"

Oron wrapped an arm around her shoulders. "It's like Darian said, not every fae gains the ability to see sprites, but since you are mated to me, it makes sense that you have the ability to see them, it will help you acclimate to our world."

Amelia practically bounced in her chair. "I can see them too!"

Izzy wiggled her fingers at Felix who was now peeking out from Meryn's hoodie. He gave her a shy smile and wiggled his fingers back at her.

"So, this Molvan jerk was acting like he didn't know what you were talking about because he didn't think you could see sprites since you were so young?" Meryn guessed.

Darian nodded. "Oron and I hid the fact we could see them when we were younger, to avoid irritating the older fae around us, now it's second nature to do so."

"What did you do to Molvan?" Amelia asked.

"I walked over and knocked his hand away from the wall where he was leaning, effectively trapping the sprite. Once free, the sprite flew away. Molvan was not only furious I had ruined his fun, but because I had also hit him. He saw me as insolent."

Amelia rubbed her mate's arm comfortingly. "What did he do?"

Darian covered Amelia's hand with his own. "He terrorized me with a dagger scaring the literal piss out of me, then used said dagger to pin me three feet above the ground dangling from the Royal Garden's perimeter wall."

"What a bastard!" Meryn exclaimed.

Darian nodded his agreement. "It had just started to dim…"

"Dim?" Amelia asked.

Darian gave her a rueful look. "I keep forgetting how much you don't know about my home. Éire Danu is called the Land of Eternal Sun because the sun never truly sets. Think of Alaska in the summer. It sort of just dims a bit in the evening."

"Serious-fucking-ly?" Meryn asked. "I go from caves, shadows, and darkness to Cancer-town? Can I get some sunglasses?"

Darian scowled at Meryn. "You will not get cancer from visiting Éire Danu. We are protected by the city's magic."

Izzy waved an impatient hand at both of them. "Back to the story."

"My apologies, little sister." Darian winked at her. "It had begun to dim, so of course, my big brother was out searching for me since I wasn't at home." He gave a soft smile. "The little sprite had gone for help and was leading him to where I was pathetically swinging in the breeze. When he found me, I sobbed my heart out and buried my face in his chest. It took him almost the entire way home to get a coherent story out of me. Once we got back to the palace, he handed me off to Cord to get cleaned up and ready for bed. Then he left. Later that night, he came to my room almost as if he knew I was still terrified out of my little mind. He got me to calm down and squeezed into my small bed with me. He told me not to be afraid, that Molvan had learned his lesson and would never come near me again. After that, I was able to go right to sleep."

"Just like that?" Meryn asked.

"Absolutely. If my big brother told me not to worry, then I knew I didn't have to worry."

Amelia turned to him. "What did you do?"

Oron gave a lazy shrug. "I used a bit of fae magic and with the help of a small sprite, we enchanted some thorny briars and pinned Molvan to the wall with the word 'bully' etched over his head." He looked over at Felix. "I believe the sprite's name was Fremi Skysong."

Felix's eyes widened and he pointed to his chest. Oron nodded. "Yes, your great- great-grandfather."

Meryn looked down at her friend then over to Darian who looked just as shocked. "Dude, Felix has saved my life and you saved his great whatever's life, so you saved me too."

Darian scowled at him. "When were you going to tell me that?"

Oron felt his mouth drop. "You mean you didn't know?"

"I was five!"

"Oh yeah. So, good work, I guess." He eyed Darian. "Did you never wonder why so many Skysong sprites moved into the royal gardens?"

Darian pointed to his chest. "Again, I was five. To me, it was a normal thing to have them there."

"After hearing what Fremi did to protect you, the queen invited the entire clan to make their home in the garden. Fremi watched over you until you were grown. There've been Skysongs in the palace ever since."

Izzy snorted and leaned against him. "I wonder what else you know that he doesn't."

Pierce sat back. "It must be nice to have a sibling. I'm also of the Hope Generation, unfortunately, in my case, not many of our leap had children right away, so I was the youngest one for close to a century."

"What is the Hope Generation?" Izzy asked.

Pierce, Darian, and Law smiled. Pierce pointed to his chest. "We're the ones born after the Great War ended. We represented the continuation of life and the hope for a better tomorrow."

Law picked up his wine glass. "It's sad that our generation now represents some of the oldest paranormals alive."

"Y'all came from somewhere, where are your parents?" Meryn asked Law.

He shrugged. "Mother is off on an assignment and we lost father in a feral attack when we were about one hundred."

Pierce nodded. "I lost both of my parents in the eighteen hundreds when a train derailed. We can take a lot of damage as shifters, but some things kill us the same as any human."

Oron looked at his brother, and they both sighed. Oron spoke for both of them. "You know what happened to our families."

Meryn was frowning. "I swear to God y'all gonna make me lose my mind." She glared around the table. "Did no one ever think of doing a census before Beth?"

Oron looked around, he wasn't the only one who looked confused.

Aiden bumped Meryn's shoulder with his own. "What did you think of now, baby?"

"Something Law said how they're the oldest paranormals now. I just think it's really odd that you have all of these supposedly immortal, fast, super strong peeps out there, some with magic and they've all had accidents? There aren't enough trains, ferals or what not to take out an entire generation."

Pierce chuckled. "I'm sure it's not as severe as that Meryn. We're also some of the oldest due to the Great War as well, we lost multiple generations in that war."

She crossed her arms over her chest. "Bet me." She looked around the room. "Hands up if you're part of this Hope Generation." Oron raised is hand along with six others. "Now lower your hand if you have lost both parents." Oron lowered his with Darian and surprisingly two others. Meryn looked at the remaining three. "Lower your hand if you have lost a parent." Law and the other two lowered their hands. Everyone looked stunned. Meryn continued. "This is called a sampling." She pulled out her phone and tapped. "Fifty-seven percent of you have lost both parents. Forty-three percent of you have lost one parent. One-hundred percent of you have lost someone from that generation. Need I go on?" she asked, putting her phone down.

Law leaned forward and set his wine glass down frowning. "The mortality rate can't be that high."

"Pierce said that not everyone in his leap or whatever had kids right away. What if a lot of them died, but since they didn't have kids, and their parents had died in the Great War, who exactly would mourn them?" Izzy asked.

Meryn pointed to his mate. "Exactly."

"That's impossible," Liam said, looking spooked.

"And chameleon shifters weren't hunted to near extinction either. And ferals didn't start banding together to create reapers either…" Meryn said, in a mockingly high-pitched voice.

Aiden stood. Meryn instantly looked contrite. "Sorry baby."

He shook his head and leaned down to kiss her forehead. "As usual you see what we don't. I'm going to call Magnus and have him throw his weight behind Beth's census project. Then you can do your magic 'tap-tap' on your frisbee and let us know what's really going on." He was pulling out his cell phone as he walked away.

Meryn smiled. "Magic 'tap-tap' huh," she sighed then looked back at her squire. "I will definitely need that coffee now Ryuu, I see databases in my future."

Pierce and most of the Vanguard looked from person to person slack-jawed. Pierce looked to Law. "Could she be right?"

Law now wore a scowl. "She's hardly ever wrong. I know we put out the order to bring in all deployed Vanguard, but we need to start putting out feelers for the Elder Generation too." He turned to Darian. "Could you speak to your queen about this?"

Darian nodded. "Of course, though, most fae live in Éire Danu, so it shouldn't be too hard to get our numbers."

Oron heard rumors of Meryn's strange ability to notice things that everyone overlooked or took for granted. But this was the first time he saw it in action. "Meryn, you're an amazing little human."

Izzy nodded. "I promise to make you whatever coffee you need while we're visiting so you can do your databases."

"I'm so falling for you," Meryn admitted.

Izzy laughed. "My coffee kung-fu is strong."

"I'm imposing a two-coffee limit for now Meryn. You shouldn't be as tired in Éire Danu as you were in Noctem Falls. You'll be getting plenty of fresh air, so let's take it slow okay?" Serenity said, holding up two fingers.

"The fate of our world could depend on my laptop and caffeine levels," Meryn countered.

Serenity smiled. "I'm more concerned about your baby, they're depending on you, not your laptop."

Meryn gave an exaggerated sigh. "Low blow, but I get it. You can monitor me then you'll see how much the nugget likes coffee."

"Deal."

"I could do a half-caf mocha with whip. It's half the amount of caffeine as in a normal double shot, but you get a little bit extra from the chocolate," Izzy offered.

"Coffee Goddess," Meryn whispered reverently.

Cameron groaned and laid his head down on the table. "We're losing our barista!"

Around the table, the men began to sulk.

Izzy looked around confused. "Why?"

Amelia placed a comforting hand on Izzy's

arm. "You'll be leaving when we do remember? But Oron doesn't live in Éire Danu, he lives in Lycaonia with us, that's where you'll be moving to."

"I'm moving?" Izzy screeched.

Oron winced at the octave. "I guess we hadn't really talked about that yet."

She turned and stared at him. "I guess we hadn't."

His mate was going to kill him.

After dinner everyone separated to their rooms saying they had an early start in the morning. Upstairs, Izzy watched as Cameron pointed to two doors. "Oron you're on the left, Izzy you're next door on the right. I'll let you figure out sleeping arrangements. Night." He quickly disappeared down the stairs.

She watched as Oron hesitated then spoke. "I'd prefer it if you slept with me."

"That's very bold of you."

"It doesn't have to be for sex," he said quickly. "I mean if you want to that'd be great, but what I meant was, I'd just like to spend the night with you and hold you, if you'll let me."

How could a man over seven feet tall be this adorable?

She held up the plastic shopping bag that held her one pair of pajamas and few toiletries she was able to salvage. "So just change into pjs, get comfy, maybe talk and sleep?"

He nodded emphatically. "Exactly."

"I can do that, though, don't hold anything I

do in my sleep against me during waking hours. I've never actually slept in a bed with someone so I may do weird shit I know nothing about," Izzy said, feeling nervous. What if she did something embarrassing like moan his name?

Oron placed his hand over his heart. "I swear to take your nighttime secrets with me to the grave and never speak of them to anyone."

"Even me," she insisted. "Especially me."

"You have my word."

"Okay. So…right." She turned the knob and stepped into the guest room. It was painted a pretty shade of blue with a very generic looking comforter on the bed. "It's nice." She went toward the door and opened it. "This is the bathroom; I'm going to change in here."

"One moment," Oron walked over and sniffed the bag. "It smells a bit smoky."

She felt her cheeks flush. "They're all I own right now,"

Oron slapped his forehead. "I am such an ass! You've adapted to our world so well that I completely forgot you lost your home in a fire today. I should have taken you shopping." He began to pace. "Maybe there's a store nearby that has women's clothing."

"It's okay, I can spray some bathroom air freshener on them," she held up the bag and winced. Then she'd smell like bar-b-que and hibiscus.

Oron snapped his fingers, then unzipped his overnight bag. He held up a long white tee shirt. "How about this?"

She put the bag on the desk and walked over.

She took the shirt from him and held it up. The hem was past her knees. "I think this will work." She brought it up to her nose, it didn't quite smell fresh, but held a unique fragrance that had her rubbing her face on it. "I love this smell, is it your detergent?"

Oron blushed to his hairline. "I uh, I've worn that one."

She grinned up at him. "I think I found one way our crystal edges fit. You smell amazing to me."

"I'm not a shifter, but the thought of you covered in my scent is hot," Oron said shifting his weight from one foot to the other, adjusting his pants.

"I'm on board with that, in fact, can I always sleep in your shirts? Used ones, but not like stinky ones."

"Gods woman!" he exhaled and closed the distance between them. Instead of leaning down to kiss her, he simply lifted her in his arms and wrapped her legs around his waist. She threw her arms around his neck and practically attacked his mouth.

She teased him back this time, loving the feel of his lips on hers. Everything about him tripped every trigger she didn't know she had. She leaned back enjoying the feel of his hands on her ass. "I could become addicted to your taste," she smiled impishly. "I wonder if all of you tastes as good as your lips."

Oron dropped his head back and breathed slowly through his nose. When he looked back at her she could see desire swimming in his eyes. "Let's do pajamas, possibly embarrassing sleep, then tomorrow night we'll be in the palace and not surrounded by roughneck Vanguard. You can find out exactly how I taste then."

She would have thought he didn't want her, but his eyes were smoldering and his hands were digging into her ass. "You don't want the men to hear me scream your name?" she teased.

His nostrils flared. "No. Not even a little. I am a jealous, possessive asshole and I want all of your screams to belong to me alone."

She shivered at the gruff tone of his voice. "I think that is sexy as hell."

"Yeah?" he asked.

"Oh yeah." She snuggled her face into the crook of his neck. There was the smell she was quickly beginning to crave.

He laughed and set her down rubbing his neck. "That tickled."

"Be right back," she said, before darting to the bathroom. Once inside she couldn't stop grinning.

She had found her soul mate, he was a fae prince and smelled like cinnamon rolls, spicy and sweet at the same time. She brought his shirt back up to her nose. She was in deep shit if his worn tee could have her legs shaking.

She quickly changed into her impromptu pajamas and washed up. She folded up her clothes and left them on the counter. They were her favorite jeans and sweater hoodie. They were probably the only things she owned that didn't smell like smoke.

Feeling nervous she opened the door to find that Oron had changed as well and looked to be wearing a shirt similar to the one he loaned her. He was sitting up in bed, leaning against the headboard. "I figure if I wear this one tonight, you can wear it tomorrow," he offered.

"You are wearing pants, right?" she eyed the covers. She couldn't tell what he was wearing from the waist down.

He nodded. "Promise you won't laugh?"

"Of course."

He stuck one leg out of the covers and she had to cover her mouth with her hand to hide the smile. He was wearing SpongeBob pajama pants. He cleared his throat. "I love this cartoon," he admitted.

"I do too. Maybe we can watch it together." She walked over to what she supposed was her side of the bed. She climbed in and was suddenly very conscious of how much she moved. Was she breathing too loud?

Beside her, he leaned over to the nightstand and turned off the light. "Temperature okay?"

"Yeah, good," she answered quickly.

"Izzy, baby, you need to relax or you'll never get to sleep."

"I'm relaxed."

"You're as stiff as a board and your hands are clenched."

"It's too quiet," she whispered.

"I actually agree with you on that. Hold on, I

have an idea." She felt him get out of bed. She peeked over and had to hold in her laughter. His pants were glow-in-the-dark.

When she saw many floating SpongeBobs heading her way, she knew that he was coming back to bed. He fiddled with something on the nightstand before soothing wave sounds began to play.

"Thank you," she said, finally feeling like she could relax. The wave sounds weren't just calming they also provided background noise so she didn't have to worry about him listening to her breathe.

"Am I weird for being freaked out because you can hear me?" she asked.

She almost jumped when his hand found hers. "I don't think so. Sleeping beside someone, being able to close your eyes and trust them while you sleep is very intimate, some think it's more intimate than sex."

"That's how it feels, like we skipped steps or something."

"I can always go next door Izzy, we don't have to do anything you aren't ready for, including just sleep."

"No, I want this, I do. But I may be weirded out for a bit, so don't think it's you."

"I won't."

They lay there in silence as her mind raced.

"Why don't you think about all the drinks you can make in the morning?" he suggested.

"That's actually a good idea."

She took a deep breath and closed her eyes.

The guys would have a drip coffee pot for sure, though Cameron did say they had an espresso machine last year when they wanted me to come out and make them coffee in the mornings. I wonder if they have any syrups?

She yawned and didn't even notice it when her breathing began to sync up with the circles Oron was lazily drawing in her hand.

Meryn is definitely an espresso woman. I bet Amelia is just whipped cream she's so friendly. I better not caffeinate Aiden too much; he has to handle a caffeinated Meryn.

I bet...Oron...likes something with fruit...

She was still thinking about different drinks when the day finally caught up with her.

The next morning Oron was still grinning at her.

"Shut up!" she said, throwing her towel at him.

"I didn't say a word," he protested, dodging the towel.

"I can see it on your face. Okay, how bad was I?"

"You told me not to tell."

"Ha! But now I know there's something, so you have to tell me."

She zipped up her sweater and put her damp hair up in a ponytail. "Well?" she demanded when he continued to smile at her.

"You are freaking adorable when you sleep. You murmur and talk and giggle to yourself. I couldn't get enough."

She exhaled. “That’s not so bad. What was I saying?”

He became thoughtful. “Something about drawing shots and sugar to vanilla ratios.”

“Oh, work stuff. I can live with that.”

He held out his elbow. She had no idea what he wanted so she bopped his elbow with her own. Chuckling he reached over and placed her hand on the crook of his arm. “May I escort you downstairs?”

She frowned up at him. “I was paying attention last night; I know the way.” He continued to smile at her. “This is a prince thing isn’t it?”

He nodded. “Sort of, more like an etiquette thing. If the men stand when we enter the room, don’t freak out, either smile or nod and take your seat. They will only sit when you do.”

“Dude.”

“You’ll be fine.”

Sure enough, the second they entered the dining room all the men rose. Feeling ten times more nervous she gave a smile and quickly sat down banging her knee on the underside of the table. “Son of a bitch!”

Oron reached over and helped her rub it. “Poor thing.”

“Coffee,” a voice croaked.

Izzy looked over to Meryn. “Has she had any yet?” She noticed that both Aiden and Darian looked a bit nervous as they kept sneaking glances at Meryn.

Aiden shook his head. “She wanted to wait for Coffee Goddess.”

"Yikes. Okay, Cam where's your machine?"

Ryuu entered from the kitchen. "If you would follow me, I have already set up the machine, ran a few test draws and put most of the supplies I could find on the counter."

Izzy stood quickly and followed Ryuu to the kitchen. "How bad is she without coffee?" she asked, as she began measuring out beans and prepping the cup.

"On a scale of Amelia to murder in the first degree… murder plus arson and torture," Ryuu admitted.

"Holy fuck! She needed this like an hour ago when her eyes first opened?"

He nodded solemnly. "Exactly."

Izzy never moved so fast in her life. After all, her mate was out there with the uncaffeinated terror.

She carried two steaming mochas into the dining room. "Here you go Meryn, try this." She placed both cups on the table and stepped back.

Looking like the girl from the Ring, Meryn lifted her head slowly swaying back and forth. She grabbed the coffee and took her first sip. "Ahhhhhh."

Aiden and Darian visibly relaxed in their chairs.

Izzy was about to return to the kitchen for the other drinks she prepped when Ryuu came in carrying them in on a tray. "You're amazing."

He simply smiled and nodded toward her seat. "Sit down, I'll be bringing breakfast in momentarily."

Liam wiped at a pretend tear. "We get a moment of pure heaven before both the squire and barista leave."

"Damn baby, what is this?" Oron asked, staring down into his glass.

"Thanks to your suggestion before bed last night, I mentally listed all the drinks I could make, I thought you'd like that one."

He took another long sip from the straw. "It's sweet, but bitter and is that raspberry?"

"It's a personal favorite of mine, a quad shot, white chocolate mocha, with raspberry syrup. Thank goodness Cam bought every coffee bar supply he could find, I had everything I needed to make it."

Oron whimpered as he continued to sip his drink. "It's so good."

All around the table, everyone enjoyed their specialty morning coffees. Izzy couldn't help but stare in fascination as Meryn slowly came online. By the end of her second drink she was upright and blinking. "Did she say quad shot?" she asked.

Serenity nodded. "Yes, she did, but you're limiting caffeine remember?"

Aiden's eyes darted to his mate quickly and instinctively he leaned back slightly. Meryn yawned and nodded. "But she said she could do a half-caf thing. If all four shots are halved, that's technically two drinks."

Serenity pointed to the mocha. "And you've already had some today."

Meryn glared at the sweet witch and Ryuu's

comparison to a murderer came to mind. "What if I just made a decaf version so you can taste it. That way later you won't waste your two drinks if you don't like it."

Aiden nodded. "That. Let's do that," he agreed quickly.

"*Denka*, as I have made pancakes and bacon for everyone, how about you try that drink after breakfast? It would give you something to sip on while we walk to the portal."

Meryn blinked. "Pancakes?"

"I know how much you like them," the squire admitted.

"Okay."

Aiden reached for his own mocha and took a drink as if it held liquor. The poor man knew precisely how nuts his mate was but loved her anyway.

Oron leaned down. "How did you know I loved raspberries?"

She rubbed noses with him. "I guess that's another way our crystals fit, they're my favorite too."

Across from them Cam leaned away from Darian. "Every morning?"

Darian looked over at Meryn to see if she heard, then nodded. "She threatened to castrate Colton the morning after she met Aiden," he whispered softly.

"He was being too loud," Meryn mumbled.

Cam turned to his commander. "Sir, you have my utmost respect."

Aiden nodded. "I appreciate that."

Ryuu came in a few minutes later and began to serve breakfast. After dousing her pancakes in syrup, she turned to her mate. "Why do we have to walk there? Isn't there a road?"

Oron shook his head. "Technically, we could open the portal in the living room and arrive directly in the queen's courtyard, but for Meryn's first visit to the fae city we decided to take the scenic route through the official city portal. It's a couple miles from here, so we'll have to walk."

Amelia waved her fork. "I can't wait. I haven't seen the official entrance yet."

Liam leaned forward. "Izzy, we found an extra backpack no one was using if you want to transfer your stuff, so it's easier to carry."

Izzy felt a wave of relief. "Thanks, I don't have much so it all should fit."

She felt her mate stiffen beside her. "Once we're in Éire Danu, I promise to take you shopping."

Amelia gasped. "That's right, you lost your home, your things." Her eyes filled in sympathy. "How could we forget?"

Izzy waved off her concern. "By making sure I didn't lose my mind yesterday when I found out about shifters and vampires and mates and stuff. Besides, I've spent my entire adult life broke, I really didn't lose that much."

Amelia turned to her mate and Darian nodded before turning to her. "Then you must allow us to spoil you a bit. It's not every day I get a baby sister."

Meryn turned to Aiden. "She gets whatever

she wants. She's Coffee Goddess." Aiden nodded. "Of course, baby."

Izzy stared down into her lap. "I don't need much."

"You need a phone, a laptop, a Kindle and definitely some more hoodies," Meryn said, ticking off items on her fingers.

Amelia nodded. "And makeup! And new outfits. I wish Beth were here, she's better at the clothes thing."

Cameron cleared his throat. "Me and the guys will get her tech gear since she's our favorite coffee girl. We'll forward it along to Éire Danu; they don't have much of a selection when it comes to human technology."

Oron reached over and took her hand. Slowly he began rubbing circles on the top of her hand with his thumb. "I'll pick out the clothes," he said. When she looked up, he winked at her. "Eau de Oron," she said giggling.

Aiden smiled. "Glad that's settled. After breakfast, we really should get going."

Meryn nodded absently, then looked over at Oron narrowing her eyes. "Did he say *walk* a couple *miles*?"

Izzy sipped her mocha. This should be fun.

CHAPTER FIVE

"I'VE CHANGED MY MIND! I lurves unofficial portals! I lurves, lurves, lurves them!" Meryn complained as they walked in the beautiful spring-like weather.

"Just a bit further baby, I promise," Aiden said a concerned expression on his face.

Serenity shook her head. "The walking is good for you."

Meryn glared at her evilly. "Meryn two-point-oh doesn't like exercise or sweating."

Izzy kinda agreed with Meryn. The weather was on the cool side, but the sun was warm and they had been walking for at least half an hour. She wasn't that much taller than Meryn and her legs were getting a workout trying to match stride with her seven-plus foot tall mate.

"Okay, break time," Izzy said, dropping her backpack.

Aiden turned to her. "Seriously?"

Meryn exhaled. "Thank god." She lifted her to-go sippy cup and began sucking down her de-caf treat.

"Yes, seriously, Bigfoot! Meryn and I are having to practically run to keep up with you giants. Have mercy on us short folk," Izzy pointed down to her legs. "I can only go so fast."

Aiden looked down at his mate. "I am so sorry baby, I wasn't thinking."

Meryn waved off his apologies. "Just give me a minute to catch my breath."

Oron picked up her backpack. "Commander."

Aiden looked over at him. Grinning Oron swept her up in his arms. "We won't have to worry about their little legs if we carry them."

Aiden brightened. "Good man!" Aiden scooped Meryn up in his arms and they resumed their stroll.

Meryn peeked out over her mate's shoulder. "I could get used to this. Giddy up, mannequin!"

Aiden simply leaned down and began to nip and nuzzle at Meryn's neck making her laugh.

Izzy yawned and snuggled into Oron's chest. She had the best mate ever.

After about another twenty minutes, Oron kissed her forehead. "We're here." She opened her eyes as he was setting her down.

Izzy looked around, expecting to see golden gates or something. There was nothing there. "Ummm?"

Oron pointed to where Darian stood holding his hands in front of him. Seconds later, a broad glowing gate appeared anchored between the two large white marble bases. He turned back to them. "Welcome to the official entrance to Éire Danu."

Oron took her hand. "Ready to see the land of the fae?"

"Absolutely!" They were about to step forward when the air around Meryn shimmered and she gave a startled yelp before her clothes morphed into a set of long dress robes in brilliant shades of gold.

Aiden looked down at her. "I'm proud of you baby. I didn't think you'd care about first impressions."

Meryn scowled. "I don't. Evidently, my gown does."

Ryuu smiled. "Well, if we're going to be fancy." He closed his eyes and his clothes also changed. He now wore formal Japanese attire.

Meryn's mouth dropped. "I didn't know you could do that! Do you have a special gown too?"

He gave her a droll look. "Of course not. Water magic is very pliable and can do many things. Did you never wonder how I got my western clothes?"

She shrugged. "I don't even think about where breakfast comes from Ryuu."

He sighed. "True."

Darian examined the hems of Meryn's sleeve and whistled. "The gown is pulling out all the stops. These are royal emblems."

Oron pulled her forward to examine the gorgeous robes. "The gown must absolutely love you," he teased.

"At least it's comfy. I prefer my sweatpants though," Meryn confessed.

Aiden straightened his uniform jacket and held

out an elbow to Meryn. “Will you allow this humble warrior to escort you into the fae city?”

Meryn placed her hand on his arm. “I’ll even let you escort me to the bedroom later,” she said, winking up at him.

“How’d she do that?” Izzy asked.

Darian turned to her. “She is wearing the Gown of Éire Danu, a famous fae relic. It was gifted to her by the previous owner.”

Around them, everyone straightened their clothes, wanting to make a good impression. Izzy looked down at her top. “Had I known this outfit would be the only one that didn’t reek of smoke I would have worn something nicer to work yesterday.”

Oron squeezed her hand. “Look at it this way, we get to go shopping together and explore the city. I’ve been a warrior for a long, long time with minimal needs to shop for. I am looking forward to finding things for you.”

Izzy’s heart melted. He even made it seem like buying her things would be a huge favor to him. “Just not sleep shirts,” she whispered blushing.

He leaned down and placed a single kiss on the side of her neck. “Never.”

“After you brother,” Darian said, pointing to the arch.

Oron nodded and started the procession into the city. Izzy walked through the portal and gasped when they emerged into a world of light. She blinked repeatedly. Everything was so bright.

“Bright light! Bright light!” Meryn mumbled

behind her. She giggled at the movie reference.

Slowly their eyes adjusted. When she looked around, she felt her excitement exploding. A bustling city unfolded before them. Under their feet, the expansive road was comprised of cream stones with gold sand between them, making the entire path sparkle. As her gaze moved up, the white and ecru buildings on either side of the road caught her attention. While most resembled Victorian brownstones, there were some stand-alone homes, however, all of them had what looked to be living trees growing through them. Above the roof line, a living canopy swayed in the breeze. Windows were framed by branches and birds sang their hearts out everywhere.

Standing off to one side, with a face like a thundercloud, a fae watched their group approach. When he began striding over to them, Izzy squeezed Oron's hand. He looked down at her and shook his head slightly.

The angry fae walked past them to grab Serenity by the shoulders. "I told you to be careful!" he shouted, giving her a rattling shake.

Micah growled and was about to pull Serenity back when she began to weep and threw herself into the fae's arms. Micah's mouth dropped. Oron took pity on the flirty witch. "Micah Sageson, meet Zachari Ri'Eldan, Serenity's older brother."

"I'm so sorry, Zach! I had to do it, it was the only way to save the children," Serenity said brokenly, hiccuping between each word.

Zachari pulled her close and squeezed her in a bear hug, his face a mask of pain. "I felt you die," he whispered. "The queen had to give me light so I did not fade from the pain of losing my baby sister." Serenity simply broke down into sobs at his confession.

Micah stepped up to the brother and sister and began to rub Serenity's back soothingly. "She is well, brother of mine. I would never let my one and only leave this world without me."

Zachari lifted his head from Serenity's shoulder. "That doesn't comfort me one bit since you stupidly died alongside her."

Micah grimaced. "I would say we're sorry, but I don't think either of us is, not really. Had Serenity not done what she did, a lot of people would have died, including children. It was scary and I hope we never get that close to the goddess again until it's our time, but I can't say we wouldn't do it again."

Serenity lifted her tear-streaked face and gasped loudly. With trembling fingers, she touched the white blond streak at his temple. "I didn't know."

Zach took a deep, shuddering breath. "Next time let me help. I was the one who opened the godsdamn portal Seri, *I* was the one who let you go to Noctem Falls. Never again will I suffer from the helplessness that overwhelmed me when I felt your soul slip away. We came into this world together; I don't know how to be in it without you."

"I promise I will never try that level of magic

alone again!" Serenity vowed, sagging against her older brother.

Zachari kissed her forehead. "Thank you." He grinned down at her. "Wait until you see mother and father."

Serenity's eyes widened and she stepped back to face Micah. "We have to see my parents the second after we've met with the queen."

Micah reclaimed his mate by pulling her into his arms. "Of course, my one and only, whatever you need." He looked up at his new brother. "Thank you for always protecting her. She's told me many stories where you defended her."

Zachari let out a long breath. "It wasn't easy, she's very contrary."

Serenity wiped at her eyes and elbowed her brother in the stomach. "Am not."

Zachari simply stared at her. "Really?"

"Zach, let me introduce my friends." Serenity turned to where they stood and started introductions. When she was done, he was smiling at everyone. "Call me Zach. Zachari makes me feel like I'm still five."

Darian walked over and they clasped forearms. "Can I assume you're our escort?"

Zach nodded. "I may have accidentally bespelled the door to Aeson's bedroom this morning so that I could be the first to see Serenity."

Serenity sighed. "You only learn just enough magic to make mischief," she complained.

Zach wagged a finger at her. "And satisfy my lady friends."

Serenity wrinkled her nose. "Never mind that."

Zach walked over and clasped arms with Oron. "Welcome home."

Oron smiled and wrapped an arm around her shoulders. "May I present my mate, Isabelle Campbell."

Serenity's brother smiled wide. "That's amazing news! The queen is going to be over the moon." He looked back at the city. "Let's show off our beautiful city so that we can head to the palace and meet with the queen."

"Great idea," both Darian and Oron said in unison.

Darian and Amelia took the lead followed by Aiden, Meryn and Ryuu. Zach looped his arm through Serenity's on one side, and Micah claimed the other. Together they slowly began walking toward the city center leaving her and Oron to bring up the rear.

As they walked, Izzy began to notice that everyone was greeted warmly, even the visiting Aiden and Meryn, but no one greeted Oron. They moved in silence down the street.

Soon, residential buildings were replaced by commercial ones. Vendors and craftsmen of all kinds filled the white and golden street. Quietly Oron would point out individual shops. All sorts of wares were displayed beautifully on marble pedestals under bleached linen awnings. Every kind of craft she could imagine lined both sides of the wide pedestrian walkway. Her eyes flew from the delicate glass figures to the intricate metalworks. She gasped at the warm wood pieces and the elegant ceramics homewares. Oron lifted their clasped hands, pointing to a brilliantly colored curtained entrance. "I'd like to take you there later. The tailor creates magicked clothing that stays pressed and clean. You'd never have to worry about smoky clothes again."

She looked into the shop's window as they passed and felt her mouth drop. The robes on display were nothing short of works of art. "Oron, I can't afford this," she whispered.

He grinned down at her. "But I can."

In front of them she noticed Meryn pointing and followed her line of sight. "What are those?"

Oron looked over. "Those are our version of streetlamps. Amber stones have been bespelled to flicker like fireflies. They are truly exquisite during the dim."

When Oron chuckled beside her, she looked up. "What?"

He nodded over to the stately looking wall coming up on their right. "That's the wall I pinned Molvan to when Darian was little."

She eyed the wall smiling at the memory of the story. The interspacing segments in front of the long, imposing wall, created immaculately designed flowerbeds that acted as a fragrant barrier between the street and the wall. At first, she thought her eyes were playing tricks on her, but soon she figured out that the slight movements amongst the flowers and bushes were sprites frolicking.

"Oron," she whispered under her breath.

Without looking, he simply nodded. "I know."

All too quickly, their magical stroll was over, and they now stood outside of some imposing gates. Oron led her to the front of their group to stand with Darian.

A fae in burnished armor stepped forward. "Prince Darian, hail and well met."

Darian nodded. "Malcom, I have the honor of escorting the Unit Commander, Aiden McKenzie, and company to meet with the queen."

Malcom gave one nod and eyed their group. When he saw her; he frowned. "That woman was not on the expected guest list."

Oron stepped in front of her. "She is Isabelle Campbell and my mate."

Malcom shook his head. "She's not on the approved list."

Izzy watched as Oron straightened. He simply led her past the guard and shoved the gate open. "Take it up with the queen," he said flippantly.

Behind them, she heard him stuttering. "Prince Darian," he began.

"You heard him, take it up with the queen," Darian answered.

When Izzy peeked back everyone was following behind them. Meryn met her eye. "Bzzzzz," she whispered.

Izzy nodded. "Totally."

Aiden looked down at his mate fear in his eyes. "Meryn, no."

Meryn smiled up at him. "What?"

Aiden looked over at Darian. "How far is it to the queen's chambers?" he asked desperately.

Darian grinned down at Meryn. "Not far. But just so you know, Malcom almost decapitated me during our last visit, so if Meryn is feeling buzzy, you won't hear a word of censure from me."

Amelia nodded. "Damn, right."

Aiden's shoulders sagged. "As long as we're not kicked out of the city; I guess it's okay."

Oron clapped his commander on the back. "No worries, sir, the queen already adores Meryn, so it's highly unlikely she'll kick us out."

"There you are! We were expecting you this morning." A tall fae female walked up to them. "Did you forget how to tell time living amongst the shifters?" she asked.

"Wonderful to see you again, Portia. Everyone, this is Portia Kilardin, the amazing palace manager I was telling you about." Darian said, greeting the extremely rigid woman and introducing her to the group.

She eyed his uniform and sighed before turning to look at the group. When she got to Meryn, she raised an eyebrow. "At least she's dressed appropriately, from the stories I heard I half expected to see her in demolition gear."

Meryn's expression flattened. Suddenly the air around her shimmered again and she was now sporting Pikachu pajamas. Izzy barely managed to suppress her giggles.

Portia's eyebrows raised to her hairline. "A sense of humor I see." She turned her attention to Izzy and Oron. "I hear congratulations are in order." She looked her up and down. "I understand you have lost most of your belongings." She unrolled a scroll. "I took the liberty of arranging for our local tailors to come to the palace to fit you for proper attire. Cord will let you know the times." She rolled up the scroll and turned on her heel. "If you all would please follow me."

Meryn sighed, and her clothes went back to her golden robes. "She's like a squire, and Beth, and Kari rolled into one."

"Portia, does mother know?" Oron asked.

Portia turned back to them and her icy demeanor melted a bit. "No Oron, I made sure that no one spoiled your surprise."

Izzy stared. The stuffy older fae liked her mate, maybe he had more allies than he thought. She brought his hand up and kissed it. He looked down at her surprised before returning the gesture.

If she thought that the fae city was impressive, she was sorely mistaken. The elegant cream and gold streets they walked seemed dull when compared to the understated, yet detailed splendor that was the royal palace.

It was golden without being gaudy. The hallway where they strolled opened on one side to a magical garden. As they walked, they passed stately marble pillars where the sprites waved and played peek-a-boo. Izzy was suddenly overwhelmed and felt tears sting her eyes. She was walking in a place more dazzling than her dreams.

Oron looked down and was smiling until he

saw her expression. He stopped and pulled her off to one side. Darian, seeing his brother stop halted their progress. Oron waved him on. Darian nodded, and the group continued.

He stared down at her for a moment before she saw a look of understanding on his face. He pulled her close for a hug. "It's beautiful, isn't it?" he asked quietly.

She sniffled and nodded. "I can't believe something like this is real and I'm lucky enough to see it."

Oron rubbed his cheek along the top of her head. "When I followed Darian to Lycaonia, it almost hurt to live there. Everything seemed dull, lifeless, and dark in comparison. It took nearly a decade for me to adjust to living outside of Éire Danu. How the warriors in Noctem Falls don't lose their minds is a miracle to me." He pulled back and looked down at her. "Never lose that sense of wonder and amazement, my love. It doesn't make you silly or weak, it proves you are alive."

She wiped her cheeks. "Come on, your mom is waiting."

His eyes lit up. "You're right. Let's go."

They managed to catch up to the group as Portia was rapping on a massive wooden door. She turned back to them. "The Queen insisted on meeting with everyone in her chambers as opposed to the throne room."

The door swung open and a scowling fae stood in the doorway. "That's because it's family visiting Portia." He looked at them and stepped to one side. "You may want to hurry along, Aleks is wearing a hole in the floor."

"I am not Brennus! Stop telling them that!" An irate female voice demanded from behind him. Brennus gave them a slow wink as Darian and Oron began to chuckle.

Darian stepped through the door leading them in. "It's wonderful to see you again, mother."

Once inside, Izzy could see that although the term private chambers had been used, it was more like a large family room. An opulent family room, but a family room none the less.

Instead of hard wooden chairs, there were plush looking sofas and loungers. Off to one side of the room, a round table and chairs sported linen napkins and fresh flowers, that softly beckoned them to sit and enjoy a brunch.

"Oron!" Izzy barely had time to step to one side before a tall woman practically plowed into her mate.

"Mother," Oron said softly, wrapping his arms around her.

This was his mother? She was gorgeous and didn't look a day over twenty-five.

Oron chuckled and stepped back, putting his mother at arm's reach. "Mother, I have someone I want you to meet." He snaked his hand around and pulled her into the nook of his arm. "This is my mate, Isabelle Campbell.

The ethereal looking woman in front of her suddenly burst into tears shocking both her sons and her own mate. "Oh! I prayed you would find mate soon, my little warrior! I hated the idea of you being alone."

Oron looked down at her, a panicked look on his face. She gently pushed him toward the overwhelmed queen. Oron took his cue from her and once again held his mother. With his free hand, he accepted the handkerchief Portia held out to him and dabbed at his mother's cheeks. "This is a happy occasion, so no more tears," he insisted. He beckoned Meryn to step closer. "Besides, I brought the little human you've been enamored with."

The queen sniffed and took the handkerchief from him to wipe her eyes. She looked over and saw Meryn hesitantly edging closer. "Oh, my dear, I am so sorry to go all to pieces on you." She held out her hand. "Let me see you." Meryn blushed and took the queen's hand. The queen looked her up and down. Izzy noticed that her eyes lingered on Meryn's cuffs. She tilted her head. "If I didn't know better, I would say that the gown is showing you off. It feels like it is having fun."

Meryn brightened. "I taught her about graphic tee shirts. I think I may have given her an addiction."

The queen nodded. "I may have to have the craftsmen start on another gown to give to Lady Fairfax. I'm certain that this particular gown won't work for anyone but you. It's almost as if you've imprinted on it."

Meryn's eyes widened. "I get to keep her?"

The queen nodded. "I think that may be best."

Meryn threw her arm in the air. "Yes!" She grinned then spotted Izzy. "Izzy, my Coffee Goddess, needs some clothes too. All her stuff burned up."

The queen's head whipped around to her. "Are you okay?" She hurried over and started to inspect her.

Izzy squirmed. "I'm good, but I lost most of my stuff, and what I do have smells like smoke."

"Cord!" the queen bellowed.

"I am right here, Aleks," a tenor voice said. Izzy looked at the man walking up to them. Unlike Darian and Oron, who had golden blond hair, Cord's was a fiery, warm hue. The undertones leaned more toward brown than blond, and he wore it well. He saw her staring and smiled. "Welcome to the family," he said, before placing his hand on his heart and giving a slight bow. "My name is Cord Danual, I am the squire for Her Majesty. If there is anything at all you need, please do not hesitate to let me know. Portia has already arranged for the city's tailors to come to the palace for your fittings."

The queen's eyes narrowed. "That means you knew he had a mate."

Cord simply smiled, then turned to the group. "Who would like some tea?" he asked as he began ushering them toward the dining table.

They walked over and Meryn turned to Cord. "Umm, your table is too small."

Izzy nodded. It looked like it was meant more for a small family than entertaining a large group.

Cord winked at Meryn then rapped on the table twice. Before their very eyes, the table expanded, and chairs popped up out of nowhere. The place settings changed from the elegant gold linen to a more serviceable cream.

"Whoa," both she and Meryn said in unison.

Cord chuckled. "I still have few tricks up my sleeves. Now, I got quite the earful from Sebastian on how you should be fed," he rolled his eyes. "I think he forgot I was a squire before he drew his first breath, but he was so worried for you, I humored him." He steered the little Meryn over to a chair. "I heard that you adore Sebastian's Vanilla parfait…"

"Magic Pudding," Meryn corrected.

Cord smiled. "Of course, Magic Pudding. Would you be interested in trying my cinnamon scones with clotted cream?"

Meryn licked her lips. "Now, you're speaking my language."

Cord turned to Ryuu. "I could show you the kitchen so you can get acclimated to the layout for your stay," he offered.

Ryuu gave a half bow. "That would be most appreciated."

Once everyone was seated, the squires headed toward the kitchen to prepare tea.

Oron took her hand under the table. She was clenching her fists again. "Mother, maybe some introductions are in order? Meryn may recognize Doran and Celyn, but my mate is new to our world."

Brennus stood. "Allow me, my dear." The

queen just smiled and he continued. "I know it may be somewhat hard to believe due to her unusual display of hysterics, but this amazing woman to my right is Queen Aleksandra…ow!" He scowled down at his mate.

She gave him a flat look. "Hysterics?"

He kept going. "The two gentlemen to my left are my younger brothers Doran Ri'Eirlea and Celyn Vi'Ailean. Doran serves in Her Majesty's Personal Guard, and Celyn is the fae Elder in Lycaonia." He barely paused before going on. "The stunning woman sitting next to Celyn has the unfortunate luck to be my brother's mate, her name is Vivian. Evidently, when they learned you were visiting, they insisted on coming as well."

"I'll give you unfortunate…" Celyn muttered.

Vivian laughed. "When I heard that Celyn was returning to Éire Danu to visit with Meryn, of course, I had to tag along." She looked over and beamed at her brightly. "And I wanted to see Felix again."

Izzy nodded absently. "I can understand that; he is freaking adorable."

The queen looked at her. "You can see him?"

Izzy froze. Had she said something wrong?

Oron squeezed her hand. "Yes, my mate can see sprites as well."

The queen puffed out her chest. "Both of my son's mates can see sprites! That will go a long way to still wagging tongues."

Meryn held up a long, skinny stick. "Let them talk smack, I'll shock the shit outta them."

Amelia and Izzy giggled and said "Bzzzzz" at the same time.

The queen looked absolutely shocked but surprised them all by bursting out into laughter. "It is going to be so much fun having you girls visit."

Aiden looked a bit ill, and Darian stared down at his mate a worried expression on his face.

Izzy snuck a look up at Oron to find he was simply grinning. "What? I want to have fun too," he admitted.

Micah chuckled. "Game on."

"Gods above give me strength," Aiden muttered.

CHAPTER SIX

ONCE EVERYONE WAS INTRODUCED, PORTIA left to tend to the day to day activities of the palace. As the door was shutting Ryuu and Cord returned ready to serve tea. The queen lifted her cup. "So, Izzy, Meryn, what do you think of the city so far?"

Izzy exchanged glances with Meryn and spoke first. "I think it's magical. I can't wait to go exploring."

Meryn nodded. "After my coffee though," she eyed her.

Izzy couldn't help but laugh. "Of course."

Serenity coughed into her balled up fist. "Limits, Meryn."

Meryn turned back to Ryuu and held up her hand. He walked behind her and gently took her wrist between his thumb and forefinger as if he were taking her pulse. "Do you have a tattoo?" Izzy asked, eyeing the blue dragon.

Meryn bobbed her head. "It's Ryuu's turkey popper for me."

Ryuu released her wrist. "Have milk instead

of tea, then you can have coffee later for exploring."

Meryn nodded and held out her cup. Ryuu walked over to the serving cart and retrieved the glass carafe of milk.

Izzy turned to Oron. "Turkey popper?"

The queen also looked bewildered. "Yes, please explain."

Oron pointed to Ryuu. "Ryuu gave Meryn that tattoo. From my understanding, it helps him gauge her emotions and tracks her health."

The queen became thoughtful. "I do not believe I would like that." She looked back at her own squire. "Though I've never had to worry about it, Cord is practically a mind reader, he's always anticipating me."

Meryn shrugged. "I have the emotional IQ of a termite, so it was kinda needed to keep me fed and alive."

Ryuu exhaled. "You have no idea."

Cord clapped him on the back. "She's glowing, and that babe looks to be thriving, so I would say you're doing a fine job."

Ryuu's cheeks tinted slightly. "She's really not that much trouble."

Meryn nodded again. "Especially now that I'm wearing Dani all the time, he doesn't even have to remind me to change clothes anymore."

Vivian giggled behind her napkin. "I have so missed you in Lycaonia."

Meryn grinned evilly. "How's Bow-wow Bowers?"

Vivian, who had just taken a sip of tea sputtered in her cup causing tea to splash up on her nose. Celyn chuckled as his mate wiped at her face with a napkin. "Meryn! You can't do that to me while I'm drinking."

Meryn shrugged. "So, did she get over the whole vaginoplasty thing?"

The queen gasped. "That was you?" she demanded.

"I neither confirm nor deny those allegations."

Even Law looked shocked. "That column has to be one of the best-kept secrets in our world, how on earth did you influence it?"

Meryn wiggled her fingers at him. "Maaagg-giiccc."

Izzy leaned forward. "What did you allegedly do?" she asked, dying to know.

Meryn gave a recap of what happened in something she called the Sewing Circle from Hell a few months ago. Izzy held up her hand. "They have a column called 'Dear Gentle Reader', like something from a Regency novel?"

Amelia smiled. "Yes, and if Meryn did what Daphne is accusing her of, then it was an ingenious power play, and it effectively shut down Daphne's barrage of hateful gossip."

Meryn poked her big sister-cousin in the arm. "Says the woman who nearly choked Daphne out."

Darian's eyes widened. "That's what happened! You said you may have to go to tribunal for an attack on a matriarch, but you never said you choked her out."

Amelia shrugged. "She was threatening my baby sister-cousin. Ryuu stopped me before she passed out," she explained.

Brennus leaned back in his chair. "I'm not sure we're ready for three spunky little ladies like this."

The queen patted his leg. "We'll be just fine. I think our people need a little shaking up and who better to do it than my new daughters."

Meryn blinked. "Me too?"

The queen nodded. "Amelia and Isabelle are my daughters given to me by Fate when they mated my sons, but I have a feeling you're more a daughter of the heart."

Meryn kinda slumped forward. "But I don't want to embarrass you," she whispered.

The queen sat up straighter. "Meryn, there is nothing you can do that would make me too embarrassed to love you."

Aiden bumped her shoulder gently with his own. "That goes triple for me, baby."

Law grinned. "Me too, but I wouldn't test the limits on that pipsqueak." She glared at him, and he held his hands up. "I've not only known you the longest, but I've also worked with you. You can be downright destructive and scary when you put your mind to it."

Aiden stared at Law with a thoughtful expression on his face. "You have known her longer."

Law nodded. "Yes, though we were out of touch the past year or so."

The queen brightened. "What did you do?"

Law froze, and he shot a desperate look

to Meryn, but it was too late she was already answering.

"We killed people." Her declaration seemed to echo through the room.

Amelia looked around. "But they were all bad," she added quickly.

Brennus tapped his chin. "Maybe an escort while they're here."

Meryn waved off his concern. "I got this. I can be good when I wanna."

Aiden pinched his nose. "But the problem is that you can go from wanting to be good to not caring if the city burns in about two seconds."

"True," Meryn admitted as she nodded.

Ryuu took pity on the consort. "I will be with her at all times and will endeavor to keep the chaos and mayhem to a minimum."

Aiden glowered at the squire. "That is not reassuring, you tend to be in the thick of it right alongside her."

Ryuu gave a lazy shrug. "I try not to stifle her creativity."

"It needs to be stifled sometimes," Aiden countered.

"I am right here you two," Meryn said, then turned to the queen. "So what do I call you?"

"What do you want to call me?" the queen asked.

"Aleks, Aleksandra has too many syllables," Meryn said, without hesitation.

The queen beamed at her. "That's perfect. I am so going to spoil you. Magnus can't have all the fun."

Aiden looked spooked. "We need to start putting parameters on these declarations. Magnus already promised her a damn flamethrower."

The queen's eyes danced with laughter. "That sounds fun!"

Izzy hesitated. "Can I call you Mama?"

Instantly the queen's eyes filled with tears. "Of course, you can." She turned to Amelia. "That goes for you too!"

Amelia leaned over to rest her head on her mate's shoulder. "I would like that."

Brennus turned to Izzy then Amelia practically pouting. "Then I insist on being Papa."

Izzy felt her heart turn over. It had been years since she lost her parents, she honestly didn't think she'd ever have another mama or papa again.

"Cord feels like a Sebastian, like a super mom," Meryn declared.

Behind them, they heard a loud crash. "Oh my, I'm sorry," Cord said, sounding flustered. Meryn turned in her chair. "I meant that in a good way," she explained.

Cord's eyes welled up with tears. "Now I understand why Sebastian fussed over you so much. He must have fallen head over heels in love with you and I have a feeling I won't be far behind him."

Meryn scrunched up her face. "But like, no sex, right? That's for Aiden."

Cord gave a deep belly laugh. "By all means, keep that for your mate, but allow us poor squires to dote on you."

Meryn rubbed her hands together. "Yummy squire food."

Ryuu sighed. "You can't be hungry already."

"I think the cinnamon woke my stomach up," she replied, then looked at him eyes wide.

Ryuu nodded. "I already spoke to Cord in the kitchen, we have arranged for a large shipment of fae cinnamon to be sent to Sebastian this afternoon."

Meryn sat back. "Thank you."

The queen sipped her tea. "I heard about your pudding addiction. Thanks to you, I hear we're getting shipments from Noctem Falls."

Meryn blushed. "Sebastian said he was going to send me pudding and meat kebobs."

Cord served his queen first then Brennus before moving around the table. Izzy smiled up at him as he placed what looked like two biscuits in front of her with some sour cream.

When he placed the plate in front of Meryn, Izzy watched in amusement as she tilted her head a bit. "What's this?"

Cord cleared his throat. "That would be the cinnamon scones and clotted cream I was telling you about."

Meryn poked at the scone with a finger before picking it up and dunking it in the cream like a chicken nugget into bar-b-que sauce. Everyone stared as Meryn took her first bite. Her eyes widened. "Oh my God," she whispered reverently. She picked up the small bowl of cream and began a rapid-fire dunking and chewing process.

Aiden who had delicately cut his scone in half

and spread the cream diligently eyed his mate in envy.

The queen chortled and picked up her scone with her fingers. "Might as well join her Commander. It looks like she found the quickest and easiest way to inhale Cord's amazing scones."

Aiden sighed in relief and picked up his treat before beginning his own dunking process.

Brennus scowled down at his plate. "Why have I never thought to do that?"

Law shook his head. "Meryn is a genius at seeing things clearly."

Meryn stopped mid-chew. "Whaaa?" she asked, her mouth full.

Izzy realized that it never dawned on Meryn that she wasn't supposed to eat it with her fingers.

Amelia patted her arm. "Nothing darling, just eat your scones."

Meryn shrugged and continued chewing.

"While you eat, I can tell you a bit about the city if you wish," the queen offered. Meryn nodded and kept eating.

"You probably saw some of the residential and commercial parts of the city when you came in through the main gate."

Izzy nodded. "The shops looked amazing."

The queen sat up a bit straighter. "They work so hard to keep the city gleaming." She held up her hands, making a triangle. "The widest part is where most of the citizens live. The middle portion of the city is where all the vendors, shops, guilds, and temples are. The point is the palace."

"Now the palace is surrounded on all sides by the Royal Garden, the only exception is the gate to enter and leave. In the Royal Garden, we have a large courtyard..."

"Do y'all have Founding Family peeps like the other cities?" Meryn asked interrupting.

The queen nodded. "Yes, they reside here on the palace grounds." She pointed behind her. "The Royal Palace acts as the anchor. Along each side opening up to the courtyard, there are six houses on the left and six houses on the right. The four closest to the palace belong to our Founding Families, the next four to our Noble Families and the last set of four to our Warrior houses."

"What are Warrior Houses? We don't have those in Lycaonia and they didn't have them in Noctem Falls either," Meryn asked.

"We've always had them," Brennus said, answering Meryn. "They are the four houses that produce the most sons who end up serving as unit warriors. Because of this, these four families have dedicated their lines to taking care of the warriors that not only defend Éire Danu, but also serve in the other pillar cities."

Amelia leaned forward. "How do you mean?"

Brennus scratched his chin then eyed Aiden. "I think in Lycaonia Byron calls the retired warriors the Old Guard. Our Old Guard is heavily involved with the warrior houses. House Erlondon acts as a training ground for our children who are too young to train as cadets. The older warriors love instructing the children and getting them started on the exercises to strengthen their bodies for future drills. House Aindin is comprised mostly of retired warriors who have taken up weaponry. They are learning to incorporate fae magic into human weapons."

Meryn turned to Aiden. "I need a super-weapon."

Aiden shook his head. "No."

"But…"

"No! You already cause enough trouble with your damn screwdriver thingy."

Meryn turned to Brennus with puppy dog eyes. "Brennus, can't I please have a weapon to keep me and the baby safe?" she asked pitifully.

The queen's consort practically melted. "Aiden, why don't you want that child to have a weapon?"

Aiden gave Brennus a flat look. "Because she accidentally shot me, she took out ferals with a sniper rifle, and she loves tasing my warriors. I'd be terrified to see what she'd do with a fae enhanced weapon."

Brennus grinned broadly. "She sounds adorable."

Ryuu preened. "I think so."

Meryn pointed to Brennus. "See, he thinks I should have one."

"No. Ask for a self-cleaning diaper."

Meryn opened her mouth, paused then turned to Brennus. "Is that a thing?"

Brennus looked confused. "Of course."

"Can I have one for the baby for when I'm watching over them?" Meryn asked.

"Hey!" Aiden protested.

She glared up at him. "You get to play in shit for cock-blocking my weapon upgrade."

"Meryn!"

"As you were saying," Meryn said sweetly.

Aiden stared down at his mate in shock as Brennus continued. "House Orthames and House Liordon help provide support to our warrior estates in the form of food preparation and house care."

Izzy was impressed, it sounded as if the city really looked after their warriors. "We're moving to Lycaonia, right?" she asked Oron.

He looked down and nodded. "Yes, I serve in the Gamma Unit."

"Could we start those warrior house things? I like the idea of y'all getting more support."

Oron's heart was in his eyes as he looked down at her. "What? You're my mate I want to make sure you're fed and are taken care of."

"But not by you?" Amelia asked.

Izzy winced. "I'm not the best person to trust in the kitchen or garage or workshop…" she sighed. "Accidents happen, buttons are my weakness."

"Sounds like Beth," Amelia said, eyes wide.

"Yeah, but hers is because of a death curse, Izzy is just curious," Meryn clarified.

"I can't help it! It's like a sickness, I have to see if stuff explodes or turns color or if alarms sound… that sort of thing."

Aiden stood, reaching for his phone; he walked away as he brought it up to his ear. "Hey Sascha, you know that plan for the biometric lock on the armory?" he walked away from the table toward the windows.

Izzy looked at Meryn. "There's an armory?"

"Just, no!" Aiden shouted his hand over the phone.

Meryn wagged her eyebrows. "Oh yeah."

Micah sat back, his hands curled around his teacup. "I have never been more grateful to live in Noctem Falls."

Darian looked over to his brother. "We're gonna die, aren't we?"

Brennus clapped him on the back. "Buck up son. I'm sure six units of warriors can handle a few innocent women."

Law tapped his chin. "I wonder if those fae warriors from Aindin could create a kinetic energy absorbing suit, you know, just in case."

Darian shuddered then turned to Meryn. "No bombs, please."

Meryn eyed him shrewdly. "Only if you promise me a fae weapon."

Darian eyed Aiden whose back was turned. "Deal," he whispered.

"Yes!" Meryn hissed quietly.

"Meryn, no weapons testing near coffee facilities," Izzy said quickly.

"Duh! Nothing can happen to muh coffee. Speaking of which," she got on her knees in her chair and turned to face her squire. "Did you order our supplies?"

"As they are vital for everyone's continued good health, of course, I ordered your coffee supplies. I'm having everything delivered to Marius and he is forwarding on to Éire Danu. As time was of the essence, I did not want to wait until I could ascertain a shipping process."

Meryn sat back down and looked at Izzy. "Coffee Goddess will get her new altar supplies soon, then I, the High Priestess of Merytopia, will commence in my new morning rituals."

The queen covered her face with her hands as her body shook. When she removed them she was wiping away tears of laughter. "She is nuttier in real life than she is on Facebook," she said between chuckles.

Meryn shook a finger at her. "You're in by the way. I processed your cult application this morning. Good job passing your Geek Life test."

"Thank you, Meryn, I have a feeling that particular group will be most entertaining."

Izzy looked around. "Is no one going to ask about the whole High Priestess, cult thing?"

Around the table, heads were shaking. Amelia answered. "We just let her do whatever she wants, for the most part, it's harmless, just a confusing lesbian message here and there."

Izzy brought out her phone. "I so have to get in on this. What's the name of your group?"

"Friend me and I'll invite you. I set the group to Super-Secret so you won't be able to search for it." Izzy scrolled through her app and fired off a friend request. "Done."

Aiden returned to his chair and sat back down. He looked at Oron. "Your unit leader may need a vacation by the time I get back."

Oron winced. "What'd Colton do now?"

"He tied Sascha to the bell tower in the drill field."

"That doesn't sound so bad."

"Then he covered every inch of rope in superglue which hardened and not only made cutting the rope near impossible, but also ensured that when he was finally cut free, he was mostly naked."

Oron shrugged. "That's what he gets for letting Emmy nearly get kidnapped and assaulted."

"What?" Aiden demanded.

Izzy watched as nearly all the blood in Oron's face drained away. "Nothing."

"Oron!"

"Shit," Darian whispered.

"She's fine Aiden."

Aiden stood again, reaching for his phone. "Hey, Colton." He walked back toward the windows.

Oron let his head drop to the table. "My unit leader is a dead man."

Izzy watched as Meryn's fingers moved a mile a minute. When she was done, she eased her phone back to the table as Aiden stomped back and sat down. "Everything okay love?" she asked.

Aiden's ire slipped a bit at her endearment. "Yes, though I can't wait to get home."

Aiden's phone dinged, and he picked it up. He read the message, sighed and sat it back down.

"Problems, sir?" Darian asked.

"Colton can't find Sascha anywhere, which

may actually be a good thing at the moment. I wonder how he knew to slip away?" Aiden mused out loud. Everyone eyed Meryn's phone then looked anywhere but at the commander.

"I bet it was his cat instincts," Amelia suggested quickly.

"Could be," Aiden agreed.

"Hey, speaking of cats, where's Rex?" Meryn asked, looking around. "I heard this was lion country or something."

The queen wiped at her eyes with a napkin. "That is mostly true. After the Great War, I opened up Éire Danu to two groups of shifters, the sun-loving lions and the wind walkers or bird-shifters. Both groups made the city their family seat. They are so well integrated into our society; I cannot imagine the city without them."

"There are bird shifters? Like robins and blue jays?" Izzy asked.

The queen shook her head. "More like harpy eagles and hawks."

Brennus turned to her. "In fact, the ranking unit of the city, Tau, has a harpy eagle shifter in their ranks, his name is Priest Vi'Aerdan."

Meryn scrunched up her nose. "Huh? A shifter with a fae name?"

Brennus smiled at her. "He was adopted."

"I told you they were well integrated," the queen said.

"One royal palace and twelve houses?" Izzy asked.

The queen gave a slow nod. "Beyond the houses, at the far end of the courtyard opposite the palace is our Sacred Arboretum or Sacred Forest. It's where the seedlings of our trees are raised to be given to extended family members so that they remain connected to their House."

"Cool," Izzy said. She had always loved trees.

"Why is it sacred?" Meryn asked.

"It isn't generally discussed outside of Éire Danu, but since you're family, I have no reservations telling you about our forest." She folded her hands in her lap. "Each Founding, Noble and Warrior house has a correlating sacred tree. My own house of EirDan is guarded by the spirit of the Oak tree. Vampires have their Books of Life that they created based on our trees, our family trees. The inner courtyard is lined with sacred trees, each one acts as the core of the Royal, Founding, Noble, or Warrior house. As family members are born branches are added, when they pass the branch petrifies to act as a memorial."

"Our house of Eirlea is guarded by the spirit of the Elder tree," Brennus added.

"House Alina is guarded by the spirit of the Holly," Darian continued.

Izzy looked up at her mate, did his house have one? He looked down at her, his eyes filled with sadness. "House Eirson is guarded by the spirit of the Birch tree, but she isn't doing well."

"She?" Amelia, Meryn, and Izzy asked together.

Oron nodded solemnly. "They are true spirits that live within their tree. Many of the sprites can also claim a flower or an herb as their guardian spirit. The sprites are closer to their counterparts though, if their flower dies, so can the sprite."

Meryn turned to look at Felix, who was perched on her shoulder. "You better make me your guardian Felix, because I ain't losing you to some accidentally sprayed Round-Up, you hear?"

Felix smiled and flew up until their cheeks rubbed together. "Together, forever," he said in a piping little voice. Felix kissed her cheek then floated over to the window to sit amongst the flowers on the ledge."

Izzy was curious to see that Brennus' eyes had taken on a sheen. "Papa?" she asked, worried for the fae.

He shook his head as if to escape his own train of thought. "The Skysong clan was a part of the palace long before the Eirleas returned to Éire Danu…"

"Return?" Amelia asked.

Doran turned to her. "Our parents were heavily involved with the humans of our village, and when the queen created the city to move us to another plane, our family chose to stay. It's why Brennus didn't meet his mate, our queen, until seven hundred years ago." He gave her a droll look. "It was quite the shock to see your older brother swing the queen into his arms and kiss her in her own throne room."

The queen sighed happily. "It was the best day of my life."

Brennus huffed. "If I had known you were

waiting with our sons, I would have returned when you created the city."

Meryn waved her hand. "What about the Skysongs?"

"Well, when we returned and I mated Aleks, the Skysongs sort of adopted the Eirleas and began looking after us as well. He looked over to Felix. "He was supposed to be with my brother, but Eamon said he was too young to go out in the human world, so he stayed behind," his voice trailed off.

"Is he okay?" Amelia asked, looking between Doran, Celyn, and Brennus.

Brennus shook his head. "He was killed by ferals. That's when Felix left the garden to go to Lycaonia to be with Celyn, he felt like he failed Eamon." He looked at Meryn. "You have given him a new purpose in life."

Meryn's eyes filled. "My poor little buddy." She turned to look at Felix and her eyes filled with anger. She popped up out of her chair and ran over to the window.

Izzy looked over to where Felix was wrestling with an older sprite his hands clutched around something at his chest.

Brennus and Aiden stood so quickly their chairs were knocked over. Meryn was already at Felix's side. She peeled the older sprite away from Felix and dropped him on the ledge. She held up her forefinger and her thumb menacingly. "Sprite or not, I will thump the shit outta you if you don't leave Felix alone!"

"Holy shit!" Izzy exclaimed.

She exchanged looks with Oron, and they both stood and rushed over to help Meryn.

CHAPTER SEVEN

"GARRICK! WHAT IS THE MEANING of this?" Brennus roared.

"That insolent youngling has gone too far!" The older sprite shouted.

Meryn held Felix close to her chest and held out her 'thump' poised fingers in front of her. "Stay back," she warned.

"Garrick you need to calm down and explain yourself," the queen ordered in a quiet voice.

The sprite hmphed and straightened his robes. "First, he allowed a member of the royal family to die, now this!"

Brennus practically bent in half to confront the sprite. "As I have told you before, if I, as Eamon's brother don't feel that Felix is in any way responsible for Eamon's death, then you as his former Chieftain have no room for complaint."

"You are fae. You are kind. Felix should have gone with Eamon. He should have died instead."

"Seriously?" Meryn demanded.

Brennus shook his head. "There is no possible

scenario where Eamon would allow himself to escape while Felix died."

"So, he's just a mini douchebag?"

Brennus eyed the chieftain. "At the moment."

"Brennus," the queen admonished softly. Her mate walked away, his hands on his hips as he tried to regain his composure.

"You said, first. Since that transgression is groundless, what other complaints do you have against him?" Izzy asked, wanting to defend the little guy too.

"He wears that necklace trying to move above his station. Only those who have earned their years like I have can appear before others, he does it at will," Garrick pointed to the small amulet around Felix's neck.

Felix shook his head bouncing his auburn curls. "No! It is gift. From friend, special friend. You never get!"

Garrick raised his long wooden walking stick, he was going to take a swipe at Felix when two darts of light flew between them.

"Finley! Feris! Get back to your flower!" Garrick bellowed.

"No!" they yelled back.

Meryn was staring down at the pair. "They look just like you Felix."

Felix drifted away from Meryn to the two little sprites and hugged them close. "Baby brothers. They were so tiny when I left, now they fly!"

"Baby Felixes!" Meryn exclaimed.

"A sword!" Garrick screeched, his face turning a deep purple.

Aiden rubbed the back of his neck. "I knew we'd eventually catch static about that."

"Whatever! If Felix is supposed to be a protector or whatever he needs a weapon," Meryn refuted.

Brennus hurried over an excited look on his face. "He has a weapon?"

Felix shyly held up his claymore. "Gift from Magnus."

Brennus whistled. "You can't be angry with him Garrick, it's a gift from the Prince of the Vampires himself."

"Abomination!"

"How is he supposed to protect people without a weapon?" Meryn asked.

"Sacrifice himself," Garrick answered angrily.

"Fuck that!" Meryn turned to Felix. "No sacrificing! You take out as many enemies as you can then you fall back and get help. That is the plan, got it?"

Felix shrugged. "I protect."

"If I lived and you died, you'd take a piece of my heart Felix. That's no way to survive. If there's a way for you to escape, then do it."

Felix stuck out his bottom lip in a pouty fashion. "I protect."

Meryn threw her hands in the air. "Fine! But we're getting you Kevlar and tiny guns."

Felix brightened. "Guns?"

Garrick began to shake. "No sprite has ever wielded a weapon, he is a dishonor to his family."

Meryn grinned. "You're kick-ass Felix."

"Kick-ass," the little sprites yelled.

Meryn's eyes softened. "You two are adorable."

Felix looked over his brothers and saw the same thing Izzy was beginning to notice. Unlike everything else in the fae city which shined and looked exceptionally well kept, these two had on threadbare clothing, no shoes and appeared to be dangerously thin.

When Izzy glanced over at the queen, she noticed her mouth was set in a straight line. She knew that the queen wanted to say something, but more than likely couldn't interfere.

"What…" Felix started then looked over to Garrick. "You said you would take care of them!" he shouted.

"Whoa, Felix, what's wrong?" Meryn asked, gathering all three in her arms. Felix had tears rolling down his rounded cheeks. He pointed to Garrick. "He punish them for my failure. Not their fault! Not their fault!" he sobbed.

Meryn realized what Felix was talking about and quietly began to cry. "They're mine."

"You're human! Don't interfere!" Garrick exploded.

"Mine!" she screamed back. "Because you can't be trusted with them."

Doran simply plucked Garrick up and began walking from the room. "I'll check on the colony to ensure no one else is being abused unjustly."

"Thank you, brother," Brennus said from between clenched teeth.

"You okay. You okay," Felix repeated awkwardly patting each brother on the forehead.

Meryn laughed and wiped her eyes. "I taught him that." She looked up at her mate.

"I don't know exactly what is going on, but if you're talking about Felix's brothers, of course they're ours," Aiden said, running his hand over her hair.

"Cord!" Meryn shouted. "They're starving!"

Izzy turned and was shocked to see the gentle looking Cord about to breathe fire. "Starving! In the Royal Garden of all places. In our own backyard!"

The queen lay a calming hand on his arm. "We can take care of them now. Meryn has invoked familial claim; they will be protected from now on."

Cord turned on his heel muttering under his breath as he headed toward the kitchen. "I will be right back with food for the youngsters."

"They're hungry?" Aiden whispered.

Felix wiped his nose with his sleeve. "Garrick punish after our parents die in flower blight. He think I bring shame to colony."

"You not bad. You not bad," the sprites said, hugging their brother.

Aiden squinted his eyes. "They are by Felix, right?"

The queen turned to Law. "May I beg a favor?"

Law swept his arm across his chest. "For you, anything."

The queen whispered in his ear, and he nodded. "Felix, can you come here a moment?"

Felix made sure his brothers were safely within

Meryn's arms and flew over to the witch. The queen took Law's hand, and Law whispered low as he reached forward and tapped the small amulet hanging from Felix's neck. When he moved his finger back, she heard two tiny clinks. Duplicate amulets fell to the floor.

Felix's eyes widened. "For brothers?" he asked reverently.

The queen nodded. "It will never make up for what they experienced, but I hope it will help them in their new home."

Felix immediately flew back to his brothers and gently slid the necklaces over their heads. He showed them how to rotate the stone.

"Now everyone see."

Finley and Feris looked around. "All see?"

"Yes, all see."

They looked at each other, then laughed joyously, making everyone around them smile.

Cord re-entered with a plate full of honeycomb, cheeses, bread, fruit, and little cakes. "Come here, little ones, time to eat."

Finley and Feris swooped down to the table looking for Felix. When they spotted their older brother, they beckoned him over. "You eat." Felix shook his head. "Not hungry, Meryn feeds me."

Meryn dipped both pointer fingers into the icing and held it out to the small sprites. "Is it okay that you stay with us?" she asked.

Each sprite gently took the sugared confection from her. "We stay."

"Good." She turned to the queen. "Oh, Aleks…"

"Yes, dearest?"

"Can you help me buy some sprite sized clothes?"

"I'd be delighted." She tapped at the crystal on the side table. A moment later, Portia's voice was heard. "Yes, Your Majesty?"

"Portia, can you arrange for a wide selection of young, male sprite clothing to be delivered to my quarters. Oh, and can you also see about getting a sprite built home sent as well, large enough for at least five."

"As you wish, Your Majesty," Portia replied, then the crystal dimmed.

Darian looked down at Felix. "Why did the colony send Felix stuff when he moved in with us if his brothers were being shunned?"

Vivian held out a spoon of honey to Finley. "I think they didn't want our colony to show them up."

"Little douchebags," Meryn said quietly.

Feris shook his head. "Not all bad. Some help."

Finley wiped his mouth on his sleeve. "When they could."

Felix picked up a napkin and handed it to his brother. "We protect Meryn."

The boys nodded. "Okay."

Meryn shook her head. "No. They are going to school or whatever baby sprites do."

Felix looked confused. "We no school."

Feris pointed to his chest. "Not baby. We is fifty."

Meryn's mouth dropped. "The babies are older than me?"

The queen looped her arm through Izzy's. "You're all babies to me."

Meryn turned to Felix. "How old are you?"

"One-hundred and forty," he chirped.

"Dude," Izzy breathed.

"That was the reason Eamon left him behind, he had only just reached adulthood when he left for his mission."

Meryn rubbed her finger over Feris' curls. "You *are* a baby."

"We help!"

Meryn grinned. "I know! You can be baby monitors!"

Ryuu nodded. "Excellent idea, *denka*."

Feris and Finley exchanged looks. "What that?"

Meryn pointed down to her rounded belly. "When my baby is born, you can help me watch after them, you know to make sure they keep breathing and stuff."

Feris and Finley flew into the air and swirled around her belly. "We help! We protect!" They wrapped their tiny arms around her barely covering half each.

"Awwww," Amelia said, reaching for her phone. She took a picture and started tapping. "I'm sending this to Beth."

Aiden cleared his throat. "Can I get it too?"

Felix tapped the plate. "Come eat."

"Ooookkkaaayy," the boys sang and flew back to the table.

As everyone sat back down the door opened and Doran returned without Garrick carrying a huge box, Portia right behind him.

Doran sat the box down on one of the smaller side tables. "I'm assuming this is for the boys."

The queen beamed. "Thank you, Portia. What would I do without you?"

Portia gave a small smile. "I came personally because we received a strange request from Cristo Bolivar."

The queen turned to Brennus. "Isn't that your brother's friend?"

Brennus nodded. "What did he need Portia?"

"One of Eamon's boxes."

Brennus, Doran, and Celyn stared. Doran recovered first. "Did he say why?"

"No, only that it was vitally important he retrieve something," she explained.

Doran and Brennus looked at each other, and Brennus nodded. "Cristo is an honorable warrior, I know that he would only request such a thing if it were absolutely necessary."

"Could be related to why I'm here. He said he had to get something first," Meryn said.

"Tell him he has our permission to retrieve anything he needs," Brennus advised Portia. She inclined her head. "As you wish." She looked down at her scroll. "We also have a Thane and Justice Ashleigh in the palace antechamber requesting to see Law."

Law grinned then frowned. "I can't wait to see my brothers, but Thane may kick my ass for calling him here."

Portia's mouth twitched as she hid a smile. "I will show them in." She turned and walked out, shutting the door behind her.

Meryn stared. "I think I like her."

Five minutes later, two warriors slightly larger than Law's impossible height walked in glowering. "Law," Thane said curtly.

He smiled warmly at Amelia, who waved enthusiastically, before his face turned frosty again when he looked at his brother.

Law smiled and stood. He clasped arms with his brother. "I'm glad to see you well."

Thane gave a terse smile before he wrapped an arm around Law's head and bent down, holding him in place.

Izzy pointed. "That's a headlock."

"Dammit, Thane, let me go!"

"You greet us with a smile as if nothing were wrong after invoking our password to drop everything and come to your side?" Thane demanded.

"It was for a good reason," Law said twisting and turning.

At the table, everyone continued eating as if the smackdown of the century weren't happening behind them.

Izzy looked at the queen who shrugged. "Brennus and Doran talk to each other like that as well."

Doran nodded. "It's a brotherly thing."

Amelia laughed. "Trust me, this is normal. Brothers tend to communicate more with their fists."

"True," Aiden agreed.

"I also hear that you fell under the influence of that spineless librarian," Thane continued.

"That's not true!"

"First he compromises Marshall and now my own brother. When I see that worthless mage, I will make him regret being born."

"Brother, I beg you, say no more," Law entreated.

Thane released Law looking concerned for the first time. "What hold does he have over you? Tell me and I will destroy it."

Law shook his head. "It isn't like that."

"This is great," Meryn said, laughing as she held up her phone.

Law looked ill. "Please tell me you didn't send him a recording."

Meryn shook her head. Law slumped forward in relief.

"It's Facetime, he watched it live," Meryn informed him.

Darian's phone dinged. With a shit-eating grin, Darian walked off to one side and opened a portal. Moments later, Izzy watched as another impossibly tall man and a laughing woman stepped through.

"Izzy that's Kendrick Ashwood, amazing witch and his mate Anne Ashwood, kick-ass nurse," Meryn said pointing to the attractive couple. "Kendrick, Anne, this is Isabelle Campbell, Oron's mate and Coffee Goddess." Anne gave a little wave as Kendrick eyed Thane and his brothers.

Law dropped to his knees his face in his hands. His actions had Thane and Justice moving to stand directly in front of him. "Whatever you have done to our brother we will revisit upon you a thousand-fold you spineless worm," Thane threatened.

"Now I'm recording. This is great," Meryn said, laughing.

Darian closed the portal and sat back down. He picked up a scone. "Meryn's right, this is quality entertainment."

Kendrick blew a kiss at Darian. "Thank you for the portal, Your Highness."

"Highness?" Several people echoed. Kendrick frowned. "You haven't told them yet? I thought that would have been one of the first things you did on this visit."

Darian shrugged. "We've been busy."

Kendrick eyed Meryn. "I'm not surprised." He turned back to Law. "You couldn't tell them?"

Law stood scowling before he walked around his brothers to effectively stand behind the queen. "I'm not suicidal."

Brennus reached behind his mate and dragged Law behind his own chair. "Please do not use my mate and the queen of all the fae as a shield."

Thane took in Law's words and pulled his fist back to punch Kendrick. Kendrick sighed and whispered a spell. "I really didn't want to have to do this, but you have left me no choice." He turned to Law. "You're not this violent."

"I would be if I thought you had done something to one of my brothers."

Kendrick rubbed his chin. “True. I’d level whole cities for Keelan.”

“Ah, Kendrick, what did you do to my brothers?” Law asked.

“They’re just frozen for the moment so I can divulge certain facts to them without worrying about one of them breaking my jaw.”

“You do know that may still happen, right?”

Thane grunted his agreement.

Kendrick shrugged. “At least this way, I can have my say, but first.” He whispered again and Izzy felt the air around them flex and her ears popped.

“What was that?” she asked.

Kendrick turned to her. “My apologies, you must be new to our world. What I just cast was a soundproofing spell, so what I tell our angry friends here stays amongst us.”

Izzy pointed to her chest. “Even me?”

Kendrick gave her a dazzling smile. “Let’s see. According to Meryn, you are Oron’s mate. Oron is Darian’s brother. Darian is mated to Amelia. Amelia is Meryn’s big sister-cousin. Meryn adopted my cousins, so that practically makes you family.”

“What!” Meryn screeched.

Kendrick looked at the group around the table, everyone wore equally stunned expressions. “Oh yeah, we forgot to mention that.”

Micah chuckled. “I got him with that one.”

Serenity punched her mate in the thigh. “How could you not tell me?”

Micah rubbed his leg. “That hurt.”

Zach laughed at his brother-in-law’s pain. “Get him, Seri.”

Serenity crossed her arms over her chest. “Any other secrets?”

“I ate your stash of Marjoram’s cookies before we left,” Micah confessed.

Meryn threw a scone at him. “Off topic.” She glared at Kendrick. “Do they know?”

Kendrick shook his head. “I was going to tell them here, where’s it’s safer, but as you know, they stayed behind.”

Meryn’s expression became thoughtful. “Cristo said something like that. That he could only tell me in the safety of Éire Danu, what does that mean?”

Kendrick waved all around them. “In our world, every wall has eyes and ears, even with soundproofing spells, thoughts can float on the wind. But here in Éire Danu, because the queen removed the city from our world, what is said here almost always stays here.”

“Makes sense,” Meryn said, going back to her plate.

Thane grunted again.

Kendrick swirled back. “Sorry about that old boy, must be my spinelessness distracting me. Now.” He walked over and placed a hand on Thane’s shoulder. “I don’t know how to tell you this, but, you are the baby daddy,” he said in a deadpan voice.

“Kendrick if you don’t…” Anne threatened.

"Fine." Kendrick removed his hand. "My name is Julian Stormhart, my father was Kiran Stormhart, and I am your king."

Thane's body trembled, and his breathing became erratic. His eyes cut to Law, who was nodding.

"It's true brother, I found out in Noctem Falls."

Kendrick whispered, and the spell freezing Thane and Justice was released. They immediately fell to the floor.

Anne scowled. "Look what you did," she pointed down at them.

Kendrick winced. "It was either freeze them or suffer a broken jaw."

Thane's head snapped up. "That may still happen," he threatened.

Justice stood on shaky legs and helped Thane to his feet. They both straightened then bowed. "Your Majesty."

Kendrick smiled. "Care to join everyone at the table so I can tell you what happened?" Thane nodded stiffly and the four of them sat at the table.

Izzy listened to Kendrick's story and felt her eyes fill with tears. His father loved his mother so much that he followed her into death. When Kendrick started explaining how babies were being murdered and how his parents were trapped as beads, she felt a sliver of ice slide down her back.

Instantly Oron was rubbing her arms. "What is it?"

"It's real. At first, everything seemed like a

fairy tale, but this darkness is far worse than drive-bys and crackheads."

Kendrick's smile was sad. "It's true that this world holds many depraved beings, but it also holds miraculous wonders as well."

"We have ferals, but we also get Magic Pudding," Meryn pointed out.

Izzy sat back. "I haven't tried that yet."

"So good," Meryn said, rubbing her belly.

"Why was no one shocked about my secret?" Darian asked, looking petulant.

"Probably because it's not really a secret, I mean, doesn't everyone know she's your mom?" Meryn asked, pointing at the queen.

"What he means dear is the fact that I made him my heir, he is the next King of the Fae," the queen explained.

You could hear a pin drop. The queen looked around. "That was the secret he was talking about, right?"

Meryn looked around then finally up at her mate who was looking anywhere but at her. "You knew?" Just like Serenity, she balled up her fist and punched Aiden in the leg.

"He's my commander Meryn, I had to tell him so he could plan my replacement."

Meryn turned to Amelia. "I'm losing you?" she whispered, eyes filling. Aiden scooped her up into his lap as she began to shake.

Amelia popped up out of her seat, cuffed her mate on the back of the head before hurrying over to Meryn. "Of course not! We're not going anywhere, what idiot over there meant was that as the queen's heir he won't be performing the more dangerous aspects of unit work."

Darian stared at his commander. "What?"

Aiden returned his flat look. "Hell yeah, I'm clipping your wings a bit. There's no way on gods' green earth will I have to report to your mother, the queen of all the fae, that I let her son and heir get hurt or killed on a mission."

"What am I supposed to do?" Darian demanded.

Aiden flushed. "I'm still working on that. But right now, the Alpha Unit is comprised of nothing but Kings, Princes and a future Elder. None of us should be doing missions." His words echoed throughout the room. Aiden paled as he realized what he said. "What in the hell is coming?"

"I feel like boss music should be playing right now, like the dungeon level in Mario Brothers," Meryn admitted.

Izzy and Amelia just nodded in agreement.

"When will you return?" Thane asked in a shaky voice.

"You know I can't, not until we figure out why my parents were driven out," Kendrick said quietly.

"I miss my brothers," Meryn said, turning to bury her face in Aiden's chest.

Amelia sat back practically beaming. "Look at you! You admitted you missed someone and asked for a hug! Oh, Meryn, I'm so proud of you!" Amelia wrapped her arms around Meryn's shoulders hugging her fiercely.

"And there's the octopus thing I kept telling Eva about," Meryn said her voice muffled from being pressed into Aiden.

Amelia sat back. "I missed you while you were away too!"

Justice pointed to them. "Do they not realize what was just discussed?"

Meryn turned at his question and rolled her eyes. "You're late to the party. I've been working on these problems since last year, so check your superiority complex. You still haven't realized that Kendrick used a combination of the Ashleigh and Ironwood names. I figured that shit out the first week or so after meeting Kendrick. He's been under your nose for like centuries."

Thane and Justice both looked like you could knock them over with a feather. "Sonofabitch," Justice whispered.

"Ha.Ha. Motherfuckers," Meryn taunted.

Law laughed outright. "Meryn, be nice."

"Why?" Her response only made him laugh harder.

"My apologies young Meryn, I didn't mean to sound rude, the part of my brain that handles politeness got shut down by Kendrick's revelation." He turned to the witch. "It's still Kendrick, right?"

He nodded. "For now."

Meryn gave Justice a thumbs up. "That happens to me all the time."

Law turned to his brothers. "She was my handler when I was overseas."

Thane and Justice stared at Meryn before

Thane placed a hand over his heart. "Thank you for keeping my brother alive."

"No worries, it was my job."

Darian sat back. "I wish Gavriel and even Colton were here. I feel like we're about to tackle a problem without any backup."

Aiden sighed and nodded his agreement. "I know how you feel."

Micah rapped his knuckles on the table. "We're chopped liver?" he asked, pointing to everyone else.

Darian turned to Micah. "You know what I mean. I almost feel incomplete without my unit."

Oron sat back, getting comfortable. "Well, my unit leader is probably hiding out in the mountains, so even if we were to head back, my unit would still be one person short."

Aiden frowned. "Why is he in the mountains?"

Darian laughed. "Trying to avoid Colton."

Aiden smiled smugly. "Colton is the second highest ranking shifter in the country, do you really think hiding in the mountains will help?"

Oron groaned. "I don't want to break in a new unit leader."

"So, do we have a boss fight to do like Meryn said?" Izzy asked, feeling anxious.

Oron shook his head. "No, we'll let Sascha face Colton as he deserves. For now, we're going to eat Cord's amazing food and get to know our new extended family."

Izzy rested her head on his shoulder. "I can do that."

Izzy spent the next hour watching the emotional ping pong happening on Thane's face. He went from pissed to shocked to jubilant to petulant, and it was entertaining to witness.

Everyone slowly had tea and discussed the events that transpired in Noctem Falls. Izzy was grateful she hadn't been trapped underground in a quarantined city as a virus ran rampant, she might have scrubbed her skin off.

She followed the conversation but paid particular attention to Meryn's running side commentary, after all, Meryn was one of her people and if she could relate to anyone at the table it was her.

She was so wrapped up in Meryn's sarcasm she almost missed Oron standing. "If you'll excuse us, I'd like to take my mate shopping before the dim."

The queen stood and went to a side table. She came over a slid an ornate golden bracelet on her wrist. "Use this darling."

She looked over to Oron who was frowning. "Mother, I can pay for the things for my mate."

The queen simply nodded. "I know dear. But this can also open portals and is equipped with a panic button that will alert the palace if she needs help." She pointed first to the yellow jewel, then the red one.

Oron sighed. "Thank you, mother."

Serenity stood. "We'll be taking our leave as well. I need to visit with my parents," she explained.

The queen nodded her understanding. "No

more putting yourself in harm's way young lady."

"Yes, Your Majesty," Serenity replied.

Brennus pulled her into a hug before handing her off to Micah and Zach, who had stood and walked over to Serenity. "She's all yours, gentlemen."

"Mine," Micah grumbled.

"Oron, hurry back, I haven't nearly enough time with you or your mate."

"Ever as you wish," he replied.

"You're such a good boy," the queen smiled at them and then went back to the table to listen in on Kendrick's take on the virus.

Once outside, she held up her arm. "What's this?"

"That is the fae version of a black credit card. It tells every vendor that you are to be treated as a personal guest of the queen and all charges are to be paid by the palace."

"Dude."

"Don't worry, we'll get a few pieces to appease my mother, and I'll pay for the real stuff."

Izzy wasn't exactly comfortable with him paying either, but she felt better about it than the queen giving her carte blanche. She noticed that her mate had skipped over the explanation about the portals and panic button. She eyed the red jewel and her fingers itched to press it, but fought the urge to see what happened. She wasn't trying to piss off her royal in-laws on the day they met.

The first shop they went to the storekeeper and tailor took one look at Oron and conveniently found odd jobs around to keep them busy. She waited exactly five minutes then dragged Oron out the door. They repeated the process for the next eight shops.

Finally looking utterly rejected Oron turned to her. "Use the bracelet, you need clothes."

She shook her head. "I'd rather go bare ass naked so they can kiss my ass easier later."

He chuckled. "Let's head to the shop I pointed out as we entered the city, it's a bit further out, but I know the owner."

Izzy braced herself for another outright rejection when they walked in.

"Oron, is that you?" An older woman called out.

"It's me Baba, I brought someone to meet you."

All over the city Izzy had seen nothing but golden, young, and beautiful people, it was almost a relief to see an older person.

Oron walked over and helped the woman to the worn stool in front of the counter. "Baba, this is my mate, Izzy. She lost everything in a fire the other day and needs some things to wear."

"And you brought her here?"

"Where else?" Oron asked, almost bitterly.

"I could have told you to come here first, the robes here are a hundred times better than the other shops we went to closer to the palace," Izzy told her mate.

Baba looked at her closely. "It doesn't matter to you that I'm old?"

Izzy didn't know what to say. "Why would that be an issue?"

Oron wrapped an arm around her shoulders. "She's human Baba, she's seen old people her whole life."

Baba cackled. "That makes sense." She wagged a bony finger at Izzy. "I bet you didn't see many like me in those other shops."

"All I saw was a bunch of assholes," she muttered.

Baba wheezed so hard Izzy was terrified she had killed the older woman. "I bet they didn't see that trinket there," she said, pointing to where the bracelet was still tucked under her sleeve.

"No, they didn't," she admitted.

Baba waved to her store. "Pick out whatever you like," she turned to Oron. "I'll charge half to your account."

Oron looked relieved. "Thank you, Baba," he said, leaning down to rest his cheek on the top of her grey hair.

"Quit flirting with me in front of your mate," Baba complained, making Oron blush.

Izzy chuckled. "You tell him, Baba!"

Baba grinned back at her. "I like her, she has spirit."

"I think she is the most beautiful thing I have ever seen," Oron said.

Izzy looked through different robes. "Do you have any that are flame resistant?"

"Get in that many fires?" Baba asked.

Izzy didn't even look up from the vast selection of brightly colored fabric. "Yeah, it's kinda a regular occurrence with me… and explosions."

Oron's smile slipped slightly. "Really?"

"Yeah, I found out the hard way that pressure cookers are not my friends." She held out a bright teal robe. "What do you think?"

Oron gave her two thumbs up. "Love it."

Slowly she made her way through the robes and fell in love with seven different colored ones, so that she had enough for each day of the week.

Oron eyed her small selection. "You should get more."

"I have one for each day, why would I get more?" Izzy asked, feeling confused.

"What about dress robes?"

Izzy looked down at her pile. "These are dressy."

Baba started folding her new clothes and placing them in a fabric bag. "Not really, since you'll be primarily visiting the palace, you'll need robes for events and balls and such."

Izzy pointed to her new robes. "Why can't I wear those?"

"Those are your everyday robes," Oron explained.

"Will I see these people every day?"

He frowned. "No."

"Then they won't know that I wear them regularly. It's silly to get a robe for people I don't see so they don't think I don't rewear my clothes."

"A breath of fresh air this one," Baba said, handing her the bag.

"Then you'd love Meryn," Izzy winked at her.

"Bring her by," Baba offered.

"I will," she promised.

Izzy made sure to take Oron's hand as they walked out.

"Thank you for my new clothes."

"I wish I could have shown you more."

"I'm glad we got my clothes from here, I'll think of Baba when I wear them, not those uppity assholes."

He twirled her around making her laugh. "Care to grab a snack?"

Izzy hesitated. She really didn't want Oron to be snubbed again.

He tapped her nose. "Don't worry about me, the street vendors aren't as picky when it comes to who they sell to, unlike the clothing merchants their products can go bad." He led her down a side street until they finally popped out into what looked to an older part of town.

The stones were worn, the cloth not quite as white, and the signs were showing their age, but the atmosphere was completely different from the more upscale streets she had seen thus far.

Boisterous laughter filled the air as a pair of older fae argued on a corner. "What is this place?" she asked, trying to take in every detail.

"The Border City. It's the part of the city that skirts the edge of the Queen's realm and butts against the Dark Forest."

"What's the Dark Forest, it sounds ominous."

"It's not, it's simply where the darker fae live."

"Darker fae?"

"Yes, like brownies and goblins."

"Why don't they live in the city? Is it because of the assholes?"

"No, it's because they don't do well in sunlight. The forest protects them with its tall trees and shadows."

"Don't goblins eat people?"

Oron started to shake his head no, then stopped. "Goblins don't, but there are creatures there I wouldn't tempt with human flesh." His eyes grew wide. "You are under no circumstances to go into that forest."

"Right." Izzy looked around. "Did you have a particular snack in mind?"

"I'm serious, Izzy, no forest."

"Such a worrywart."

Oron placed both hands on her shoulders. "You're forgetting, I dreamt of you, I know how your curiosity is."

"Food," she said simply, still ignoring him.

His shoulders slumped forward. "Fine, but if you get eaten, I will be very put out with you," he threatened. He took her hand and they wove between the people on the bustling street.

When they stopped, Izzy looked up. "Is this a tavern?"

Oron nodded and pushed the door open. "Dav, you in?"

They stepped inside, and it took a few moments for Izzy's eyes to adjust to the dark interior.

"Oron! Well met! What'll you have?" a male voice called out.

"Hey Dav, I'll have a pint and some of your beer-battered fish." He looked down at her.

"What about you?" he asked, as he lifted her onto the stool at the bar. Everything in this city seemed to be giant-sized. She never considered herself short, but she was starting to feel puny. "I'll have the same." She smiled up at the barkeep. He was handsome, with more character on his face than most of the too beautiful fae she'd seen.

Dav winked at her making her blush. "Who are you pretty lady?" he flirted.

Oron wrapped an arm around her shoulders. "My mate."

Dav stepped back and held up his hands. "No offense intended." He eyed her closely. "But I will say this, she's too beautiful for your ugly mug."

She felt Oron move his hand, and Dav laughed at whatever gesture Oron had done behind her back. "Dav Li'Filrien, meet Isabelle Campbell. Izzy, Dav is a retired unit warrior, he opened up this tavern so us poor grunts had somewhere to go when our unit leaders let us off our leashes."

"Izzy, can I call you Izzy?" Dav asked. She nodded. "Izzy, welcome! How do you like our city?"

She played with one of the small cloth napkins at the bar. "I like this side of town more than the other side."

Dav scratched his chin. "Seems more real? Friendlier? More human?"

Izzy stopped and thought about it. "Yes, to all of it. Why is that?"

Dav chuckled. "Border City is slightly older,

we don't keep up appearances and aren't as picky about what people wear or who they're related too. Many human mated couples move here because we seem more open, which of course led to the majority of people being a mixture of human and fae, and in turn, made them more open and friendly, drawing in more human or shifter mated couples. Over several generations, the result is what you see."

"I like it." She looked up at Oron. "Even your mom's room didn't feel as homey as this," she indicated to the tavern.

Dav burst into laughter. "What a fine compliment! Better than the royal chambers! I should put that on a wall plaque."

"Quit embarrassing her," Oron said, kissing her temple before moving to stand behind her. He wrapped his arms around her as if he were making himself her shield.

Dav quieted. "She meant that?"

She nodded. "His mom is really nice, but her room still felt kinda cold, maybe it was all the marble. But it feels warm here and inviting." She ran her hand over the worn wood of the bar. "I feel like the happiness of this place has seeped into the wood and it's radiating from within like a happiness air freshener."

When she looked up from inspecting the bar, she found that not only Dav but the other patrons at the bar were staring at her. "What?"

Dav turned to Oron. "Did you tell her?"

Oron wore a broad grin. "Haven't had time. I only met her yesterday. That's when she found out about our world by the way. She got thrown into the deep end."

"Impressive lady you have there Oron. Are you sure she's human? I've known many talented witches who have yet to notice the spell that Malachai put on the bar," a deep voice complimented from their right.

"Thanks, Priest. As far as I know, she's human, but from everything I've observed in Lycaonia from the influx of human mates, is that our understanding of them is woefully inadequate." He nodded his head. "Izzy, this is Priest Vi'Aerdan."

Izzy snapped her fingers. "The harpy eagle adopted by fae parents, he's the one your mom was talking about, right?"

Priest's eyebrow rose. "The queen was talking about me?"

"Yup! She said that your adoption showed how well integrated the bird shifters were to the city."

Dav gave a bark of laughter. "That's one way to look at it."

Priest gifted her a wry smile. "My adoption was somewhat of a huge upset when it happened. I'm glad that the Queen can now use it as a positive example of how much our city has grown."

"Well said," Dav remarked, tossing his towel on the bar. "Let me go put your order in, be right back." He disappeared behind a swinging door.

She bopped her head backward onto Oron's chest to get his attention. "What spell?"

"I knew you were going to ask that." He kissed

the top of her head. "Back when Dav opened the tavern he asked his fellow unit brother Malachai to cast a spell on the bar to absorb the happiness and laughter of the place and release it to help destress the warriors when they come in for a break."

Izzy wanted to rest her head on the bar. "That's amazing. I wonder if you could do something similar to children's desks in school."

Priest shrugged. "We don't have many schools. Most of us are taught from home."

Izzy snapped her fingers. "What if you could make happy pencils?"

Priest smiled and nodded. "Now that's something I wouldn't mind having, especially for my report write-ups lately."

Dav came back through the door. "What write-up?"

Priest rolled his eyes. "We keep getting reports from people about shadows. Personally, I think the citizens are bored out of their minds and crave the excitement a unit of warriors can bring."

Izzy gave a single nod. "Happy pencils."

Dav blinked and she watched his facials expressions as he figured out what she was referring to. "Can I use that idea?" he asked.

"Sure, but if you end up making them, I want some," she countered.

"Deal."

"How's Ari?" Oron asked Priest.

Priest raised one eyebrow. "His older brother is visiting for a while, so he's pretty much living at the estate." He started chuckling low. "Though

I heard he shocked the hell out of Ari when he held out his hand for a fist bump."

"Meryn taught him that," Oron said.

Priest shook his head. "I don't know what she did to him, but Rex seems more approachable now."

"You should see how she changed Prince Magnus," Oron countered.

"Is it true he gave her a Noctem Falls Regalis card?" Dav whispered.

Izzy looked back at her mate. He nodded a single time and Priest gave a low whistle. "What's a Regalis card?" she whispered.

Oron leaned down. "It guarantees that the recipient is treated as a Royal of Noctem Falls. That should anyone insult or injure her they would face the wrath of the entire vampire race."

"Wouldn't Aiden or Ryuu kinda do the same thing?" Izzy asked.

Dav leaned over the bar. "Someone might be crazy enough to anger Aiden, though he is impossibly strong and an amazing fighter he is still a single man. That card promises retribution from every living vampire," Dav explained.

"And his mom likes her," she added.

Both Priest and Dav laughed. "It's no secret that the queen follows little Meryn on Facebook, hell, half the city does. She's hilarious."

Izzy sat up straighter. "I'm her Coffee Goddess. She's getting me an altar and everything."

"Coffee Goddess?" Dav asked.

Oron tickled her neck. "She's an extremely talented barista."

"Gods! Coffee! We don't have a decent place here," Priest practically whimpered.

Izzy eyed the long wooden bar. "If you order equipment, I can show you how to make drinks," she offered.

Dav froze. "Are you serious?"

"Yup, no one should be without coffee, that's like, criminal," she shuddered at the thought.

"And she'll only require ten percent of your profits from the coffee sales," Oron tacked on.

Dav pursed his lips together. "Worth it."

Izzy turned around to face her mate. "I wasn't going to charge him."

Oron smiled. "He can more than afford it and you are jobless. Tell me you wouldn't feel better with a small bit of money coming in for yourself?"

Izzy chewed on the side of her thumbnail. "I could get my own stuff then."

"You know I would buy you anything you would want or need, but you like the idea of your own money."

"Doesn't everyone?"

"You've got yourself a rare woman there Oron," Dav said.

Oron squeezed her close. "Don't I know it."

"Are the rumors we heard true? Are all the warriors getting mates?" Priest asked.

"Twelve warriors, including myself, have dreamt of and found their mates. That's about ten percent of the current roster finding their mates in under six months. I think it's safe to say we're all getting them," Oron informed them.

"Twelve?" Priest repeated? "I heard of the Eta unit finding their mates, who else?"

"Warrick Fortier, I attended his mating ceremony myself."

Priest gave him a funny look "Isn't that personal."

Oron threw a napkin at him. "Not the claiming you dolt. Because Warrick had just taken over as the Founding Family head, they had a ceremony so more people could see both him and Avery."

"What's she like?" Dav asked.

"He," Oron corrected.

"I didn't know Warrick was gay," Priest said.

Oron laughed. "Neither did Warrick from what I hear. But you almost can't be in the same room as the two of them. It's like Avery is the sun and Warrick rotates around him."

"Good for them," Dav said, passing them their beers.

Izzy accepted hers and took a sip. "Wow, I usually don't drink beer, but this is amazing." She took another healthy gulp.

"It's my secret recipe," Dav bragged.

"So how long are you all visiting?" Priest asked.

Oron shrugged. "No idea. Cristo Bolivar asked Meryn to come here and we're still waiting for him to find something, maybe a few more days."

"Is the Unit Commander going around to the different units while he's here? I think it's the first time in recorded history that an active Unit Commander has visited Éire Danu."

"He seems to be racking up quite a few

firsts with Meryn at his side. He was the first commander to visit Noctem Falls as well. He enjoyed meeting with the men, so I'm sure he'll be arranging either drills or meetings while he's here."

"Aiden has to be one of the best Unit Commanders we've ever had," Priest said.

"Here, here," a few other voices echoed throughout the room as the men lifted their glasses.

Izzy raised her beer and drank with the rest. Though she had never served with Aiden, she knew from what she'd already seen that he genuinely cared for each man who served in the units, and the men knew it.

After eating the best fish she had ever had in her life she and Oron lazily walked back to the palace. The sky wasn't nearly as bright as this morning signaling that it was almost evening. She couldn't remember the last time she had enjoyed a simple afternoon. Usually, she worked from sunup to sundown to make rent, today was a true gift.

This time when they went to go through the gates, Malcom didn't try to stop them. As they turned into the hallways of the queen's private chambers, they saw Aiden carrying a large dollhouse down the hall.

"Where are you heading Commander?" Oron asked.

"Meryn wants the sprites' house in the room adjacent to our guest room so they are close by.

She said she doesn't trust Garrick and she wants to be able to defend Felix should the need arise."

"You don't seem too upset over that," Oron pointed out.

Aiden gave a one-shoulder shrug. "She battled that damn tunnel escort on a regular basis in Noctem Falls, I'm pretty sure she'll be okay taking on a sprite."

"Has Thane Ashleigh laid out Kendrick yet?"

Aiden smirked. "Not yet."

"Think he will?"

"Probably. He's not known as one of the most ruthless witches ever born for no reason."

"We're gonna head to our quarters, if you see everyone before we do, let them know we'll be at dinner."

Aiden nodded. "Will do."

When the large commander walked away, she looked up at her mate. "Our quarters?"

He blinked slowly. "You did want to move in with me, right?"

"I'd like to be asked," she said, crossing her arms over her chest.

Oron set her shopping bags down and got down on one knee. "In the human world, a male usually goes to one knee to ask the female to marry him. Since you are literally the woman of my dreams, and I can think of no one else I'd rather spend the rest of my days with, would you do me the honor of sharing my quarters with me? I swear to always put your needs above my own and will tend, nurture and grow your hap piness so that you will never know another day of sorrow."

Izzy covered her mouth with a trembling hand. She would think that he was teasing, but the sincerity in his eyes was her undoing. "I think I love you," she whispered.

The love in his eyes transformed his face into one of pure joy. "That means you aren't fighting the mating pull and you want to be mine." He stood and swept her off her feet whirling her around the hallway. "I swear Izzy, I swear I will make you happy."

She laughed and wrapped her arms around his neck. "You make me happy just by being near me," she confessed. "You're the first person in a long time to care about me." She felt herself blushing horribly. "I'm glad Fate chose me for you." She thought of another being given to her mate. "If you were with someone else, I'd punch her in the face."

Oron set her on her feet and took her hand. "I have a set of quarters here in the palace and my own suite at the Gamma estate in Lycaonia." He had them turning left then going down another hallway. "I think I'll copy my commander and have you move into the Gamma estate instead of having you live in the city."

"Where you go, I go," Izzy said. "Whose idea was it that the warriors lived in one place and their mates another, that's stupid."

"Meryn thought so too, so she ignored centuries of practice and moved into the Alpha estate. At the time, I thought she'd be a distraction, but she's helped us out a lot. Plus, Aiden doesn't have to worry about what she's doing if they live together."

"And I have to make coffee for Meryn," Izzy reminded him.

"Gods forbid that woman doesn't get her coffee," Oron said in a sober tone.

When he had them stop at a wide wooden door, she eyed it carefully. "That is a very impressive door."

Oron shrugged. "Brennus helped me update mine, Darian's and mother's. They are reinforced with a steel coating spell and have an aura lock on it."

"Aura lock?"

"Place your hand in the center of the door."

She lifted her hand and laid it flat against the door. Oron placed his hand above the locking mechanism and whispered a phrase. For a second, her hand glowed and then the light dimmed. "What was that?"

"The spell registered your aura to act as a key. You now have access to the room." He turned the knob and pushed the door open. "Welcome home, Izzy."

CHAPTER EIGHT

IZZY LOOKED AROUND AS ORON shut the door behind him placing her bags on the floor. She didn't know what to expect, she hadn't been in many men's rooms, so she wasn't sure why she was surprised at Oron's simple, yet elegant decor.

"What were you expecting?" he asked.

"I don't know, more bachelor-game-room-man cave I guess."

He shook his head. "Not really my thing."

She ran her hand over his duvet cover. It wasn't cotton, nor silk, but seemed to be a blend of the two. She walked past the bed to the wall by the bathroom. Portraits of every shape and size covered the large wall. Some were of Brennus, him frowning, scowling, laughing and even one of him rolling his eyes. There were many more of the queen. Like the ones done of Brennus, each portrait seemed to be dedicated to a certain expression, even one of her crossing her eyes and sucking in her cheeks. But it was the ones next to those that brought tears to her eyes. The sketches of the tiny baby were more amateurish but no less stunning. As the child grew, the portraits became more detailed. She turned to stare at her mate. "You did these," she said.

Oron gave a slow nod. "After my family was sent away, I realized I was having a hard time recalling certain details about my mother, my birth mother. I never wanted to forget Darian, so I started drawing."

"Why not take a picture?"

"Cameras hadn't been invented yet," he reminded her gently.

"Oh, yeah."

She went back to the wall and as she moved she watched Darian grow up. She ran her fingers along the frame of one of the last ones. "His eyes are different now," she observed.

Oron walked up behind her and wrapped his arms around her waist. "This was drawn before he left for Lycaonia, before he suffered and knew darkness. This is how both mother and I still see him."

Izzy saw the light shining from Darian's eyes in the picture. Here was a young man who knew only love and happiness. "He seems stronger now."

"He is."

She turned in his arms. "Did you do any self-portraits?"

Oron blushed and nodded slowly.

"Where are they? I'd like to see them."

Oron sighed and shuffled over to his massive bed. He reached under the bed skirt and pulled out a box. He walked over and set it on the table by the window.

She hurried over and lifted the lid. As she lifted each picture from the box she couldn't stop the tears from falling. Every portrait he had drawn of himself made him look dark and sinister. It was nothing as overt as a forked tongue and horns, but there was a clear difference between the laughing Darian and the solemn Oron. This was how he saw himself and it couldn't be further from the truth. Carefully she placed the drawings back in the box.

"Why do you weep?" he asked, wiping away her tears.

"I wish I could draw you as I see you, it's nothing like that," she pointed to the box.

"Will you be my light," he whispered.

"No. You are your own light, but I will be your mirror so you can see it clearly."

"Can I make love to you, Izzy, will you let me claim you?"

"I don't think I have ever wanted anything more in my life," she admitted.

Slowly Oron stepped forward and lifted his hand to her face. He traced her lips with his thumb and ran it down the column of her neck. She shivered at his touch.

He walked her backward until the back of her legs hit the mattress. Ever so slowly, he undid every button and zipper. Each movement was tender and done with a single-minded focus that was leaving her breathless.

When she stood before him in her bra and

panties, he stepped back and began to undress himself. With her eyes locked on his hands, each action was done with precision, nothing was hurried or rushed. She could almost feel him savoring every single second of them coming together.

When he slipped his boxer briefs down his legs, she had to reach out a hand to grasp the bedding to steady herself. Standing before her, completely nude, her mate seemed more like a dream than reality. No human could ever look as beautiful. Her mind stalled, he wasn't human, he was fae and he was all hers.

She reached behind her back and unclasped her bra and shimmied out of her panties, letting them both drop to the floor. She found herself growing impatient at his slow progression. "Come to me, my mate," she said, holding out her hand.

In a single stride Oron was at her side and taking her hand, which he placed over his heart. Under her palm, she could feel it beating out of control. "It's a little worn and broken, but all the pieces are yours," he promised.

She reached down and brought his hand over to cover her heart. "Mine is a little battered, smoky, missing parts and impulsive, but if you want it, it's yours," she whispered.

Oron lifted her up and gently lay her on the bed. Before she could blink, he was lying beside her. He carefully began to run his hands down her chest, over her belly, across her hips until he cupped her mound. The heat from his hand had her squirming. With an evil grin, he curled his pointer and middle finger so they slid between her folds. She closed her eyes and enjoyed the pleasure that he was building within her. She expected him to breach her, but he never did. He just steadily rubbed either side of her clit until she was clutching the blankets with both hands. "Oron," she whispered harshly.

"Let go," he ordered.

She lifted her hips against him and her orgasm crashed through her. When she was done shuddering, he placed the tip of his finger on her clit and pressed down firmly. "What are you doing?"

"You'll see." He leaned down and teased her lips with his own. When she was thoroughly distracted by his kiss, he lifted his finger and she groaned at the new sensation. Again, he began his steady slide up, then down. "Oron, I can't…" How could she explain that she had never come twice like that? "Let's take care of you," she started to reach for him when he suddenly moved his hand a bit lower and began a circling motion directly under her clit. "Oh god," she breathed. "Please be ready Oron, I don't want to come again without you."

He simply nodded then moved between her legs. While on his knees, he opened her wide and draped her legs over his thighs. "Tell me right before you fly," he commanded.

She thrashed her head from side to side as a new pressure built. Just when she thought she was falling apart she screamed out his name. "Oron!"

With a primal roar, he reached down and plunged deep into her body. "Please, please, please," she begged.

He lifted his hand from her body and leaned down, so they were nearly chest to chest. "Kiss me Oron, I want us connected in every way," she gasped each word.

Oron didn't hesitate a moment. He captured her mouth and his tongue began to mimic his cock. He entered her slowly then teased, before thrusting back in.

She dug her nails in his back and met him thrust for thrust. They weren't just having sex; this was beyond making love. He made sure he knew every inch of her body and he was welding them together.

When he slammed to the hilt, the bite a pain triggered her pleasure. He threw his head back and yelled her name. He slowly withdrew from her body as two balls of light lifted from their chests, swirled, merged, then separated. They then drifted down and settled back within their chests. The ball of light that came to her carried with it a piece of Oron. She knew then she would never be alone again.

Izzy practically danced around the bathroom as she got ready. The connection created with Oron was unlike anything she had ever experienced. She found herself rushing when getting ready for dinner so that she could return to his arms. She rolled her eyes in the mirror. Her happiness caused her to act ridiculously.

She pulled her favorite robe from the bag and slipped it on over her freshly perfumed body. When underthings appeared and slid into place, she yelped. Looking at herself in the mirror, the intricate embroidery along the cuffs and hems mesmerized her. The woven designs looked as if the flowers were simply resting on her sleeve.

She chose to wear the teal one Oron liked so much in the shop. She artfully arranged her damp curls into a cascade down her back. Right now, her hair looked brown, but she knew as it dried it would brighten to a deep auburn. She didn't have much make up with her, so she made full use of what little she did have. Bronzer doubled as eyeshadow, lipstick doubled as a blush and she used some mascara coated floss to apply eyeliner. All in all she thought she did an impressive job.

When she stepped out of the bathroom, Oron stood from the chair where he had been waiting for her and his mouth dropped. "Iz, you look…" he shook his head, but his eyes went right back to her. She loved that he hadn't even been able to complete his sentence.

"Like?"

"No, love. That teal is amazing on you." He walked over and cupped her face with his hands. He gently kissed her lips, then stepped back. She scrunched up her nose at his lukewarm greeting.

"If I kiss you the way I want to, we won't make it to dinner."

She turned back and eyed the bed longingly.

"Come on Iz, don't tempt this poor warrior, I am only so strong."

She laughed and this time when he held out his elbow, she placed her hand on it and allowed him to escort her to dinner.

She thought they were heading to the queen's chambers, but instead, he steered her down a different hall. "Where are we going?"

"We met in mother's chambers earlier for privacy. But I can guarantee you Cord has pulled out all the stops, so we're heading to the smaller more intimate dining room."

"Smaller dining room?"

Oron grinned. "The larger one is meant for balls and can seat nearly one hundred people. The smaller dining room can seat up to fifty, but the table can be shortened by adjusting the spell."

When they walked in, every man at the table stood. Once again feeling nervous and as if she were on display, she hurried to her chair. She sat and allowed Oron to scoot her chair in.

"Izzy that color was meant for you," Amelia said by way of greeting.

Meryn looked disgruntled. "My dress still wants me in robes. I'd kill for sweatpants. I had some really cool tee shirts lined up to show Aleks too."

Izzy hid her smile, but had to admit Meryn looked stunning in her evening robes. The contrast between the deep brownish-gold and shimmery pale gold made the entire ensemble look stunning. "At least they're comfortable," she said. And they were too. Nothing chafed or was too tight.

Meryn exhaled. "True."

Aleksandra turned to her. "How did you like your excursion into the city? Did you find a lot of clothes to buy?"

Izzy looked down at her hands, then up at her new mom. "I liked the Border City; they were like normal people."

Meryn brightened. "Border City."

Izzy turned to her future cohort. "Yeah, it's next to the Dark Forest where there's brownies and goblins."

Meryn stared at her. "Wicked."

"No, Meryn," Aiden started.

Izzy gave her a serious look. "Yeah, Oron said I wasn't allowed to go there." She kept a straight face and shook her head.

Meryn met her eyes and she swore she could almost hear her agreeing to sneak off to the forest with her. Meryn looked over to Oron. "Well, if Oron said we shouldn't go, then it must be too dangerous."

Izzy nodded. "Absolutely."

Amelia didn't look convinced. "Right."

Izzy turned to Meryn desperate to change the subject. "How are Finley and Feris?"

"They're good. Aiden and I got them settled in the little room next to ours. You would have thought we'd given them the moon when we told them that it was their new room." She glanced down. "Another reason I miss my hoodies, there's no room for Felix in my robes."

Izzy looked at her questioningly.

"He rides in the boob pocket to stay warm," Meryn answered. "These robes smush everything up and together, so I don't have a pocket for him. If I had known I would be stuck in these robes for an indefinite period of time, I would've brought the scarf Aiden's mom knitted for me over the holidays, she added a pocket for Felix," she paused. "Shit! Where will Finely and Feris go? I only have so much space down my shirt."

Izzy looked around the table. She was pretty sure that conversations like this had never happened at the fae royal dining table before.

Cord walked up behind Meryn and dished out her soup. "What if you had a vest with multiple fur lined pockets? Each sprite could have his own space, then maybe have a larger pocket where all three could be together," he suggested.

"Kick-ass idea, Cord. Once Dani is done being all formal, I'll see if we can work that out. No wonder you're a super squire!" Meryn exclaimed.

Cord looked down at her. "Super squire?"

"Yeah, Sebastian said that you've been serving here so long that you've forgotten more recipes than he's learned."

"He's such a good lad. For that, I'll send him some fae honey as well," Cord said, looking pleased at the compliment.

"Any word about Pip's progress?" Aiden asked.

Meryn shook her head. "They must be busy getting him all used to the sky."

"What do you mean Meryn?" Aleksandra asked.

Meryn took a deep breath and launched into the story of how she met the twins and Pip and how they were her brothers now. When she explained how Pip had gotten frightened by the open sky, Izzy felt terrible for the poor little guy. "But Nigel and Neil are helping Sebastian and Magnus to get Pip ready, so they can catch up to us soon," Meryn explained. She rubbed her chest. "I miss them. Like a lot. This shit sucks."

The queen's expression was unreadable. "And the animals who mistreated him?"

Meryn gave her a satisfied smirk. "Sebastian is handling it."

Izzy turned to Doran. "Speaking of assholes. What about Garrick? Please tell me he hasn't gotten away with what he's done."

Doran practically growled. "I pulled the whole colony onto the garden lawn and explained that the queen would not abide, nor tolerate the way the boys were treated. They were very contrite, though some were just more concerned about being caught." He turned to his sister-in-law. "You may have to issue a city-wide decree stating that although we as fae do not interfere with the running of the sprite colonies, they still need to follow our laws and guidelines and allowing their young to starve is unacceptable."

The queen nodded. "I will have Portia circulate an edict tomorrow, first thing."

"Why do they have separate colony hierarchies, don't they all report to you?" she asked.

The queen shook her head sadly. "When I created this pocket world, I asked the fae creatures of Earth if they wanted to join us. Some followed contingent on being able to keep their own species sovereignty. I am queen, but the only one who reports to me amongst the sprites, for example, are their chieftains. I cannot directly discipline one of their people."

"Sounds complicated," Meryn commented.

The queen sighed. "They did not want to trade one prison for another. Earth was becoming a dangerous place for magical creatures, but many stayed behind rather than be under my rule even in the slightest. I have heard nearly all that stayed behind have perished."

"Ultimately, I have the final say in matters, but their leaders still handle the day to day administration of their people."

Brennus grinned evilly. "I tend to encourage people to listen. It makes things run smoother."

Meryn stared. "That's right, you're the unit leader for the Tau Unit as well as Royal Consort."

Brennus looked from Meryn to Aiden. "Ari Lionhart tends to act in that capacity more than I do, to be honest."

"Lionhart? Rex's baby brother?" Meryn asked.

Aiden wrapped his hand around the back of her neck. "No, Meryn."

Meryn scrunched up her face. "No, Meryn. No, Meryn. No, Meryn," she repeated.

"Who's Rex?" Izzy asked.

Meryn fanned herself. "Awesome Elder with

amazingly defined biceps. He's Ari and Declan's older brother and like a super politician. He came with us to visit his parents for a while."

"When do I meet him?" she asked Oron who was giving her an amused look. "Why do you need to meet the Elder?" he asked sensibly.

"Because as an Elder I bet he could explain your world from a unique perspective," Izzy answered.

Brennus chuckled. "She's got you there, son."

"You can talk to Byron McKenzie when we get home. He's just as knowledgable and safely mated." He looked around. "Where is Cristo? Wasn't this whole trip his idea?"

Brennus frowned. "He evidently hasn't found what he is looking for amongst my brother's things. He said he will continue in the Eirlea vault tomorrow, then if he still hasn't found whatever he's looking for, he will seek permission to enter the EirDan vault after that."

"Y'all just letting him chill in your vault?" Meryn asked.

Brennus smiled sadly. "Cristo, along with Thane, Rio and Ange served together with Eamon in a Vanguard squad. If I can't trust one of the men Eamon considered a brother, I'm not sure I want to face the world that would be."

"Do you know what Cristo is looking for?" Thane asked.

Doran shook his head. "No, he hasn't told us."

"Eamon also left some things with us over the years," Thane laughed suddenly. "I asked him one time if the fae vaults would be safer and he said that if anyone got past us to steal his things, they were welcome to them."

Brennus chuckled. "That sounds like him."

"Hey, do you have any sprite sized Kevlar in your vault?" Meryn asked Brennus.

Brennus' mouth twitched fiercely as he clearly fought to smile. "Meryn, I don't think sprite Kevlar has been invented yet."

"Oh." She frowned. "Why not? They need extra protection being so little."

"I'm not sure."

"Can you make some?"

Brennus shook his head. "I'm afraid I only wield weapons, not craft tools. But I'm sure you could probably find a willing craftsman in the city."

Aiden patted his mate on the back. "Don't worry Meryn, we'll commission some for the boys before we leave. Felix proved himself to be an invaluable warrior in Noctem Falls, he deserves to be outfitted as one."

Meryn blew kisses at Aiden then swiveled in her chair to face the queen. "Random question."

"By all means, dear."

"Is your sun a real sun? Would it hurt a vampire who has a severe sun sensitivity?"

The queen lifted her wine glass. "Our sun isn't the actual sun. It is the core of fae magic, as such, it provides us with not only warmth but also light. But it sounds as if your vampire friend is reacting to UV rays, which aren't present here. All of our plants have adapted to grow under the light of our false sun," she explained.

"So Vivi and Etain can come visit." Meryn pulled out her phone and sent a text.

The queen set her glass down. "You were asking for Vivian Vi'Aerlin?"

"Yup, she gets wicked sunburn."

"That is excellent news! Allia and Alain have been begging me to convince their brother Etain to visit. I knew he was reluctant to do so since he had just mated, but I had no idea she had such a severe reaction to the sun. I know that Etain's mother will be thrilled to see her son again."

Meryn's phone dinged and she picked it up. "She said they would schedule a visit later. Magnus keeps threatening to go on an around the world cruise, so she's had to hold the fort down while Beth keeps Gavriel from choking him."

Aiden groaned. "It will be years before Gavriel returns to Lycaonia."

Meryn smiled slyly. "When we get back, I'll have Sebastian install Magnus in his office and shove Gavriel through the portal. We'll be fine."

Aiden brightened and set his spoon down as he had finished his soup. "Thank the gods you got on Sebastian's good side."

"How'd you do that?" Thane asked.

"Murder," Meryn said bluntly.

Law choked then glared at Meryn. "I know you keep doing that on purpose, Meryn. Quit trying to kill me."

As everyone laughed at Law, Izzy noticed that Meryn hadn't been joking. It just confirmed the fact that she needed Meryn in her life because she was turning out to be crazier than she was.

She was slightly tipsy as Oron steered her back to their room. "She has sooooo killed people."

Oron laughed. "Probably."

"I loves her."

"I know."

"What we doing tomorrow?"

"Well, while you were enjoying your third glass of wine, Ryuu let me know that your coffee supplies arrived. I imagine you will be getting your new coffee station set up."

"Not coffee station." She shook her head.

"What then?"

"My altar! I am Coffee Goddess rawwrrr!"

Oron opened their door and ushered her inside. "Come on, it's time for good Coffee Goddesses to get to bed."

"You gonna sex me up?"

"Not tonight, baby."

"I like your penis."

Oron chuckled as he unbuttoned her robe. "I'm glad. He likes you too."

"He does?" she asked, as she tried to get a rogue hair out of her eyes.

"Yes, immensely." He hung up her robe, then removed his own.

She looked down. "I'm naked."

"Yes, you are." He hung his own robe up and kissed her nose.

"No sexy time?"

"No baby, not while you're tipsy."

"But I thought your penis liked me."

"He does and he also respects you."

"You're gonna make me cry, you have such a kind penis."

"Yes, love, I know. Now, climb into bed."

Izzy tried to climb on, but seemed to lack the coordination. "Push my butt, but not in a sexy way."

Oron laughed and did as she asked. She landed on the covers and started giggling. "You bopped my butt."

Oron pulled the covers out from under her then rolled her onto her pillow. He gently tapped a glowing crystal, plunging the room into darkness before she felt the bed dip as he climbed in. He pulled her into his arms and covered them with the blankets.

She wiggled a bit and felt something hard behind her. "Your penis *does* like me!"

"Izzy! You're killing me," Oron groaned.

"You called me 'love', no take backs," she said, before yawning.

"I'd never, ever take that back, Isabelle."

"I love you too, Oron. Never been in love before, glad it's with you."

Oron arms tightened around her. "You're saying that again tomorrow when you haven't been drinking."

She yawned again. "Okie, dokie, Mr. Pokie," she giggled as she pushed back against him.

"Dream of me," he whispered.

"Sounds like a plan," she said, right before she fell asleep.

Chapter Nine

"OH MY GOD, I HATE you! How could you let me ramble on like that!" Izzy wanted to lock herself in the closet. She was barely able to function this morning as she pulled on her new robe. This one was fuchsia. All she could hear echoing through her head as she pulled on her new clothes was her voice telling him that she loved him and some stupid nonsense about his penis.

Her sexy mate was all smiles. "You were adorable."

"Did I really say I loved your penis?"

He shook his head and she felt a moment of relief. "You said you *liked* my penis and that you loved me," he clarified. "But I'm not counting that as your first declaration of love, you have to say again while not under the influence of three glasses of my mother's best wine."

Izzy headed for the closet, but Oron intercepted her. "I love you, Izzy. I don't want my first declaration to be from when you were drinking either."

She looked up at. "I really do love you, but it scares me."

"Why?"

"Because I loved my parents, and when they died, I almost got lost in myself."

"How did they die?"

"A stupid drunk driver. He clipped them causing their car to go off the road and slam into a tree. He walked away without a scratch and didn't serve any jail time since it was his first offense. He only had to do community service."

"How old were you?" he asked, holding her close.

"Twenty-one. I had to sell the house and most of its contents to pay the bank. I packed a few bags and have been on my own ever since."

"You and Meryn impress the hell out of me. You had to take care of yourselves at such a young age."

"What about you?"

He rubbed their noses together. "I had mother, Cord, and of course Darian, I wasn't alone."

"Have you ever shown him his baby pictures?"

Oron blushed furiously. "Of course not. It would be embarrassing for him to see my chicken scratch."

Izzy stepped back and headed to his wall. She had taken the second picture down when he placed a hand on her arm. "What are you doing?"

Izzy held up the picture that showed baby Darian with a beautiful woman and tall man. "Those are his parents, right?" He nodded. "Don't you think he'd like to know what they looked like, hell, what he looked like? As you said, this was before cameras Oron."

Her mate turned his head away. "They're not very good."

"They are exquisite. Now, grab the one where Cord looks like he's about to strangle Darian in the kitchen." Izzy gathered a few more and they headed to the smaller, more intimate dining room for breakfast.

She noticed the closer they got to the dining room the slower Oron walked. "Hurry up!" she said excitedly.

This time when she entered, she ignored all the men standing and went right to Darian. "You know how you didn't know that the Skysongs moved here because Fremi saved you, but Oron did because he was older?" Darian nodded slowly, taking in her ramble. She was about to continue when she noticed Oron lingering at the end of the table. "So help me…" Oron trudged over to stand next to them. Instead of handing the picture of Darian with his parents to him, she passed it to Oron, then stepped back.

Without saying a word, Oron handed Darian the small framed picture.

Darian looked down, confused. "What is this?"

Amelia gasped as she looked down. "It's you," she whispered, tears in her eyes. Of course, his own mate would recognize him.

Darian looked up at his brother. "Oron, is she right?" Oron just nodded. Darian looked back down at the picture. He kept swallowing over and over again as tears ran unchecked down his face. “Are these, are they…” he couldn’t even finish the sentence.

Oron just placed his hand on top of Darian’s head. “It’s your mother and father. You had just started to crawl in the garden and they were so proud.”

“What?” Aleksandra asked, before popping up out of her chair and racing over with Brennus and Cord.

When she looked down and saw the picture, she covered her mouth with both hands. “How?”

Oron shrugged. Izzy knew that this was an important moment for her mate, so she slipped her phone from her pocket and began taking pictures.

The queen turned and grabbed both of Oron’s hands, snatching the one from Darian’s head. “These hands did this?” He just shrugged again. “All these thousands of years, why didn’t you tell me you were this gifted?”

“I’m not, I’m just a warrior,” he said.

The queen pulled him into her arms. “You Oron Vi’Eirson are not ‘just’ anything. You are my son. You are the best brother any boy could pray for. You are kind and your light shines so bright it threatens to eclipse others. Your hands can create *and* defend, you are not *just* anything,” she said fiercely.

“Aleks, look!” Brennus said, holding up another picture.

When the queen saw what the picture held, her knees gave out, so Oron had to support her. Heedless of her condition, she still reached for the sketch. It was of her, giving baby Darian a bath while a laughing Cord supervised. The queen's hair was falling out of her immaculate braid, her sleeves were pushed up to her elbows and she looked to be soaked from head to toe.

Brennus handed Cord the one where Darian had destroyed his kitchen. Cord accepted the picture and turned his back to the room while his shoulders quaked.

Oron looking positively terrified, helped his mother to a chair while she cradled the drawing in her arms like a newborn.

"You are a unit warrior when you can create such masterpieces?" Aiden demanded.

Oron spun. "But sir, they're not that…"

Meryn held up a hand. "Oron, they look like freaking pictures, like from a camera. Trust me, they are beyond art."

Darian stood and simply wrapped his arms around his brother's neck. "I already owed you my very life, even if I were to live as long as our mother, I could never repay you for what you've preserved." When he pulled back and looked up into Oron's face Darian's composure cracked. "I never knew what they looked like," he sobbed, clutching at his shirt like a small child.

Oron's back straightened and there was no panic on his face now. He wrapped an arm around Darian and rubbed his hand over his hair. "Shuush, Dari, it's okay."

"I just can't," Amelia sobbed into Meryn's shoulder at the sight of her mate so undone.

Meryn awkwardly tried to mimic Oron's

actions and wrapped her arm around her big sister cousin's head.

Izzy set her phone down, feeling satisfied with her work. She plopped into her chair and looked around for the coffee.

"Allow me," Ryuu said, a kind smile on his face. "You, more than anyone, deserve it." Ryuu poured her a fresh cup of coffee. She sat back and enjoyed her mate's moment of glory.

"I can't believe you've had these for thousands of years!" Darian exclaimed a bit later once he composed himself and started looking through the other pictures.

"Looks like your honeymoon period is over," Izzy teased.

"Can I go put them back now?" Oron asked.

The word 'no' echoed throughout the room.

Meryn was giggling uncontrollably. "Even thousands of years ago you guys did bathtub pictures," she said, pointing to the picture of the toothless Darian grinning up at his soaked mother. "Look Felix, baby Darian."

Izzy watched as Felix appeared from Meryn's lap. He looked down at the picture and smiled. "Baby," he repeated.

Izzy noticed that, unlike the previous day, Meryn now sported a graphic tee and jeans. She wondered if she'd have to wait until they left to get more jeans.

"I wish I had something like this from when I was a cub," Pierce said, looking over Meryn's shoulder. As usual, Pierce hadn't strayed too far from Ryuu.

"Oron, I have no right to ask, but may I please have this one?" Cord asked, holding the picture of Darian covered in flour as if it were the most valuable thing on earth.

"Of course, Cord, you're like a father to Darian and me, there's nothing I'd deny you."

Cord dashed away his tears. "It was one of my most cherished memories even before I saw the picture."

Darian turned to them, looking surprised. "Really? Because all I remember from that day is that it took me forever to sweep up all that damn flour."

Cord smiled. "You were trying to help me make dinner since I had accidentally slipped and bruised both my ego and my tailbone. When you tried to explain yourself, you started crying because you didn't want me to be hurt."

Kendrick chuckled. "The crybaby ended up with a crybaby," he teased.

Anne whacked him. "Hush."

Cord placed a hand on Oron's arm. "Are you certain?"

"Yes, I'm certain, I have a ton more pictures under my bed, I'll just frame one of those for my wall to replace it," Oron explained.

"More?" Aleksandra gasped.

"Wall?" Darian asked at the same time.

Oron groaned and let his head fall back as his queen mother and heir apparent brother tore from the room, heading down the hall unceremoniously. "Dammit!" he exclaimed.

Thane gently traced the edge of one of the pictures then stood. He walked over to Oron. "Oron, if I were to put an image in your mind, could you draw something for me, something like those?" he asked, pointing to the table.

Oron's mouth dropped. "You want me to draw you something?"

Thane just nodded quietly. "You can name your price."

Oron shook his head.

Thane frowned. "I guess it was too much to ask."

"No, what I meant was I could never charge you money for doodles," Oron explained.

Thane studied Oron's face. "I want you to look at me and really listen." Thane pointed to Oron's hands. "I am not an overwhelmed mother or brother. I tell you this with objectivity and with no sense of bias. What you have is an extremely rare and gods-given gift, Oron Vi'Eirson. I would happily pay any sum you would name to have even one picture done to this quality. In fact, I will be personally petitioning Aiden to remove you from service immediately to protect these irreplaceable hands."

Aiden grunted but didn't argue.

Oron turned to her and she could see that he was getting overwhelmed. She stood quickly and went to him. She wrapped an arm around his waist and winked at Thane. "I think those hands are magical too."

He blinked, then laughed at her double entendre. “I imagine that to be true.”

She just rubbed Oron’s back. “No decisions have to be made right away. Personally, I’m looking forward to living in Lycaonia. I hear that Meryn needs my skills as she works on databases.”

“I’ll do it, but I won’t accept any money. I will barter for a favor to be redeemed by my commander should the occasion arise,” Oron said, extending his hand.

Thane looked relieved as he shook hands with Oron. “Aiden is an honorable man. I have no problem promising a future favor to him, as I am certain he would never ask me to do something that would go against my own conscience.”

Aiden’s cheeks tinted. “Thank you both Oron and Thane, I pray that we never find ourselves in a scenario where I would need to cash in such a favor.”

“Oron! I am going to kick your ass all over this realm!” Darian threatened, as he walked back into the room, struggling under the weight of a large box.

His mother was walking beside him a sketchbook under one arm. “And I will cheer him on. How could you not share these?” she demanded.

“I didn’t think they were any good,” Oron admitted.

Darian dropped the box on the table and began pulling out sketchbooks and loose pictures. “I think I have a hernia,” Darian complained.

"Good, now you can't chase me," Oron said, flicking his ear.

Darian absently rubbed his abused ear and continued flipping through pages.

"Oron, may we have a few as well," his mother asked, unable to take her eyes off the pictures now scattered on the table.

"Any that you would like are yours," he replied.

Breakfast morphed into a stroll down memory lane. Everyone took turns eating to keep the food away from the pictures. Izzy was enjoying her coffee until she saw Brennus quietly consoling his mate as she wept into her hands.

Neither Darian nor Oron had noticed yet. She stood and walked over to sit beside her new in-laws. When she looked down and saw why the queen of the fae was weeping, she felt her own tears gather.

It was a book of self-portraits. The queen now saw how Oron always viewed himself. Finally, around the table voices quieted as both Oron and Darian saw their mother weeping. Moving quickly, they knelt on either side of her. She watched as Darian noticed the pictures first. He flipped page after page, the blood draining from his face. He stood, his mother's tears forgotten as he came face to face with Oron's pain.

Oron saw which book it was and quickly grabbed it from Darian. He was halfway to the fireplace when Darian tackled him.

"Thane, get the book!" Darian yelled.

Thane raised his hand and shouted. "*Venito*!"

"Asshole!" Oron muttered, as the book flew to Thane.

Thane looked down and saw what was on the first page. "My request can wait. To ensure I am one of your favored clients, I offer you a gift. I will copy images from the minds of the queen, Brennus, Darian and Cord, images of you, for you to draw. I will store them in a crystal so that you can see yourself as they do."

Izzy jumped from her chair and plowed into the witch, wrapping her arms around his waist. "Thank you!"

"Hey!" Oron shouted.

Izzy giggled as he raced over. She slapped Thane's ass causing him to yelp in an undignified manner before she ran around to the other side of the table, avoiding her mate.

"Izzy! Get your adorable behind over here," he ordered.

"Catch me!" Every time he'd go left, she'd go right. In the end, her brother-in-law betrayed her and carried her over to Oron.

She smiled up at him. "I'm glad he caught me, I was running out of breath," she wheezed.

Meryn walked over and handed Oron her phone. He looked down and blinked. "That's me?"

Izzy could have kissed Meryn. The picture was one she had just taken showing a joyous Oron poised to dash right. True happiness spilled from his image.

Darian looked over his shoulder. "That's how I've always seen you. When I was younger, I felt like you always surrounded me in your light to keep me safe. I have no idea who that man is that you have drawn, I've never seen him before a day in my life."

His mother came up on his other side and nodded. "That smile is so very precious to me," she stood on tiptoe to kiss his cheek. "Oron, the memories you have frozen in time for us to cherish and share is a gift. You cannot share a light you do not have son and your light is there for everyone to see," she pointed to the table.

"You always called me your little warrior, so I didn't want to disappoint you," he admitted.

"I called you a warrior because I was proud of what you had done. I wanted you to know that your actions were noble and that your family's shame was not your own." She cuffed him upside the head. "Had I known the gods gave me a genius artist I would have bought you every medium under the sun and called you my 'little artist'," she said, before kissing his arm.

"I'm not giving up being a unit warrior," he said stubbornly.

"Good," she heard Aiden mutter under his breath.

The queen turned to Thane. "About that crystal."

They were still looking over pictures when Portia entered. "Your Majesty, Cristo and Stefan Bolivar," she announced, holding the door open. Two dark-haired men hurried into the room. "Brennus, I found it!" The taller one called out.

"Cristo, I'd be more excited for you if I knew what 'it' was," Brennus said flatly.

Cristo held up a square, wooden box and looked like he was about to answer when he turned to the Ashleigh brothers and Kendrick. "The strongest soundproofing spell the four of you can manage please."

Kendrick exchanged shocked expressions with the brothers and the four of them extended their right hands forward until their fists were touching. When they released the spell Izzy's ears popped and she felt like she was going to puke. She didn't know a thing about magic, but she knew without a shadow of a doubt, that she just experienced the strongest soundproofing spell ever cast.

"Whoa," Meryn exclaimed, swaying in her chair. Both Aiden and Ryuu helped to keep her upright. Izzy was interested to see that where Ryuu's hand rested on Meryn's shoulder, a blue light glowed.

The queen clutched at her chest. "The next time you release enough magic to stall the sun, could we get a little warning." She eyed the door. "I assume a barrier is up as well."

Kendrick winked at her. "Of course."

She opened her mouth repeatedly as if to pop her ears. "I hope none of the servants need us until you take that thing down." She shuddered. "It's almost like a living breathing entity."

Meryn looked at the door, her eyes ablaze with curiosity. "Cool!"

Cristo placed the box on the table. "We were

looking for Eamon's communication spheres!"

"What's a communication sphere?" Izzy asked.

Thane ground his teeth together. "Eamon created a magic that allowed him to basically record a video in a sphere and send them home. He used them for reports that were too sensitive to trust to paper. The sphere would simply appear here in Éire Danu and could only be opened by Brennus."

Izzy thought Brennus was going to be ill and not because the super witches' had cast the soundproofing bubble.

Cristo looked around. "Good! Doran and Celyn are here as well."

Brennus stared at the box. "Why would you possibly need them? They've gone untouched for nearly forty years."

"Because, I think I can finally open them," Cristo announced.

"Cristo, I have never wanted to punch you more than I do at this moment," Thane threatened as he stalked forward. "How dare you rip open a wound that has long since healed."

"Justice, Law, leash the maniac for the time being," Cristo ordered, completely unfazed by Thane's threat.

Law and Justice each grabbed their brother by the shoulder. Thane stared at them. "Since when do the two of you take orders from someone and against me?"

Law and Justice each pointed with the hand that wasn't restraining their brother. "It's Cristo," they said together. Thane simply growled but stopped his forward march.

"What do they mean, 'It's Cristo'?" Izzy asked.

"Yeah, what she said," Meryn echoed.

"What they mean, is I am Thane's Vanguard squad leader," Cristo explained.

"We're not Vanguard," Thane protested.

Cristo turned to him and held up his fingers in air quotes. "Fine, we're 'Guardians'. Happy now?" He immediately turned back to the box.

Thane squinted at the handsome man. "Why haven't I killed you yet?"

"Because secretly you want me to have your love child," Cristo said, without even looking up from the box.

Kendrick pointed to Cristo. "You like him because he reminds you of me."

"You mean I want to wrap my hands around his throat and throttle him because he reminds me of you?" Thane corrected.

Brennus laid a hand on the lid Cristo was about to open. "Are you sure?"

Cristo nodded. "My nose has never failed me."

Brennus lifted his hand. "What does that have to do with anything?"

Cristo turned and faced the large group. He clapped his hands together. "Okay boys and girls, gather round, it's story time."

Brennus rolled his eyes then sat down next to his mate and the man Izzy assumed to be Stefan sat down next to Meryn.

"Once upon a time, there were five strong, handsome warriors. They didn't like the way certain groups were being led, and tended not to play well with others, so they joined forces to combat evil." Cristo pointed to his chest. "There was a sexy wolf-shifter, Rio Suarez a coyote-shifter, Thane Ashleigh a rage-filled sarcastic witch, Ange Belanger a directionally challenged vampire and Eamon Vi'Eirlea, a golden child of the fae." Cristo's eyes drifted to the box. "Now, these five men managed to accomplish amazing feats, all while not murdering each other in their sleep."

"Get on with it!" Thane ordered.

"As I was saying," Cristo huffed. "They worked together beautifully, until one day, when Eamon had to take a mission from his queen, leaving his friends behind. The other four heroes believed that the mission would only last a few months, then the heart of their group would return, but as the years passed they all wondered what had become of their brother." He tapped his nose. "So, the brilliant wolf-shifter tracked down his friend and made a discovery so secret that his friend Eamon made him take a blood oath never to speak of what he learned outside the protection of Éire Danu." He drew in a deep shuddering breath and it was then Izzy realized that the flippant tone was a form of self-preservation, to make the telling of this story easier.

Thane stood and walked over to Cristo placing a steadying hand on his shoulder. "I swear whatever you have to say, I will help you to bear it," he promised.

Cristo's eyes shined. "Surly asshole," he said,

though his voice held no venom. He turned back to the group. "He discovered that in the process of investigating for his queen, his best friend had found his mate and they had a child together."

Brennus stood, reaching for Cristo rage etched in every line of his face. "Lies! Our tree did not show any branch extending from Eamon, nor any child!"

Thane stepped between the two. With a whispered spell, he calmed the angry fae warrior and gently sat Brennus in a vacant chair. Doran and Celyn were by their brother's side in a moment.

"Our brother speaks the truth, Eamon had no mate, no child," Doran insisted.

"For five years Eamon stopped sending these," he opened the case and lifted out a pulsating sphere. Inside Izzy could clearly see a dozen more just like it. "You see, his mate had the gift of premonition and in every instance, if someone outside their tiny family learned of their existence, their child would die. Eamon used fae magic to hide his bond with his mate and removed the light of the fae from his child. He stopped sending these spheres because he had used them to document the time spent away from his family, so they wouldn't miss anything."

He turned to Brennus. "Did you never wonder why we were unable to open the last barrage of spheres we received?"

Brennus nodded. "It is because we tried opening them after he died."

Cristo shook his head. "If that were truly the case, the light within the sphere would have dimmed." He looked at Brennus then Doran. "Do you remember what he said he would use as a key before he left?"

Doran looked away as Brennus answered. "The blood of his closest relative."

Cristo held out the sphere, Brennus went to take it but Cristo walked past him to stand in front of Meryn and extended it to her. "Brennus, you were no longer Eamon's closest living relative because he left a daughter behind."

Izzy looked around for a second before the sound of shouting voices exploded all around her.

Chapter Ten

IZZY COVERED HER EARS AS everyone seemed to be speaking at once. She turned to see Ryuu begin to glow blue, then lift his fingers to his lips and release a piercing whistle, the silence that followed such chaos was deafening.

"Quiet yourselves," he said in a dangerous voice. He pushed Cristo a step back and glared at him. "She is with child; how could you spring it on her that way?"

Cristo met the squire's accusing eyes. "What would have been the less traumatic way to tell her? Because no matter how it's said, the truth doesn't change."

Ryuu released a very impressive hiss and knelt beside his charge. "Breathe *denka*, all is well. We are with you," he said in gentle tones.

Aiden wrapped an arm around her as Stefan quickly stood so that Amelia could sit and hold Meryn's other hand.

"You knew with Amelia that she was my family, what about them?" she asked, pointing to Brennus.

He shook his head. "I can feel no tie to them, *denka*," he replied.

Aiden looked at Cristo. "You must be wrong."

Cristo held up the orb. "There's one surefire way to find out. One single drop of her blood will tell us everything. Either it will drip off the way Brennus' blood did or the sphere will open and you will know I tell the truth."

Meryn looked to Kendrick. He hurried over and knelt beside Ryuu. "What is it darling?"

"I trust you almost as much as I trust Aiden and Ryuu, could me giving up a drop of blood do anything hinky, magic-wise?"

Kendrick went to answer then stopped. "As usual you think of things I do not, that's quite a feat, young lady." He stood, then began to pace back and forth.

Brennus went to ask him something, but Anne stopped him. "Leave him. He's mentally running through every spell he knows to see how a single drop of her blood could be used against her."

Thane stepped beside Cristo. "Cristo would never endanger you, Meryn."

Meryn nodded. "I know, he's a shield. But who's to say someone didn't tamper with that thing before it showed up here?"

Kendrick stopped in his pacing and held out a hand. "Cristo if you would allow me, I would like to ensure that nothing outside the original spell is affecting the sphere."

Cristo hesitated. "It won't harm the sphere?"

Kendrick shook his head. "There's no power behind it, just a revelation spell."

Cristo took a deep breath then handed it over to Kendrick. Kendrick held it at arm's length. "*Revelare*." It flared yellow for a moment, then the light faded.

He handed it over to Meryn. "There's nothing on this sphere that would cause you harm."

Meryn looked from Cristo to Brennus and back. "Just a drop of blood, right?" Both Cristo and Brennus nodded.

She held her hand out to Ryuu. "Can you do the blood thing?"

Ryuu took her hand that held the sphere gently between his. Meryn grimaced and turned away. Ryuu smiled as one nail lengthened to a sharp black point. He quickly tapped the tip of Meryn's finger.

"Ow!" Meryn complained, before allowing a single drop of blood to fall on the sphere.

When light flared out around them, Oron used his body as a shield putting himself between Izzy and the room.

"Gods!" someone whispered.

In the middle of the chamber, as if being projected on a movie screen a video-like image began.

"Uncle Eamon," Oron whispered.

Brother, my queen, I pray that this finds you well.

The handsome man rubbed his hands over his face as he sat at a wooden desk. From the bookcase in the background, Izzy thought he was in an office or library.

I hope to make this my last report as I have decided to return to Éire Danu.

Eamon, darling...

Izzy heard a woman's voice from off-screen.

I just started this recording, now I'll have to destroy it and start over.

Behind him, a beautiful woman came into view, tears streaming down her face. She threw herself onto his lap.

Whatever is the matter, my love?

He looked around frantically.

Where's Meryn!

Around Izzy, more than one person gasped.

The time we both feared is upon us. Oh Eamon! She wailed.

I had to leave her with my mother! She sobbed between each word. *I tried calling Lily so many times while I sat in the car, but the headaches I got from the premonitions made my nose bleed. Mother was the only place I saw where she'd be safe, the only place I saw where she'd have a future.*

Eamon ran a hand over her hair. *We'll leave everything behind and go to Éire Danu, we'll come back and get Meryn the second we can.*

The woman shook her head.

They're here. Just beyond the property line.

Eamon took a deep breath.

Darling, fetch that bottle of fae wine we were saving.

She nodded then rose to her feet before disappearing to one side.

They watched as Eamon pulled out a pouch

from his desk drawer. Eamon turned to face the sphere.

Brother, there is so much I wish to tell you, have told you actually, I just haven't sent them on to Éire Danu…

The woman reappeared. It looked like she had washed her face and fixed her hair. She smiled at him and handed him one of the two glasses before curling up in his lap.

It's okay to tell them now. I don't know why, but I know it's safe, I don't see this recording harming Meryn.

How much time do we have?

Twenty minutes, at the very most.

Eamon carefully measured out a black powder and mixed it into their wine. They smiled at one another, the love between them as clear as crystal. He raised his glass in a toast.

To Meryn, may you know only happiness and love all your days.

The woman raised her glass.

May you stay safe.

Beside them, Brennus sobbed. "No! Don't drink it!"

Together they drank deeply before setting their glasses down on the wooden desk. Using a key Eamon unlocked the top right drawer, retrieved a small wooden box and set it down in front of them. He carefully lifted each sphere and released it in the air. It blazed for a moment before disappearing. He slowly started releasing one after another.

Brother, I am sending you about a dozen

recordings where I explain and show you almost everything. I know you must have so many questions, but we don't have a lot of time, so I will answer the one you're probably demanding of me. Who is this beautiful woman at my side and who is Meryn?

Eamon released the last stored sphere and nuzzled the woman's neck.

This gorgeous creature is my mate Violet and Meryn is our daughter, she's five, Brennus, and gods! She's so amazing. She reminds me of mother. She's so kind and loves helping. Brother, you must watch over my daughter. She is with a human, my mate's mother, her name is Estelle Camden and she's dreadful.

Eamon!

She is! Why Fate thought that she'd be safe with that harpy, I'll never know. He sighed. *Brennus, you have to protect my baby girl.* Eamon stumbled on the words 'baby girl' and even Izzy could see how painful it was for him to say.

I have named Thane Ashleigh as her athair. He chuckled. *That should surprise him.*

At the end of the table, Thane gasped, and wept at the declaration.

Violet wiped her eyes. *This is too hard! Knowing that she will barely remember us is breaking me. All I ever wanted in life was to be her momma. I wish I could see her one last time.*

Quietly she began to weep as Eamon held her close and spoke a prayer.

Dear gods, please let her remember us and how we loved her. How everything we did was to keep her safe, to ensure she had a future, even keeping her existence a secret.

Violet sat up and gasped.

Eamon.

What is it, my love?

I can see something.

He placed his fingers over her heart and his light shone brighter.

It's my brothers and my queen. Gods, even Thane, Cristo and young Stefan are there.

"Kendrick?" Meryn asked, in a wobbly voice.

Kendrick covered his mouth with a shaking hand. "I think your mother is having a premonition of this exact moment, of us watching the sphere."

Eamon gasped. *Is that my baby girl? Meryn, is that you?*

Meryn nodded, hiccuping as she wept softly. "Yes, Daddy, it's me."

Oh Eamon! Look! She's pregnant! We did it! We really did it! She made it! Violet's joy made her beautiful features shine that much more.

That's Aiden McKenzie, the Unit Commander, unless I'm mistaken.

"No sir, I am Aiden McKenzie. You have given me the most precious gift in the world. I will fill every second of her life with happiness and she will want for nothing," he promised, his voice cracking. He held on to Meryn tightly.

Damn right I have and you better keep her safe too.

"I swear to you on my life, I will always keep her safe," Aiden vowed.

Violet reached out a hand as if to touch Meryn. Meryn extended her hand toward the sphere.

Darling, we love you so much. We're so sorry to leave you all alone.

Eamon reached out as well.

My Meryn, my little Merriment.

Violet laughed and pointed.

Look, she's wearing a shirt with that ridiculous box on it from that TV show you watch with her.

I knew she liked it!

Violet turned back to the sphere.

Were you happy my little love? Did Brennus and Doran raise you well?

Izzy saw just a second of hesitation before Meryn beamed up at her parents. "I couldn't have asked for a happier childhood. You don't have a thing to worry about, they didn't spoil me too badly." Meryn turned and pulled Ryuu toward her. "I have so many people who take care of me. Ryuu is my squire, he feeds me awesome food." Ryuu nearly bowed in half at his charge's parents. Meryn lifted the hand that still clasped Amelia's tight. "Momma, look! This is Amelia, she's my big sister-cousin, Lily's daughter, she's mated to Darian!" She looked down. "Felix do your thing," she begged. Felix fumbled with his necklace and rotated the stone. "I even have Felix to watch over me."

Eamon looked puzzled.

Of course, Felix is with you.

Violet stared.

Oh Amelia, darling look at the two of you

together. Eamon, Amelia my niece mated to Darian, your nephew. Our families are tied together even more.

Like most of the people in the room, Darian had tears streaming when he stepped behind Amelia. "I swear to you uncle, I will protect them both."

The sphere flickered. "I love you, Momma, I love you, Daddy. I think of you every day!"

Violet blinked slowly.

I have loved you from the first moment the pregnancy stone glowed for me and I will carry that love with me when I go.

Eamon moved his hand as Violet closed her eyes.

The vision is gone.

Violet's head slumped forward and he pulled her back against him gently.

"No! Momma!" Meryn screeched.

Eamon sat back.

With my death, the recording will end. My queen, my final report to you is as follows. Last week I was finally able to track down the ones I feared were killing our people.

He paused.

Oron, son, I'm so sorry, but it's your family. They didn't fade honorably as they should have. Most turned feral and have been hunting fae for vengeance. They are the ones who tracked us here.

He sniffed the air.

They have set fire to the house thinking to smoke us out. As if I'd let them take us alive. My mate is beyond their terrible reach and I'll be joining her soon.

He struggled to draw breath.

My little Meryn, kind as ever. Thank you for the beautiful lie. You made your mother's final moments filled with love and hope and peace. But you are my child and I saw the way pain filled your heart at the mention of your childhood. You must have suffered so much before my brothers found you. Believe in your uncles and your athair, my little Merriment...

He closed his eyes.

They will avenge your sorrow and our deaths, which stole so many years from us.

He opened his eyes.

Brennus, Doran, one of the spheres I sent contains Meryn's light. To keep her hidden, I had to remove it the moment before she was born. I am entrusting you both to return it and keep her safe.

He closed his eyes once more as the edges of the picture began to dim.

There they are!

Oron inhaled and ground his teeth together at the sound of the stranger's voice. "My father," he whispered.

You're too late. Eamon wheezed.

He then smiled.

We will watch over you, never doubt our love.

They watched as hands grabbed Violet dumping her to the floor in their effort to reach Eamon.

Eamon roared and released a blast of burning pure light. His attackers screamed in pain. He struggled, but carefully lifted Violet in his arms before collapsing back into his chair.

You have failed in your mission to capture us alive and my brothers will hunt you to the ends of the Earth.

He smiled beatifically.

Hello, my love, were you waiting long?

Just as the image collapsed on itself an arm with a fiery, red tattoo appeared, reaching for Eamon.

And then the recording ended, leaving nothing but grief in its wake.

"Meryn!" Ryuu called out urgently, as the woman passed out in her mate's arms. Anne rushed over to assist.

"Please tell me they're okay," Aiden begged.

Ryuu held up her wrist, then exhaled. "Her mind shut her entire body down to protect itself." He looked over to Kendrick. "We need Sacred Chamomile."

Kendrick nodded, then began digging into the small bag at his waist. Izzy watched in amazement as he brought out first a book, then another smaller pouch from the tiny bag. He caught her staring. "It's called the Bag of Wishes, I can store anything I need in here, and good thing too. Ryuu!" he called.

Ryuu looked up from his charge and raised a hand. Kendrick tossed the bag to him, which he effortlessly caught with one hand. Pierce promptly took the bag from the squire. "You stay with her, even I know how to make tea." He turned to Kendrick. "I think we can take at least the barrier down."

The queen stood. "I'd like for all of us to adjourn to my private chambers. It will be more comfortable there, for everyone." Unlike earlier, she was now supporting her mate. Brennus and his brothers looked absolutely wrecked.

Anne stood when Ryuu scooped Meryn up in his arms. He was keeping a blue light shimmering over her. Amelia had her eyes squeezed shut and her hands over her ears. Justice and Law were murmuring low at her side, their hands glowing as well. Izzy remembered that Amelia was an empath, she had to be getting grief and pain from every direction and Law and his brother were doing what they could to help.

Kendrick raised his right hand to the ceiling and a pulse wave swept the room as both the barrier and soundproofing spell was released.

Slowly everyone made their way to the queen's chambers and collapsed into any chair or sofa they could reach. Pierce and Cord headed to the kitchen to start the tea as Izzy stared out over the room.

"Meryn, sweetheart, it's okay," Aiden whispered as Meryn's eyes began to flutter open.

She looked around then up at her mate. "It was real?"

Aiden nodded. "Yes, baby, it was real."

Meryn turned her head and her eyes roamed until they landed on the chaise where Brennus sat with his mate and brothers. She smiled softly. "I guess you are my Uncle and Aunt," she announced. She gave everyone a wobbly smile. "He called me his Merriment, not Menace. I'm not bad," she whispered.

Brennus' eyes widened and he stood. He went over to kneel down in front of Meryn. "I have a baby niece."

"*We* have a baby niece," Celyn reminded him. "Thank the gods I'm the Elder for Lycaonia, I get to visit her whenever I want," he bragged. Vivian swatted his arm. "Celyn, that's not nice," she smiled. "Even though it's true."

Meryn looked over to Amelia. "Is she okay?"

Darian nodded as he continued to rub Amelia's back. Kendrick was now the one standing at her side. He placed a hand on her shoulder and slowly her face became less pained. Finally, she exhaled and opened her eyes. "It was a bit intense there for a moment," she said weakly.

"I could have done that," Thane groused, shooing Kendrick away from Amelia.

Kendrick pointed down. "My godsdaughter."

Thane pointed. "My sister."

Kendrick shrugged. "Fine, I'll go help Meryn."

Thane growled. "That's my godsdaughter."

Kendrick threw his hands in the air. "And she's my…" He paused and turned back to Meryn. "What are we anyway?"

Aiden collapsed back on the sofa looking drained. "Gods, they are alike. That sounded like a Meryn question."

Meryn looked up at Ryuu. "How does this work?"

Ryuu rubbed his chin. "You adopted his cousins as your brothers, but your tie to him was established before you met the twins."

Amelia clapped her hands together excitedly. "Oh! I know! He's your big brother-cousin!"

Meryn nodded. "Okay, that is kinda perfect. Let's do that. You're my big brother-cousin."

Kendrick gave Thane a shit-eating grin. "I'm her big brother-cousin."

"What does that make Thane and Kendrick?" Meryn asked.

"An asshole," they both said at the same time.

Cord and Pierce came back in with trays. Cord looked around. "There's enough for everyone."

When Pierce brought a tray around, Oron shook his head. Pierce looked at her and she gave a quick shake as well. If he wasn't having any, neither was she.

"Oh, I like this. It's stronger than the Blessed Chamomile," Meryn said, leaning back into Aiden, holding her cup.

Ryuu's pinched features relaxed as he released her wrist. "You're doing much better."

Meryn closed her eyes. "That was my mom and dad, huh?"

When Oron stood and walked over to Meryn, Izzy followed.

Meryn peeled one eye open. "What?"

Oron knelt down and bowed his head. "Meryn, I am so sorry."

Meryn handed her cup to Aiden and had Ryuu help her up. Once standing Oron looked up at her, Izzy could see the fear of condemnation in his eyes.

Meryn took a deep breath and slapped Oron across the face, the cracking sound silenced the room. Aiden quickly stood and set the cup down on the table. Like Aiden, Izzy was about to step in when she noticed the look on Meryn's face.

"Don't you dare say you're sorry as if you were somehow responsible for any of this. My Dad loved you, he called you son, so don't you belittle yourself that way. We're family."

Oron's eyes streamed tears as he stood. He took a single step back before placing a fisted hand over his heart and bowed low.

"Meryn, I swear to you by all our gods, that I will see my family pay for the pain they've caused."

Thane, Justice, Law, and Cristo placed their hands over their hearts. "So do we swear," they repeated.

Oron looked shocked. She tugged on his sleeve. "What?"

Aiden answered. "They have also taken on his oath; they are promising to help him see it through."

Thane nodded. "So will Rio and Ange, if their dumbasses ever find their way here."

Oron turned to him. "You didn't have to…"

Thane held up a hand. "We will complete Eamon's mission. He died getting us this information, we will finish what he could not."

Izzy rubbed her nose back and forth on his upper arm. "Just say thank you," she suggested.

"Thank you," he said, his voice catching.

"Can you replay spheres?" Meryn asked in a small voice.

Brennus smiled. "Yes, we can watch it again whenever you wish."

Aiden made Meryn sit back down and joined her. He handed her the tea and snuggled her close. "Why don't you just rest for now?"

The other men returned to their chairs and this time when Oron sat down, he chose the loveseat closer to his family. He pulled her down to sit next to him and tucked her close to his body.

The queen tapped the crystal near her chair and a few moments later, there was a knock on the door and Portia entered.

"Yes? Your Majesty."

"Can you take the following announcements down?"

"Of course," Portia unrolled her scroll and it hung in mid-air as she readied her quill. "Ready when you are."

"Please announce that I am calling all my children home. This is an order and not a request. We will make every effort to make the relocation as painless as possible, but time is of the essence."

Portia nodded and the queen continued. "We are also announcing that Darian Vi'Alina has been confirmed as my heir, he will be the next king." Portia nodded as if she had been expecting that for some time. "I'd also like to add the following birth announcement. Thirty-five years ago, Meryn Eirlea was born to Eamon and Violet

Vi'Eirlea. Meryn was raised in the human world and has recently mated to Aiden McKenzie. She will be designated second in line for the throne."

Portia's eyes bulged as she dropped her quill.

Darian dropped his head back on his shoulders. "Mother, can't we just keep this to ourselves for a while longer?"

Brennus rubbed his chin. "Should she be Meryn Vi'Eirlea?"

Doran shrugged. "Makes little difference to me who carries the title of head of household. Just let me know if I should be Li' now."

Meryn sat forward. "What the what?" She set her tea down. "If y'all are making major announcements and stuff I need coffee, not coma tea." She turned to Brennus. "And never mind about the Vi' thing. I'm Meryn McKenzie."

Aiden gave a single emphatic nod. "Exactly."

The queen turned to Meryn. "Darling, fae royalty outranks a possible Elder status for Aiden."

Meryn crossed her arms. "I like being a McKenzie."

Aiden beamed. Meryn continued. "The alliteration is cool. Meryn McKenzie, two m's."

Aiden looked crestfallen. "That's why?"

She shrugged. "Besides loving you to pieces? Yeah."

The queen turned to her mate. "She really doesn't care about rank."

Brennus looked confused. "Months of following her on Facebook and you're just now figuring that out?"

Portia picked up her quill. "Should I still make

that announcement?" she asked, sounding more composed.

The queen nodded. "Regardless of what name she ends up with, I want the world to know she is tied to our family. I want her to have every layer of protection her station affords."

Behind them, Celyn had collapsed to one side laughing uncontrollably. Vivian looked down at her mate, open-mouthed. "Celyn, what on earth?"

Every time Celyn went to speak, he just began laughing again. Finally, he calmed down enough to speak. "Renee is going to swallow his tongue the first time he has to call her Lady," at the declaration he exhaled. "I can't wait to get back."

Meryn began to giggle. "Elder Vi'Ailean, you're awesome."

Celyn sat up frowning. "That's Uncle Cel to you, young lady."

Meryn covered her mouth with her hands. "Kick-ass," she whispered.

Aiden stood. "Meryn, will you be okay for a little bit?"

She nodded. "Why?"

"I need to tell mom and dad before the announcement goes out."

Her eyes widened. "Good idea."

Aiden leaned down, kissed her forehead, then walked to the far side of the room for his phone call.

"I don't mean to bring up something painful," Izzy started. "But didn't her parents say they did everything they could to keep her a secret?

Should we be making an announcement?"

Meryn shrugged. "The bad guy knows who I am, so I don't think it matters at this point."

Thane scowled. "What bad guy?"

Meryn smiled. "The demon that almost killed me when I interrogated DeLaFontaine in Noctem Falls. He took me into a dream state, stopping my heart, but in the end, he said he thought he liked me and that playing with me would be fun." She beamed at everyone.

Izzy may have been new to this world, but even she knew that Meryn had just dropped a bomb of epic proportions.

Kendrick just chuckled at Meryn's clueless-ness as everyone else began to unravel.

Portia turned to the queen. "I will make the announcements you have specified and leave you to figure out the rest," she said, looking wan.

The queen nodded absently and Portia quickly left the room. The queen then stared at Meryn. "A demon said you were fun?"

Meryn shrugged. "Yeah, what a weirdo."

Amelia crossed her arms. "Forget to tell me that?" she asked fuming.

Meryn gave her big sister-cousin an exasper-ated look. "Do you have any idea the amount of shit we had to deal with in Noctem Falls? I would have told you sooner, but then we had Avery's ceremony, then leaving, then going to the camp, then coming here. We've been fuck-ing busy."

Izzy looked up at her mate. "Demons are real?"

Oron looked a bit spooked himself. "Evidently."

Aiden returned looking exasperated himself. He glowered at Celyn. "My mother is pissed at you by the way."

Celyn looked gobsmacked. "What could I have possibly done to anger your mother?"

Aiden sat beside Meryn. "You're here, which means my father is stuck in Lycaonia so that Renee isn't the only Elder in the city. And of course, since my father can't come, neither can my mother and she wants to hug Meryn." He sat back and closed his eyes. "I'd rather face ferals than my mother right now."

Vivian chuckled. "I'll call her later to let her know we hugged Meryn in her stead and I'll forward along a nice gift from Éire Danu. That way, my mate will have a fifty-fifty chance of being mauled when we go home."

Celyn looked at his mate. "I thought you were on my side."

Vivian gave him a sweet smile. "She's one of my best friends, I'm on both your sides."

Stefan turned to Darian. "Darian, can you open a portal for me? I'm going to head back to Noctem Falls and update Magnus personally." Darian nodded.

Meryn held up a hand. "Hold up mutt. You're not going anywhere until you explain how you knew me."

Brennus turned to Cristo. "How did you know to look for the spheres?"

Meryn crossed her arms over her chest. "Get to talking."

CHAPTER ELEVEN

CRISTO SMILED AT MERYN. "STEFAN knew your scent because he had met you before, we both have." He held his hand up about two feet off the floor. "You were about this big when Stefan and I found your father. My little brother decided to tag along when I went searching for my friend, that's how he ended up meeting you, Eamon and your mother."

Meryn scowled at Stefan. "Why didn't you say anything?"

Cristo held up a finger. "Because he never knew your name. Your mother said it was safe for us to meet as long as we never knew your names. In fact, she said it was important that Stefan met Meryn, she said it would help her later."

Kendrick sighed. "I wish I could have known Violet Vi'Eirlea. I have never met anyone, witch or no, who had so many detailed and accurate premonitions."

Stefan looked confused. "Why was it important that I meet her?"

Cristo took pity on his brother. "Why is Meryn

sitting here? Why did I go to Noctem Falls?" Stefan blinked and Cristo continued. "You acted as the link between Meryn and me. Between the past and the present. You knew her scent, but couldn't place it but you also associated it with me, which had me curious. So, I go to Noctem Falls and I remembered exactly where I knew her scent from because she smelled like Eamon to me. I wasn't one hundred percent sure you were Eamon's child, but I couldn't say anything since Eamon made me swear not to discuss you or your mother to anyone outside of Éire Danu."

Brennus' face was like a thundercloud. "You could have damn well told us!"

Cristo stood anger in his eyes. "Told you what exactly? Oh, hey Brennus, I know you are mourning your older brother, but guess what? He also had a mate and the most beautiful baby girl I've ever seen, and gee they also died in the fire." He pointed a finger at Brennus. "You didn't know! You didn't mourn them!" He pounded his own chest. "I did!" He let his arm fall to his side. "You were hurting enough, I couldn't add to your pain," he said, hanging his head.

"But I didn't die," Meryn said.

Cristo looked up. "The ones responsible for the fire spelled it so that when it burned, there were no remains. We had nothing to entomb, so I assumed you had perished with them. The enemy even left a few dead ferals in the yard to make us believe they died in a random attack. I swear to you Meryn, had I even the slightest inkling that you lived I never would have stopped looking for you. I would have come to Éire Danu, told your uncles, rallied an army and launched a worldwide search for you," he vowed.

"Her disappearing saved her life. Had she come to Éire Danu, that demon would have found her," Kendrick hypothesized.

Aleksandra looked at him. "What makes you say that?"

Kendrick pointed to Meryn. "The demon told her that witches warned him of her, that he'd been searching for her. Had she come here and taken on a royal name; she never would have lived past ten years old." He grimaced and turned to Meryn. "I know you probably don't want to hear this, but going to your grandmother may have also been another layer of protection. By ignoring you, she kept your very name out of the ether, you couldn't have been more hidden."

Meryn gave a slow nod. "Until I met Aiden."

"Yes, until you were claimed and took your place in our world. That is when it seems the wheels began turning," Kendrick surmised.

"It also explains why my Aunt Lily didn't know about me even though she met up with my mother after my birth." She looked at Cristo. "Why in the hell did she say her name was Evans?"

Cristo laughed. "They pulled it from a hat. Vi'Eirlea is an obvious fae name if you know what to look for, and since House Eirlea was tied to the throne, they couldn't even use that abbreviated version."

"I had a fake fucking name my whole life?" Meryn exclaimed.

Izzy shrugged. "Evans isn't a bad name though. You could have gotten stuck with something weird."

"Or the name of a family known for treachery and murder," Oron whispered.

Meryn snapped her fingers. "I know! Make him Vi'Eirlea instead of me," she said, pointing to Oron. "My dad obviously cared about him and Darian, he even called Oron son. I don't think he'd mind."

Brennus stood and looked to Doran who was grinning from ear to ear. "Meryn, that is a brilliant idea!" He frowned. "Why did we never think of it?"

Oron tensed under her hands. "You can't be serious," he whispered.

Brennus whipped around to face him. "Of course, I'm serious. Your mother is making Darian her heir. I will adopt you into my family and make you head of our house." He jerked his thumb to his chest. "I'm the queen's consort. I'm basically eye candy for her and I snarl at anyone who needs to step back in line."

The queen pinched between her eyebrows. "Brennus, really."

He continued. "The rank of head of house is wasted on me." He pointed to Doran. "He is blissfully happy being in charge of the royal guards and eschews all forms of responsibility."

"Sad, but true," Doran confirmed.

Brennus walked over and pulled Oron to

his feet. "Meryn has already declared she will remain a McKenzie, so you take nothing from her. I feel like I have done nothing for you as your adopted father. Please let me do this," he pleaded.

Oron stared. "You're begging me to take your name? One of the most respected and venerated names in our world and you're begging me to take it." Oron looked back at her. She stood and took his hand. "It's your choice, my love. You'll always be Mr. Pokie to me."

Oron stared at Brennus, then her words sunk in. He leered down at her. "You *do* remember last night."

She winked. "What do you want to do? What would make you happy?"

Oron turned back to Brennus. "Are you certain? I would be more than happy with Li'Eirlea."

Brennus pulled him into a fierce bear hug. "Of course, I'm certain! And given what our future looks like, you need the higher rank more than either me or Doran do."

Oron rested his forehead on Brennus' shoulder. "I would be honored to be a part of your family."

Brennus stepped back and cuffed him. "You're already family, son."

Oron glanced over to Cord who gave a nod. Taking a deep breath, Oron looked Brennus in the eye. "May I call you father?"

Brennus gave an undignified whoop and began to repeatedly pound Oron on the back.

"Damn right, you can. Aleks! He wants to call me father," Brennus announced.

Aleksandra dabbed at her eyed. "Yes, dear. I heard." She stood and pulled them both into a fierce hug. "Go make it official before I call Portia back to make the announcement."

Brennus took Oron's hand and began to drag him toward the courtyard. "We'll be right back!" Brennus called back to her, as Doran and Darian raced after them.

Izzy and Amelia exchanged looks before Izzy asked. "What are they doing?"

Aleksandra sniffled. "He's going to cut Oron, so he bleeds onto the Eirlea Elder tree and add him to their family line. By doing so, they will be merging House Eirson and House Eirlea. The Eirlea Elder tree will give strength and support to the Eirson Birch, which will allow her to endure until Oron and Izzy have children and more light feeds into both trees. This is the perfect solution." She looked at Meryn. "You are a true wonder."

Meryn shrugged. "I guess, even though I do most of this shit by accident."

"Accident or destiny?" Kendrick asked.

"We need to find your light," the queen announced.

Cord carried the wooden box over to the queen. She carefully lifted each sphere until she smiled. "This one is the warmest." She walked over and sat on the ottoman in front of Meryn. "Ryuu, can you get another drop of blood from Meryn?"

Ryuu held out his hand. Meryn sighed and

reached out to him, turning her face away. He pricked her and she yelped. The queen dabbed her finger on the sphere and it opened. Unlike the other, which contained a recording, this one opened to reveal a small ball of light.

"Meryn, this may be a bit disorientating."

"I'll still be me, right?"

"You may gain some new abilities, but you will remain who you are," she promised.

"Okay, hit me." Meryn pushed out her chest and closed her eyes.

The queen chuckled and gently pressed the small ball of light into Meryn's heart. Both she and Aiden clutched at their chests. A moment later a tiny bead popped out of Meryn and dove into Aiden.

The queen blushed. "I forgot about them sharing since they are mated."

Aiden grunted and rubbed his sternum. "How do you feel baby?"

Meryn opened her eyes. "Still hate people and love coffee. Shouldn't I be all 'light and happiness' now?"

"I told you Meryn, you would remain who you were. You have a lifetime of experiences that make up your personality, adding your light doesn't change that."

"Holy shit!" Everyone's heads turned to the sounds of startled male voices.

Darian and Doran raced back in, looking as though they had seen a ghost. The queen stood and rushed over. "Son, whatever is the matter?

Where's your brother and Brennus?" Darian pointed to the door.

Slowly Brennus and Oron backed into the room. In front of them, an ethereal form floated in from the courtyard.

"Wicked," both she and Meryn said at the same time.

The queen smoothed out her dress before dropping into a beautifully executed curtsey. Seeing the queen giving this entity deference made everyone in the room stand to attention and either bow or curtsey.

The form solidified into the shape of a remarkably handsome man. Unlike the fae, he had long jet-black hair that was tied back at his neck with a winding vine. He did wear robes, but unlike anything Izzy had seen in the city. His sleeves were gossamer so you could see his muscles move and flex beneath the thin fabric. More than anything, he wore power, pure and simple.

"Dude," Izzy whispered.

"I know right," Meryn whispered back.

"Abraxas, you honor us with your presence," the queen said in the form of a greeting as she stood.

"How could I not come? Nothing happens to my family for thousands of years, then within the space of five minutes, you add a son, a daughter, three mates, and a bud on the way." His bright green eyes scanned the room before landing on Meryn. He strode over only to be brought up short by Ryuu. Izzy was terrified that the squire was going to get himself killed.

"Abraxas," Ryuu said curtly.

"Sei," Abraxas replied, just as shortly. "Step aside."

Ryuu shook his head. "She belongs to me."

Abraxas' body took on a green glow. "She is of my line, move aside."

"Ryuu, don't get murdered by the hot tree guy," Meryn ordered, as she peeked out from around her squire.

Abraxas' light dimmed almost immediately. "Hot tree guy?"

"She meant no offense," Brennus said, moving to try and stand between him and Meryn.

Abraxas inhaled and then exhaled. Everything and everyone around Meryn was pushed aside, except for Ryuu.

"Kick-ass," Meryn whispered.

Abraxas smiled. "Come here, little one, I will not harm you."

Meryn popped out from behind Ryuu, causing him to shake his head. She walked up to Abraxas and held out her hand. "Meryn McKenzie, please to meetcha."

Amelia wasn't the only one to cover their face with their hands at that greeting.

Abraxas took her hand gently. "You're Eamon's daughter."

She gave a slow nod. "I just found out though. He died when I was young."

The handsome spirit tilted Meryn's head back to stare into her eyes. Meryn blinked. "Hey, we have the same eyes! I thought I got them from my Aunt Lily, but they match your green better."

"Your father was one of my closest friends. He would sit in my branches and tell me wild tales of the things he had seen and done. When his branch turned to stone, I felt my heart hardened as well." He released Meryn's chin and rested a hand on her belly. "Such a strong life." He threw an irritated look at Aiden. "Even though you are mated to the furball, will you come to visit often so that I may know you and your child?"

Meryn looked surprised. "Of course." She paused, then asked. "Does your tree have a swing?"

Brennus released a strangled sound. Behind Abraxas, Oron and Darian were waving their hands back and forth and shaking their heads.

Abraxas kissed her forehead. "I will add one, just for you and the baby." He stepped back and looked at Ryuu. "Nothing better happen to her under your watch. No flowing about, leaving her unguarded."

Ryuu glared at him, "You must be mistaking me for one of your kind who only sits back and watches, stagnating in place."

Abraxas turned to Meryn. "There were no other squires you could have chosen?"

Meryn hugged Ryuu around the waist. "I wouldn't have anyone else. He loves me and I love him. He feeds me and lets me act crazy even though he knows Aiden will give him shit. He allows me to be free."

Abraxas' facial features softened. "I guess he's allowed in my garden then."

Meryn exhaled. "Good. Because he's in charge of diapers."

The tree spirit extended out his arm with his fist closed. "Hold out your arm, Meryn."

Meryn held out her arm, her palm facing up. He circled her wrist with his fingers and when he removed them, a beautiful wooden bracelet was left behind. "You have my blessing."

Meryn slid it around on her tiny wrist. When she tried to remove it, it wouldn't budge. "You could have told me it was permanent."

His mouth twitched. "Oh, I don't know. I think I timed that just right."

Meryn slowly turned to stare at Ryuu. "Where have I heard that before?"

On his way to the door, Abraxas clapped Oron on the shoulder. "I will care for her, don't you worry. She will not suffer because you chose to be happy." He waited for Oron to look up at him. "I've been waiting thousands of years for you to find your way to me. Welcome, son." When he lifted his hand, a wooden torc circled Oron's throat. Though it had an opening, like Meryn's bracelet, it wasn't meant to be removed. He walked out into the courtyard and disappeared.

Brennus plopped down onto an ottoman. "I need a drink."

Aleksandra shoved a cup of tea at him. He sighed. "Not what I meant, but it'll do."

Izzy went over and wrapped her arms around Oron's waist. "I was scared to death when he touched you."

Oron kissed her forehead. "He's our guardian, he would never hurt us."

She pointed to Brennus. "Then why did he practically try to throw himself in front of Meryn?"

Brennus downed his tea. "Knee jerk reaction."

She reached up and touched his necklace. "There's weird letters on it."

"It says 'Son of Eirlea'," he said, reaching up to run a finger over the smooth wood.

"How could you possibly know that?"

He shrugged. "No idea. I just know that's what it says."

Izzy turned. "What about you, Meryn?"

"Mine says 'Daughter of Eirlea' and some kind of warning."

Ryuu looked at her bracelet. "Loosely translated it means 'Harm her if you dare.' He has always been overly dramatic."

Meryn eyed her squire. "If you knew him, how come you didn't know I was part fae? You knew Amelia was my cousin, but not that Brennus, Doran or Celyn were my uncles."

He tapped her chest. "You didn't have your light."

Aiden reached down and tugged on the bracelet. "I am not a damn furball!"

"So, does that make Oron Meryn's big brother?" Izzy asked curiously.

Darian just started laughing. Oron flipped him off.

Meryn looked hurt. "You don't want to be my brother?" she asked.

Both Izzy and Amelia crossed their arms and glared at their mates.

Oron walked over and ruffled Meryn's hair. "Meryn, we're laughing because we're already your brothers remember? Amelia mated Darian making him your big brother-cousin and I'm his brother. I guess we're just linked in more than one way."

Meryn smiled smugly. "My Christmas list is massive now."

Stefan walked over to Darian. "Can I get that portal now? If Portia is half as efficient as she seems, that announcement will be going out any minute now and I really owe it to Magnus to alert him to everything that's happened, so he doesn't hear it third hand."

Brennus walked over to the crystal and tapped it. It took a few moments, but just as before, there was a knock on the door before Portia entered. "Yes, Your Majesty?"

The queen smiled. "We may have a few tiny announcements to add."

"I may not make it through the day," Portia murmured. She took out her scroll and quill. "What are we adding?"

"Brennus Vi'Eirlea has officially adopted Oron into the house of Eirlea and has passed on his head of house position to him, furthermore, the Eirlea Guardian Abraxas has blessed both Oron and Meryn acknowledging them as son and daughter of Eirlea. Brennus will take on the new title Ri'Eirlea and Doran will be now known as Li'Eirlea."

Portia had long since stopped writing. She was staring at Meryn. "You do cause chaos wherever you go."

"What can I say? It's a gift."

"Portia, I want these to go out today please," the queen requested.

Portia added a final note then nodded. "I had the other ones finished and spelled; it won't take me a half an hour to add this." To her surprise, the meticulous woman turned to look at her. "Lady Isabelle, the tailors will be coming by today for interviews. Speak with each one and chose who you think you can work with for fittings."

"Thank you, Portia." The poor woman simply nodded and walked out.

"Ewww, fittings. Those suck, well, unless it's Sebastian. He was really nice about letting me take breaks," Meryn said sympathetically.

Izzy plucked at her robe. "I have seven brand new robes; I don't need more."

"I feel ya on that," Meryn said.

"Whenever you're ready, Stefan," Darian announced.

"Do we have to go to the main entrance?" he asked.

Darian shook his head. "I can open a portal here, and I'll send you right to the Grand Hall."

Stefan looked relieved. He turned and hugged his brother. "Don't be a stranger."

Cristo pounded his back. "Take care of the pack."

"Always do." He walked over to where Darian

opened a regular sized portal. He gave a quick wave, then stepped through.

When the portal closed, Meryn quickly turned to Kendrick and Aiden. "Five bucks says he goes straight to Kari, tells her everything and has her update Magnus."

Kendrick grinned. "You're on. This is the news of the century, I bet you he can't wait to spill the beans."

"Aiden?" she asked.

He shook his head. "No way am I taking that bet. That pup is most definitely going straight to Kari. He hates meetings."

Meryn turned to Cristo. "You in?"

He threaded his hands behind his head. "I'll do you one better. I bet you ten dollars he goes to Kari, tells her everything, then has her sit in on the meeting so he doesn't forget anything."

"Deal," Meryn and Kendrick said.

Aiden bopped his mate's head around. "How are you doing?"

Meryn held out her arms and allowed her mate to settle her in his lap. "Still kinda in shock, I think. I love them because they were my parents, but I don't miss them as people because I didn't know them. I cried because I was sad, but I think I'll be okay."

Ryuu stared down at her. "Your ability to compartmentalize is frightening."

"Don't hate on my coping mechanisms."

"Do you need a nap?" Aiden offered.

"No, I'm still kinda wired."

There was a knock at the door then Portia stuck her head in. "Lady Isabelle, your interviews are here."

Izzy turned to Meryn and jerked her head subtly. "Wanna help me?"

Meryn gave her a puzzled look but stood anyway. "Sure."

"Have fun," both Aiden and Oron called out.

Izzy waved as Meryn, Ryuu, and Pierce followed her out. Once in the hallway, Meryn turned to her. "What are we really up to?"

"If these tailors are who I think they are, revenge."

"Awesome."

Portia was waiting at the end of the hall to escort them to a large waiting room. "Portia, how many interviews do I have?"

"There are five tailors waiting."

"Thank you." When she and Meryn got settled in a loveseat, she leaned in and whispered. "Ignore them if I do." Meryn gave the barest of nods as the first person entered.

Izzy recognized the person from her shopping excursion with Oron. She took out her phone and set a five-minute timer.

"Lady Isabelle, what a privilege it is to meet you."

Izzy stared down at her phone.

"Lady Isabelle?"

Again, she didn't respond.

"Is the poor child deaf?" The woman asked Meryn, who just swung her feet and smiled up at her. For the next five minutes, the woman just stood there. Finally, when her phone beeped, she looked up and said. "You may go."

The woman gave a nervous titter before she quickly left the room.

Meryn frowned. "That was awkward."

"Why were you grinning at her like a serial killer?"

"It's my intimidation technique."

"Not bad, you looked like a psychopath."

"Awesome."

The next four interviews went pretty much the same way. When they were done, Izzy sat back, feeling satisfied. She was about to suggest they go back to their mates when Portia walked in. "Lady Isabelle, I had the five tailors complain to me that you didn't interview them. They are very upset."

"Where are they?" she asked, standing.

"In the salon."

"Show me to them."

"As you wish," Portia guided her and of course nosy Meryn with her squire and squire's flirt in tow.

The second she entered the room they all began talking at once. She held up her arm, showing them the bracelet that the queen had gifted her the day before. They quieted almost immediately. She lowered her arm. "The reason I needed new clothes wasn't because I wanted a new look. I lost all of my belongings in a fire and all I had were the clothes on my back and a few in a shopping bag that reeked of smoke. I was desperate not to embarrass my mate, so he took me clothing shopping yesterday.

You may not recognize me since you all took one look at my mate then either disappeared or became so busy with what you were doing you ignored us. I waited exactly five minutes for you to acknowledge that we were there, but none of you did. Today, I simply took my five minutes back. You're all dismissed," she said, pointing to the door.

Portia stiffened. "You heard her. And don't think for a single second that this won't affect your standings with palace orders."

Izzy felt like cheering; she knew that older woman liked her mate.

As the final tailor was walking past her, she heard him mutter. "Traitorous bastard."

Izzy didn't waste a second. She jumped up and wrapped her arms around his neck. She clung to him with her left and began punching him anywhere she could with her right, mainly his ear."

"Kick his ass, Izzy!" Meryn yelled.

"Get her off me!" the tailor screamed.

Within moments guards flooded the room, but they stood there awkwardly, not knowing what to do.

"Izzy!" she heard her mate call out her name.

"I'm not stopping until I see blood!" she screeched.

She really hoped she saw blood soon; her knuckles were killing her.

"Izzy! Jump clear!" she heard Meryn order.

She let go and jumped back. She saw Meryn

dart forward and tap the guy with her little stick, he went down like a sack of potatoes.

"Yes!" Izzy said. She ran over and high-fived Meryn.

"Meryn!" Aiden roared as he ran into the room.

"I'm okay."

"I know you are. Why did you tase this man?" he demanded, looking her over.

"I don't know."

"What do you mean you don't know?"

Oron rushed to Izzy's side. "Did he attack you?"

She shook her head. "No, I kinda attacked him."

Meryn shrugged her shoulders. "I buzzed him because Izzy was hitting him."

"Do you know why she was hitting him?"

"No."

"Then, why?"

"Because I'm a ride or die bitch."

"You're not dying! And you're not a bitch." Aiden looked down at the unconscious man his canines dropping before his murderous gaze lifted to the other tailors. As one, they stepped away from the enraged commander. With a growl, he looked down at the incapacitated man. "Did he call you a bitch?"

Pierce stepped in. "Sir, what she means is that since Izzy is her friend, she, of course, would step in to help, no matter what."

Oron turned to her. "Okay, then why did you attack him?"

The man at their feet groaned and struggled to get up. Izzy kicked him. Oron physically lifted her up and carried her over to stand next to Meryn.

"Can you please tell us what in the hell is going on?" he begged.

"He called you a 'traitorous bastard'."

Meryn lifted up her stick again and went to step forward. Aiden blocked her way. "No one disrespects my big brother-cousin," Meryn growled.

One of the other tailors inched forward and helped the man to stand. The queen and Brennus walked up behind them, Portia right at their side.

"Listen up. You better start circulating some rumors real damn fast. My name is Lady Vi'Eirlea, my mate is Oron Vi'Eirlea, and I am extremely protective of my mate. I will make it my life's mission to torture anyone who threatens his happiness." She pointed to Meryn. "And she likes electrocuting people." Meryn held up her stick and used it to draw an imaginary line across her throat. The entire group eyed the doorway.

"And who exactly would be threatening our son's happiness?" the queen asked in a deadly tone.

"The exit is this way," Portia informed them and led them away.

Oron was simply staring down at her with his mouth hanging open.

"Damn Izzy, how'd you jump high enough to reach his head?" Meryn asked.

She shrugged. "No idea. I think I got so angry, I blacked out for a second."

"Maybe you should bring your mate to the training field," a male voice suggested.

"Fuck you, Malcom, my mate isn't going anywhere near the training field." Oron groused.

Izzy began to bounce on her feet, throwing jabs. "Fighting in robes suck." She looked back at Oron. "I need fighting clothes."

"You do not need fighting clothes!" he roared.

Aiden suddenly broke out into a wide grin. "It's not just me!" he crowed.

Meryn elbowed him. "What does that mean?"

"No fighting," Oron ordered.

"No, because I love you, and I won't let anyone hurt you anymore," she declared.

"Awww, I want one," one of the guards teased.

"I like the little one with the taser."

Aiden and Oron glared at the men.

The queen walked between them and wrapped an arm around each of them. "Why don't you girls take a relaxing walk?" she suggested.

"Mother! What if they get into another fight?" Oron asked.

"I'm pretty sure they'll win," his mother assured him.

"That's not the point."

Izzy grabbed Meryn's arm and they made their escape.

Chapter Twelve

THEY SLOWED DOWN WHEN THEY turned the corner, trusting the queen to run interference. Of course, Ryuu and Pierce were right there with them.

"So, what now?" Meryn asked.

"How adventurous are you feeling?"

"That depends on the level of exercise said adventure will require."

"Leisurely stroll."

"Where to?"

"The Dark Forest."

"I'm in."

Pierce turned to Ryuu. "How are you not dead by now?"

Ryuu simply smiled. "She adds a spice to life."

Izzy led them down the side street to the Border City. Meryn's eyes were wide. "This is a thousand times better than that other marketplace."

"I thought so too," Izzy agreed. She was looking for the tavern Oron took her to when, in their heads, they heard Portia's voice. It was the announcements that the queen had wanted to be sent out. When it was over Meryn and Izzy were rubbing their ears. "Yours itchy too?"

"Yeah," Meryn complained.

Ryuu placed a hand on Meryn's head and she smiled. "Thanks, Ryuu."

"Though an effective way to communicate, telepathy isn't for everyone," he said.

Out of the corner of her eye, she saw the familiar swinging sign. "Come on Meryn, this place is run by warriors and it's really great." She took her hand and dragged her through the door.

"Look what the wind blew in. We just heard the announcement about the two of you," Dav called out.

"Hey Dav, I wanted to show Meryn your amazing bar," she said, trying to climb up on the stool. After the third failed attempt, Pierce lifted her up and sat her down. "Thanks."

Ryuu did the same for Meryn. "Thanks, Ryuu," she said, reaching for the menu. When her bracelet grazed the top of the bar, there was a cracking sound and the floor under them began to move. Ryuu scooped up Meryn and Pierce grabbed her.

"What the hell did you do little lady?" Dav demanded.

"Nothing! I just wanted some damn french fries," Meryn said, looking confused.

When the noise stopped, everyone was staring at the bar. Along the wall, it had sprouted branches that climbed to the ceiling and underfoot roots twisted around the floorboards. Pierce set her down gently.

Ryuu cleared his throat. "That bar wouldn't be made of elder, would it?"

Dav nodded absently then his eyes widened to stare at her bracelet. "You were just blessed this morning, weren't you?"

She nodded. "I thought this was like a friendship bracelet."

"Looks like it's a bit more than that," a warrior said from behind them.

"No shit," Meryn said. "Can I get those fries to go? I'll wait until I talk to Uncle Bren about this bracelet before I come back."

The woman at Dav's side looked to Izzy. "Anything for you?"

"Fries and chicken tenders for me, extra ketchup," Izzy answered.

"Oh yeah, ketchup. And could you add extra tenders for me? The kiddo loves protein," Meryn said, pointing to her midsection.

The woman's eyes softened at the sight of Meryn's rounded belly. "We just had both come out of the fryer, give me a moment to get them bagged up for you," she said, then disappeared into the kitchen.

"I'm sorry about this Dav. Meryn had a rough morning, so I wanted her to experience your happy bar," Izzy dropped her head feeling like a failure, again.

"Is that what that was?" Meryn asked.

Izzy looked up. "What?"

"Like I'm still kinda upset about what I learned, but it's like it somehow got wrapped in cotton, not even the Sacred Chamomile did that."

"Sacred Chamomile?" Dav asked. Izzy noticed that the men around them were standing almost at attention.

"Sacred Chamomile is exclusively used for intensely traumatic events, sweetheart, are you well?" Dav asked, concern written all over his face.

Meryn nodded. "I'll be okay."

"No one is after you, is there?" one of the warriors asked.

"I don't think so," Meryn paused. "Though, that tailor is probably super pissed at me."

"Who on earth would get mad at a sweet thing like you?" Dav asked.

"It was the tailor from Elegant Expressions, I jumped on his back and beat on his ear and then Meryn tased him," Izzy explained.

The men's faces turned murderous. "Did he assault you?"

"No, worse. He called my mate a traitorous bastard," Izzy said, still feeling kinda angry about that.

Meryn nodded. "I was gonna tase him again until he pissed himself, but Aiden was getting growly, so I couldn't reach him."

"Oron and Aiden are two lucky bastards," one guy said. He looked up panicked. "I meant that in a good way."

Izzy laughed. "We know."

The waitress came back out and handed Izzy a cloth bag. "Here you go, dear."

Izzy shook her bracelet. "Can I charge it to this?"

Dav laughed. "It's not like a credit card, it basically tells shop owners that you have permission to send the invoice to the royal palace to be paid."

Meryn eyed her bracelet. "Do you think we could buy some fae weapons?"

Dav's laughter boomed. "Little lady, if you have a taser that took down a full-grown fae, you have a damn good weapon."

Meryn looked disappointed. "But there's no blood when I tase people," she complained.

"Lucky bastards," another guy repeated.

The waitress handed Izzy a tiny pouch. "I saw that she has a sprite, so I packed a couple tiny vials of honey for him."

Meryn smiled brightly. "Thank you!"

Izzy passed Meryn the tiny pouch who handed it off to Felix.

They waved goodbye then headed out into the street. Once outside, Ryuu set his charge down.

"It's too damn bright here," Meryn complained.

"Aren't you half fae?" Izzy pointed out.

Meryn went to answer then stopped. "I guess I can't say I'm human anymore."

"Why not? You may be half fae, but you're definitely human."

"How does that work?"

"Well, you grew up human. You rode the bus, watched cartoons, did late night taco runs, that sort of thing, your experiences make you human. Being half fae is like having dark hair and green eyes."

Meryn tilted her head. “I get that.”

Izzy looked around until she saw a sign that said, ‘Dark Forest’, it pointed away from the city.

“Seriously?”

“What?”

“Check it out.” She nodded to the sign.

“I thought no one was supposed to go there.”

Izzy bit her lip. “Actually, Oron said humans shouldn’t go there.”

“Oh. So, in this scenario, am I half fae?”

Izzy nodded. “Works for me.”

“Come on!”

They had only been walking away from the city for a few minutes when a large wooded area loomed in front of them.

“Did he say what was in here?” Meryn asked.

“Besides brownies and goblins? No.”

Meryn munched on her chicken tenders. “These are freaking awesome.”

Izzy popped a fry into her mouth. “The fish we had almost made me cry.”

Meryn looked over at Ryuu. “I want fish before we leave the city.”

Ryuu nodded. “Of course, *denka*.”

Pierce pointed to the forest. “I can’t tell you how many times I’ve been to Éire Danu and I never thought to come here?”

“Why?” both she and Meryn asked at the same time.

“Because we’re not supposed to,” Pierce explained.

"Boring," Izzy replied.

When they walked into the forest and the canopy overhead shaded them from the sun, they both sighed in relief. "This feels so good," Meryn murmured.

"I want to take a nap right here," Izzy said, pointing to the line of sunlight on the ground. "Hot? Roll over into the woods. Cold? Roll back and warm up."

Meryn practically whimpered. "That sounds so good."

Izzy looked around. "I feel like we should be leaving breadcrumbs since we're on the way to Grandma's House."

Meryn giggled. "It does have a fairy tale feel to it, doesn't it?"

"Halt! What are two humans doing in the Dark Forest?" a deep voice demanded.

"Ha! He said human," Izzy pointed out to Meryn.

"And I thought we both decided I'd be half fae in the forest."

"Oh yeah, sorry."

They both looked over when the stranger stepped from the shadows. Izzy could only stare, he was green and massive. She could see he was green since most of his skin was showing, as he only wore a loincloth leaving every muscle clearly visible. His pointed ears peeked out from his shaggy black hair, but his eyes were his most breathtaking feature. He had double irises in two different shades of green.

"Whoa," she said, exhaling slowly.

Meryn took a deep breath. "God, you're freaking beautiful."

The creature looked taken aback. "It is dishonorable to lie."

Izzy couldn't answer, she could only stare. There was no way in hell this was a goblin. She hadn't heard one damn story growing up about green sex gods.

"Fucking Grimm brothers were jealous," Meryn muttered.

Izzy could only nod. That had to be it. Human men had felt so threatened by these creatures that they had turned them into twisted nightmares.

"Why are they staring? Are they casting a spell against me?" the stranger demanded.

Ryuu cleared his throat. "I do beg your pardon, but you have quite simply stunned my charge and her friend. She wasn't lying when she said she thought you were beautiful. They are both overwhelmed by your appearance, so could you give them a moment to gather their thoughts?"

The stranger was so shocked at Ryuu's words he dropped his spear. "They truly think I am beautiful."

"Man, if I weren't mated," Meryn whispered.

"Ditto," Izzy repeated the sentiment.

Meryn shook her head. "I mean, I love my mate with everything in me but I…" her eyes drifted back to their new friend. "Damn."

Izzy smiled. "I am so sorry I was staring. But how could you not know how…" she pointed up and down. "Everything you are."

"I don't think that made sense."

"Shut up, Meryn, I'm surprised I remember English at this point."

The stranger's cheeks darkened to a deeper green. "My name is Gilheim."

Izzy pointed to her chest. "My name is Izzy, this is Meryn."

He blinked. "Meryn and Isabelle are the names of the women in today's announcement."

"You got that too?" Meryn asked.

He nodded. "Everyone in the realm did." His skin tone lightened to an almost mint green. "You mean to tell me that you are the mate of the new head of the Eirlea House and you are Meryn McKenzie, daughter of Eamon and second in line for the throne."

"Which answer won't make you freak out?" Meryn asked wisely.

"Why would you be here of all places?" Gilheim asked.

Meryn sighed. "Can I be honest with you, Gilheim?"

"Of course, honesty is always best."

"Well, we were curious because we were told we shouldn't come here and I wanted to get out of the damn sun." Meryn pointed overhead. "The shade feels so good."

"But you are half fae. You are related to royalty," he stammered.

"This half fae woman loves the shade."

When he smiled, his green toned skin made his teeth glow bright white. "You should come to see my village. May I escort you there, daughter of Eamon?"

Meryn nodded. “That sounds awesome.”

He turned to lead them, then remembered his spear. He bent over to retrieve his weapon and both she and Meryn whimpered.

He looked back at them, exuding the excitement of an eager puppy. “I will show you the way.”

“It’s raining men…”

“Meryn!”

“Hallelujah!”

Izzy laughed. “Stop it, missy!”

They gladly followed behind Gilheim and Izzy had to hand it to Meryn, she had only tripped over her feet twice, both times when a breeze shifted Gilheim’s loincloth. Luckily for her, she simply froze, so she avoided any spills.

“Elder Tanir!” Gilheim ran ahead of them to a longhouse.

“Gilheim, welcome back, my boy.”

“Run into anything exciting?” a jeering voice asked.

“Thank you, Elder. Actually, Telk, I did into something very interesting.”

“Do tell us,” Telk teased.

“I had the honor of escorting…”

“Some pigs back to the pasture?” Another voice taunted. Male laughter echoed all around.

“No, I…”

“You smell of swine Gilheim, can’t you yell your report from outside?”

Izzy watched as Meryn marched into the longhouse as if she owned the place, Ryuu right behind her.

"Ride or die," she said, looking up at Pierce.

"Ride or die." Together they walked in after her.

"I see that being a douchebag isn't restricted to just vampires. I have to admit, this is my first time meeting green douchebags," Meryn said, smiling sweetly at the group of males sitting on the floor in a circle.

"Bitch, this is a leader meeting," the asshole from early started.

"Good. I'm just in time. What are we discussing?" Meryn asked.

The green man with a head full of white hair chuckled. "Gilheim, this wouldn't happen to be who you ran into during your patrol, would it?"

"Yes, Elder. This is Meryn McKenzie, daughter of Eamon. She wanted to see our village," Gilheim explained.

"Lies! No fae comes here willingly. Even when we trade, we have to do it during the deepest part of the dim," Telk yelled, rising to his feet. He took a step forward to tower over Meryn.

Gilheim immediately moved between them. "You would dare approach one such as she in anger?"

"As if you would do anything," Telk sneered.

Gilheim placed his colossal hand on Telk's chest and pushed. Telk flew backward, hitting the ground hard.

The Elder stood. "Have you found something worth fighting for Gilheim, son of Gilliad?"

Izzy watched in fascination as a tiny winged being fluttered around Telk trying to help. It wasn't a sprite, because, like Gilheim, he was also green, but instead of flat teeth, he had a mouth full of sharp teeth like a shark. When Telk backhanded the tiny creature, she rushed forward to pick him up. Telk ignored them both as he walked back to Gilheim.

"I have Elder. I will not allow Telk to harm Eamon's daughter," Gilheim declared.

"I challenge you Gilheim, for the insult you have paid me," Telk spit as he yelled.

"Accepted. I will wait for you in the challenge circle," Gilheim said, turning his back to Telk to walk out of the longhouse.

Grinning, Telk reached under his vest to pull out a sharp blade.

"Meryn! Tase!" she yelled when she saw the knife.

Without hesitating, Meryn pulled out her stick and a blue spark lit up the interior of the longhouse right before Telk collapsed, sending the blade spinning on the ground.

"He would cheat?" Gilheim asked, sounding shocked.

Meryn laughed. "Look at you, now look at him. You're like twice his size, of course he was trying to cheat."

Gilheim turned to the Elder. "I can wait until he wakes to continue."

The Elder shook his head. "As you were willing to fight and die to defend Meryn, daughter of Eamon, she was also willing to fight to save your life. I rule this challenge to be forfeited by

Telk. What would you take that is his? Maybe his leadership position?"

Gilheim ducked his head. "I enjoy a simple life Elder. He can keep his position."

Izzy looked down where the tiny creature hid behind her fingers. "Can we have him? I don't know what ties he has to Telk, but he was trying to help him when Telk hit him," Izzy explained cuddling him close when he began to shake.

Gilheim turned to Meryn. "Is that acceptable to you?"

Meryn met Izzy's eyes, and she nodded. "Yes. I hate bullies."

The Elder walked forward and took Meryn's hand. "I knew another fae who hated bullies. He would run in the shadows and sleep in the shade. He saw creatures for who they were, not what they were."

Meryn's eyes filled. "My dad?"

The Elder nodded. "He saved Gilheim when he was just a young gobling from a pack of wild wolves."

Izzy walked forward. "Is that why he was willing to fight for her?"

The Elder nodded. "Eamon was raised amongst humans and ran a bit wild. He had no preconceived notions when he came to Éire Danu fully grown. Eamon Vi'Eirlea has many friends in the Dark Forest."

"I just found out about him today," Meryn admitted.

"You are welcome back anytime to sit in our

circle and hear stories about him," Elder Tanir offered.

He looked at Gilheim slyly. "Let us go announce your victory over Telk. I know of a certain goblette who would be very interested to hear about your win."

Gilheim turned an impossible dark green color. "Elder," he hissed in embarrassment.

Meryn giggled, then stopped. She sniffed the air. "Food. Real food! Not vegetables!" She practically ran out of the longhouse, Ryuu and Pierce right behind her. The men laughed at her enthusiasm.

She tapped the Elder on the shoulder and leaned down. "I don't want to be rude, but what is he?" she whispered, holding up the tiny creature.

"That is a house brownie, a very, *very* young one. Telk managed to trick this one's guardian into pressing Creelee into service when Creelee's parents were killed by an owl. I am very delighted you saved him."

"Can he go into the sun?" Izzy asked.

The Elder nodded. "Of all the creatures in this Dark Forest, brownies and goblins are the least susceptible to the fae sun. Creelee will do just fine returning with you. But if you prefer, I can take care of him," he offered.

Izzy looked down to see a pair of bright blue eyes staring up at her. With his mouth shut he looked adorable. He smiled, showing off his razor-sharp teeth. Who was she kidding? He was adorable even with the teeth.

"You have to listen to what I say." He nodded. "I'm new to the palace, so I'll do my best to keep us both out of trouble." He nodded. "To be honest, I'm a bit of a mess myself, so I may get us both in trouble despite trying to be good." He nodded again. "Well, okay then. I guess we're a team." She held out her finger for him to shake and he promptly bit her. "Ow, Creelee!"

The Elder laughed. "He just sealed your agreement in blood. He's yours for life now and can never be returned to Telk."

Izzy stared down at the tiny brownie nuzzling the tip of her finger. "I think we're gonna do just fine."

"*Denka*, we've been away from the palace for hours. I think it's time we head back," Ryuu suggested.

Izzy groaned. "Can't we just stay here?"

The goblins laughed. "We can build them their own longhouse," one of the females suggested.

Meryn was reclining back, patting her stomach. What she smelled cooking was an entire roasted wild boar. "I'm so full."

Gilheim looked down at her in satisfaction. "You fed well, that is good, for you and for your youngling."

"Stay, stay, stay," the goblings chanted as they played with Izzy's hair. They loved that it was red and kept bringing her flowers.

"Okay Ryuu, help me up," Meryn asked, holding up her hands.

Ryuu easily lifted her to her feet. Izzy took

the braided flower crowns she was working on from the children's gifts and began passing them to ecstatic children who immediately ran off to show their parents.

Izzy looked on her shoulder and Creelee was fast asleep. She ran her bitten fingertip over his hair and he practically purred in his sleep.

Pierce helped her to stand and Gilheim joined them to escort them safely to the edge of the woods.

"If I had to live in Éire Danu, I'd live with the goblins," Meryn announced out of nowhere.

Gilheim stumbled. "But, you get to live in the palace," he said, sounding confused.

Meryn shrugged. "It's pretty and all, but your village felt more like a home."

Izzy felt movement by her ear and saw that a sleepy Creelee looked out at the world from his perch. She reached into her bag and offered him a left-over chicken tender. It was just a bit smaller than he was. His eyes widened before he decimated it. "Do you want another?"

"Nother," he chirped.

"He is so freaking cute," Meryn gushed, then looked over at Felix. "But not as cute as you," she added quickly.

Izzy handed Creelee another tender. She watched him closely afraid he was swallowing the pieces whole, but he wasn't. He was chewing with those sharp teeth of his.

He looked up at her with huge eyes. "Nother?"

She held out the last piece. "This is the last one I have with me, but if you're still hungry when we get to the palace, we can order you something, okay?"

"Otay," he replied before devouring the third tender.

As they were walking, she realized she had nothing for the little brownie. She looked over at Felix. "Hey Meryn," she called.

"Yeah?"

"Do you think we could use some of the sprite stuff for Creelee?"

Meryn shrugged. "They're about the same size, that should work."

"He stay with us?" Felix asked.

"Yeah, he's returning with us," Izzy answered.

Meryn shook her head. "I think he's asking if it's okay for Creelee to stay with him and his brothers in their house."

Felix nodded emphatically.

"Oh." She looked down. "Would you like that? Play with young Finley and Feris in the evening, sleep in their sprite sized home, then spend the day with me?"

Creelee looked a bit overwhelmed. "You."

Poor little Felix looked so rejected.

"Creelee, we're going to be together no matter what. We are Team Izzy and Creelee, don't doubt that. I just want you to be comfortable while I get your own home set up. Felix has a smaller sprite sized house that will fit you. If you meet his brothers and are still nervous, we'll figure something else out. But if you meet his brothers and decide you'd like to get to know them better, you won't hurt my feelings at all if you stay with them at night."

Creelee brightened now that she had reaffirmed that they were a team. "I try."

"I'm very proud of you, Creelee. When we're not together, you listen to Felix okay? He'll watch out for you like I would."

Creelee nodded. "He older."

Felix puffed out his chest. "I help."

"You're just like Oron, an excellent big brother," Izzy complimented.

Felix turned bright red and ducked down Meryn's tee shirt.

"You know, after visiting the goblin village, this morning doesn't seem real. I wish we could just enjoy the simple things like they do. Like those flowers or that freaking amazing pork," Meryn licked her lips.

Ryuu ruffled her hair in a rare display of affection. "Some live to be thousands of years old and never realize that true happiness exists in the small things."

When they reached the edge of the woods, everything looked darker as the dim began for the evening. Out of the corner of her eye, she thought she saw a shadow move, but then it was gone.

Gilheim scuffed his foot. "Will you visit again, Meryn, daughter of Eamon?"

"You bet! Can we bring our mates next time?"

He smiled wide. "It would be an honor."

"Til next time," she said waving.

He waved then began to jog back the way they came.

Meryn looked at the fae city and sighed. "It is pretty, I guess."

Izzy giggled. "Can you imagine his reaction if we talked the queen into coming?"

"I bet he'd faint." Meryn laughed. "Elder Tanir would bow so low he'd get mud in his hair," Meryn continued.

"Telk would say something horrid, then Brennus would have to bury him," Izzy added.

"Aiden would spend the entire time with his hands over my eyes to prevent me from checking out Gilheim's ass," Meryn said, placing her hands over her eyes. "Meryn!" she roared like her mate. Izzy could barely see as she walked, she was laughing so hard.

Slowly they walked back to the city, predicting each goblin's reaction to meeting the queen of the fae and the rest of their family.

CHAPTER THIRTEEN

IZZY KNEW THEY WERE IN trouble when the first guard that saw them after entering the palace screamed the word 'found!' and ran off.

"Fuck," Meryn groaned.

They trudged their way back to the queen's chambers and opened the door. Izzy watched as Meryn changed tactics going from being defensive to cute. She bounced into the room and ran to her mate. "I had the most amazing time ever! I can't wait to tell you everything," she said brightly.

Izzy watched the cascade of emotion flow over Aiden's face. He went from relief, to anger, to frustration, to resolution, to puzzlement and finally settled on adoration. "Baby, we were worried sick," he said, placing her in his lap. Izzy realized she was in the presence of a master. Because she knew, that Meryn knew, that there was no way Aiden would say or do anything to burst Meryn's happy bubble.

Oron stalked toward her, his eyes narrowed. She knew she'd never get away with the cute thing so she tried something else. She remembered the way Oron's body looked without his robes and let the heat rise in her.

Her mate stopped and stared. She closed the distance between them and ran her hands over his chest. He leaned down to nuzzle her neck. "I missed you," she whispered.

"Owww! Something bit me!" Oron yelled, standing back holding his cheek.

Her seduction plan flew out the window as worry for Creelee took over. "Creelee, honey, it's okay. This is Oron, my mate," she cooed.

"He eat you!" Creelee cried, tears of fear on his little cheeks.

Behind her, she heard Meryn mutter. "Not yet."

She shot a glare at the little nut, then turned her attention back to Creelee. "That was just a kiss, he was happy to see me, so he kissed me. It doesn't hurt at all." She lifted him to her lips and gently kissed the top of his tiny head. "See, not scary."

Oron watched on. "Is that a brownie?"

She held him close. "Yes, I adopted him."

Aiden began laughing. "That happens to me too."

Oron ignored his commander. "Where did you find a brownie in need of adoption?"

"In the Dark Forest," she replied.

His right eye developed a tic. "The one place I begged you not to go."

"I am in no way responsible for this Oron. You knew my personality when you issued that decree. You practically forced me into going by ordering me not to go. It's your fault."

"Yeah! What she said!" Meryn chimed in.

"You were with her?" Aiden asked, in a quiet tone.

Meryn turned in his lap. "Yup! And I got to meet a ton of goblins who knew my dad! They had just finished roasting this huge boar and let me eat all the pork I wanted. And I made a new friend. His name his Gilheim and he's super sweet."

"Gilheim? Isn't that the name of the gobling Eamon saved?" Doran asked.

Meryn bobbed her head. "Yes! He totally defended me against that dick, Telk."

"Defended you?" Aiden asked, a flush working up his neck.

Meryn waved off his concern. "Just your normal run of the mill douchebag action, evidently they come in all colors, including green."

Oron approached. "Creelee, I want you to know that if my mate promised to take care of you, that means that I will too. If you need anything and she's not around you can come to me. You're our family now."

Creelee's eyes got huge. He flew forward to hover in front of Oron. "Fam-ee"

Izzy watched as her badass mate melted on the spot. "That's right, family."

"Fing-er"

Oron held up his finger. "It only hurts for a second," she advised.

He looked at her. "What does? Oww!" He swung his eyes over to Creelee.

"That," she said, pointing at the tiny teeth mark on his finger. She held up her own healing digit. "I think it's how he cements his bonds."

Izzy watched as Aleksandra eased forward. "He's very young for a brownie."

"His parents were killed by an owl," she explained. "That's when Telk made him a servant. But that all changed when Meryn tased Telk helping Gilheim win their duel. The Elder said we could ask for anything of Telk's, so we saved Creelee."

Aiden glared at Ryuu. "She had to tase someone else?"

Meryn nodded. "He was gonna shank Gilheim."

Thane pointed to Meryn. "She does this all the time?"

Law nodded, taking a sip of his wine. "I heard the unit warriors are getting together and buying Aiden antacids for Christmas this year."

"Real fucking funny," Aiden growled sourly.

Brennus held a hand to his own stomach. "I may need to get in on that gift," he muttered, sitting down.

The queen rolled her eyes. "She's a grown woman, I'm pretty sure she can handle herself."

Aiden nodded. "She can. She can also handle ferals, reapers, demons, sniper rifles, hand grenades, homicidal tunnel escorts, a city of infected vampires and evidently goblins. Eventually, her luck will run out."

Even the queen paled at that. She turned to Meryn. "How long have you been in our world?"

Meryn looked up as if she were counting. "About six months."

"Lord girl, you've been busy," Izzy said, feeling impressed.

Meryn grinned and pointed down. "All while growing a person!"

"Now that we have found the girls, are we ready for dinner?" Cord asked completely unruffled.

"Yes! Squire food!" Meryn said, hopping off of Aiden's lap.

"Didn't you just eat like half a boar?" Izzy asked.

Meryn shook her head. "No, the baby did. Now *I'm* hungry."

Instead of going to the dining room, it looked like Cord had simply enlarged the table in the queen's chambers again.

Everyone got seated and Cord with Ryuu's help began to serve.

Meryn took a long drink of her water and set her glass down. "The goblins heard Portia's announcement, that's how Gilheim knew who I was."

The queen smiled. "They are my children too, Meryn."

Meryn smiled. "I liked them a lot."

"I imagine you would. They are simple and down to earth. They enjoy the small, yet precious things this world has to offer. I love them dearly."

"Then why are they stuck in the forest?" Meryn asked.

The queen looked a bit surprised. "Their ancestors had me create the forest for their protection. They were not sent there, they chose to be there."

"Oh. It just seems weird that the fae have this huge city and they live in longhouses in the forest," Meryn mumbled.

"And yet, who seemed happier?" The queen challenged.

Meryn went to answer then stopped. "The goblins, though I think if you were just looking at the fae, then the people in the Border City are better off."

Brennus stared. "You think that the people in the Border City are better off than the people who live in the city proper?"

Meryn nodded.

"Why?" he asked.

"Because the people in the Border City were talking to their neighbors, yelling at their kids and laughing. The people in the city proper didn't greet anyone or stop to chat with friends. They simply went about their day. A truly rich person has friends, because if you have friends, then you always have what you need," Meryn explained.

"What do you mean?" Doran asked.

"Well, if you have friends and you need a cup of sugar, you can ask to borrow some. If you're alone and you need something, you go without."

She looked at her uncles. “I’m just learning about friends.”

“And brothers,” Aiden added.

Meryn nodded. “And sisters and uncles and aunts and family. I’m kinda lucky that I grew up alone. I think it makes me aware of how special family is.”

Brennus’ eyes shined. “Is there anything that you’ve always wanted? Something we can give you?”

Meryn mumbled something so unintelligible that even Aiden looked puzzled.

“You’ll have to repeat that darling,” Brennus coaxed gently.

Meryn sat up straight and looked at her uncle. “Hugs.”

Brennus blinked. “Hugs?”

Meryn shrugged and stared down into her plate. “I was never hugged before meeting Aiden. I want hugs and bedtime stories and fishing trips and…”

Brennus stood quickly and pulled Meryn out of her chair into a massive hug. “Meryn, please, you’re breaking my heart,” he begged.

Doran walked up behind them and simply laid a hand on her head. “We can’t replace your childhood, but maybe we can create memories similar to the ones you always wanted while you’re here. After all, to most fae, you are a child.”

Meryn hesitantly wrapped her arms around her uncle and held on. After a moment everyone heard the muffled question. "How long are hugs supposed to last?"

Brennus chuckled and released her. "Until your heart is full," he answered and steered her back to her chair. When he sat down again, he looked from Darian to Oron to Meryn. "Girls are sweeter, but I never felt gut-wrenching fear for the boys the way I did for Meryn this afternoon."

"Sorry, Uncle Bren," Meryn said.

Aiden's mouth dropped. "Why didn't you tell me you were sorry for worrying me?"

Meryn tilted her head. "I would always be apologizing."

"Oh gods," Brennus murmured.

"Plus the boys were over four thousand years old when we met them," Doran added. "Meryn is just a baby."

Brennus snapped his fingers. "That must be why."

After Cord filled their plates, Oron lifted a small piece of beef out of his stew. "Creelee, would you like to try this?"

Creelee looked up at her and she nodded. "Remember, he's family too."

Creelee landed in the space between Oron's chest and his bowl. He looked down. "Mud."

Oron chuckled. "It's stew." He placed the piece of beef on the edge of his bowl. Creelee picked it up and in two seconds flat it was gone. "Whoa," Oron said, his eyes wide. He looked very impressed.

"He's a great eater," she said proudly.

Oron was grinning and looked like he was having the time of his life as he fished pieces of beef out for Creelee and watched him devour them.

As the dinner continued, Oron offered Creelee everything that was served. As Izzy guessed, Creelee tended to like meat the best, but had surprised her when he discovered he loved pasta and pickles. By dessert, her tiny man was laid out under a napkin with an engorged belly. He had a smile on his face as he rubbed his tummy.

"I hope he doesn't get sick," she fretted.

"Nah, he can handle it," Oron said like a proud papa.

Izzy looked across the table and nearly laughed out loud. Meryn reclining back in her chair with her pregnancy belly looked like Creelee. "Eat too much?" she asked.

Meryn just smiled. "I'm so full."

"I made chocolate pies for dessert," Cord said, as he entered the room with the serving cart full of pies and after dinner drinks.

Meryn struggled to sit up. "I have room for pie," she clarified.

Creelee heard Meryn's declaration, rolled to one side and sat up. "Room for pie," he repeated, causing everyone to chuckle at his antics.

When Cord set the pie down in front of them, Izzy's mouth started watering. She could smell the sweet aroma of chocolate.

"Mud?" Creelee asked Oron, tugging on his sleeve.

"No, Creelee, this is chocolate. It's sweet and

tastes good. Try a little bit, then see if you want more," he suggested.

"Cord, did you have to give him a whole piece? It's almost bigger than he is," Izzy said, watching worriedly.

Cord just smiled as he walked around with the coffee.

Creelee stuck one tiny finger in and licked it. Before she could stop him, he literally dove into his piece of pie. "Creelee!"

She could barely see him in the thick layers of chocolate and cream. Oron looked at her and she shrugged. Was this normal? Seconds later, the piece looked smaller. In fact, it kept shrinking until all that was left was bits of cream and crust.

Cord walked over and instead of handing her a cup of coffee, there were two large cups of warm water, a bar of soap and a fresh tea towel. "Thank you, Cord."

"Creelee, in the cup."

Swaying on his feet, he made his way over to the cup. She gently lifted him up and dunked him in like a tea bag.

"Warm," Creelee said.

"Wash off all that sticky mess," she ordered.

Creelee ducked under the water and when he popped back up, most of the chocolate had come off. "Rub your hands on the soap." She held up the bar. He rubbed his hands on the bar until bubbles started to form. Giggling, he began playing with the bubbles. She didn't mind because he was basically washing himself.

"Okay, Creelee, let's rinse you off." She held

out her finger and he held on. She lifted him up and into the fresh water. She had to hide a smile when she saw that he was now buck naked. His loincloth was probably somewhere on the pie plate. Once he was rinsed, she helped him out of the warm water and wrapped him up in the fluffy tea towel. She gently ran the towel's edge over his head, drying his hair. When he yawned, Felix flew over and held out his arms. "I can take him."

"Creelee, Felix is going to put you to bed. Is that okay?" she asked, not wanting him upset.

Creelee rubbed at his eyes and nodded. She passed him, towel and all to Felix, who flew off with the newest member of her family.

"You're going to be an amazing mother," Oron said softly. She could plainly see the love in his eyes. "Let's get Creelee to the stage where he doesn't eat pie by jumping into it, then we'll talk about kids."

"Whatever you say, love," he replied, lifting her hand to kiss it.

"Meryn, what's wrong?" Aiden asked.

"I think I'm jealous."

"Oh honey, do you miss your mom?" Aiden looked down at his mate anxiously.

"Huh? Oh yeah. But that wasn't what I was talking about."

"Then what."

"I want to jump into pie and eat it too," she sighed.

"Meryn, I love you," Kendrick announced, shaking his head.

"An enlargement spell?" Justice wondered out loud.

"It's doable," Law agreed.

Thane blinked at Meryn. "Gods, I think I want to try that too."

As the debate raged on how to make a slice of pie large enough to jump into, Oron leaned down and whispered four of his own magic words. "Let's go to bed."

"Did you really have to go to the Dark Forest?" he asked as they were undressing for bed. Even though she had spent the afternoon ogling half-naked buff goblins, the sight of her mate's bare skin still wreaked havoc with her body.

"Yes, at the point you told me not to go, it became a physical compulsion; besides, it wasn't even dangerous," she pointed out.

"When did you meet up with Gilheim?"

"Right after we entered under the shade, he was running patrols."

"So, you were basically escorted the entire time?"

Izzy climbed under the covers as she thought about that. "I guess you could say that."

Oron lifted the covers and slid in next to her. "I wasn't exaggerating the dangers, my love. The goblins may not have been a threat, but the other creatures there are. They aren't feral, attacking you would be in their nature."

"Like wolves?"

"If they felt like you had invaded their territory, yes."

"I can only promise to go with an escort," she said, turning in his arms to face him. This was how she liked him best, completely open to her.

She reached up her hand and touched the wooden necklace. "Does it hurt to lay on that?"

Oron touched his torc. "I forgot it was there to be honest. I don't even feel it."

"Your neck is lying on a piece of wood," she pointed out.

"But it doesn't feel that way. It's very comforting to me."

"Meryn's bracelet caused Dav's bar to grow branches and roots; evidently, it was made of elder."

Oron stared down at her. "Seriously? Good to know."

All throughout dinner, she noticed the slight change in her mate. He had sat a little straighter, met everyone's eyes, and spoke up more. It was as if he had been freed from the weight his old family name.

"Look at me, I'm being absolutely scandalous. I'm in bed with this Oron Vi'Eirlea. Who is this brilliant stranger who has slipped into bed to seduce me?"

His normally honeyed brown eyes darkened. "Seduce you, eh?"

She could only nod as his eyes seemed to devour her. He moved quickly, throwing back the bedding and covering her body. She could feel that he was hot, hard and dripping already. He pinned her arms over her head and leaned down to whisper in her ear.

"What do you need Izzy?" he asked, in a rough voice.

There was no hesitancy in his touch, he knew he owned her body and soul and she could feel it.

She looked into his dark brown eyes. "Just you."

"Perfect answer," he growled. He rolled her until she was on her hands and knees as he knelt behind her. "Keep your hands over your head," he ordered. She pressed her chest into the mattress and raised her hips so that she was offering herself to him.

"Gods, Iz, you're so damn beautiful," he said, trailing his fingers down her spine.

He tested her and she knew he found her ready. He plunged two fingers deep, causing her to moan. "Please Oron, not slow. Not tonight."

Oron gave a masculine chuckle. "As you wish my love." The next moment his fingers were gone and she felt the blunt head of his cock pushing inside her body. "Yes," she hissed. Somehow he managed to ignite every point of pleasure in her body. She rested her forehead against the sheets as he slammed into her over and over again. Slowly her body began to coil as he managed to caress that elusive spot inside her. She tilted her pelvis until every single thrust has her gasping. "There!" she screamed.

Her desperate need propelled him to new levels of urgency as his fingers dug into her hips. "Gods Iz, there's no one like you. No one has ever loved me the way you do," he groaned as he snapped his hips.

She was afraid to move her upper body and change the angle, so she turned her face instead. "And no one has ever accepted me the way you do. You know exactly how chaotic I can be and you claim me as your own anyway."

"Only me, you're mine, Iz. My solace in a world that hates me."

"As you are mine."

When he plunged deep enough to slam her cervix; she was about to flip him when her orgasm caught her unaware. One moment she was about to tap out, the next she was screaming.

She felt his hot seed fill her before he collapsed, taking her to the bed at his side.

"Love you," he gasped.

"How…can…you…talk?" She was trying to remember how to breathe and her mouth was dry from yelling. He simply laughed and held her close.

When he pulled away, she felt him slip from her body and gasped at the sensations it wrought. She managed to open one eye to watch him stumble toward the bathroom like a newborn foal. She was still giggling when he reappeared washcloth in hand. He ignored her mirth. "At least I can move," he teased, as he wiped her clean.

"Mr. Vi'Eirlea, you have done your job well."

He kissed her shoulder before pulling the duvet up to tuck her in. She began to drift away when he slipped in beside her.

“Goodnight, my love,” he whispered.

“Goodnight, my everything,” she replied and his arm pulled her close. Feeling like everything was perfect in her world, she gave in and slept.

CHAPTER FOURTEEN

THE NEXT MORNING IZZY HAD fun showing Cord how the espresso machine worked.

"That was much easier than I thought it would be," Cord admitted.

"Are these ready for *denka*?" Ryuu asked, walking in from the dining room.

Izzy nodded and handed off the two mochas. "Has she threatened anyone?"

"Not as of yet, but I'm pretty sure it's a close thing," he lifted the two cups and walked out of the enormous kitchen.

Izzy had felt intimidated when she first entered Cord's domain. But he had been so eager to show her how he had set up all the equipment she found herself caught up in his enthusiasm.

He was such sweetheart to set all of this up for her, sacrificing a portion of his counters to create a mini coffee bar.

"Head out to the table dear, I'll be bringing out breakfast in a moment," Cord said, steering her toward the door. How he had managed to watch her like a hawk and still prepare a full breakfast was nothing short of a miracle.

"Thanks Cord." She walked out and when she entered the dining room, the men stood. Instead of making her feel awkward, she felt special.

"Good morning," she said brightly.

A round of greetings sounded off, but her attention was on Meryn. The little nut was sitting back in her chair, eyes closed, clutching her cup of coffee.

"Iz, Iz!" a tiny voice called.

"Good morning, Creelee!" She held out her hand and he flew right to her. "Did you have a good time with Feris, Finley and Felix?"

"Nice," he said, rubbing his cheek along her finger.

"Creelee is fun," Feris chirped.

The sprites had made their way over to Meryn and were sitting on her shoulders. Every time Feris went to poke Meryn's cheek, Felix stopped him, shaking his head.

"Thank you for looking after him, Felix."

Felix blushed and nodded.

She looked down and noticed that the boys had also given Creelee some of their clothes. The sleeves and pants were cuffed, but he looked adorable in his brown pants and cream tunic.

"Boys, thank you for giving Creelee some clothes, that was very kind of you."

Finley nodded. "Stay warm."

As everyone enjoyed their coffee, her eyes strayed to the newcomers. She nudged Oron with her elbow.

He smiled down at her. "We were waiting on you to make introductions, especially considering Meryn hadn't had any coffee yet and would have probably been a wasted effort."

Meryn simply nodded her agreement, eyes still closed.

"So who are these handsome devils?" she asked, watching Meryn.

Meryn's eyes popped open. "Handsome?" she looked around and noticed the new men at the table. She turned to Aiden. "Warrior peeps?"

He nodded. "Baby, I would like to introduce you to Ari Lionhart, the Tau Unit's acting unit leader, also Rex and Declan's brother." Ari smiled at them. "Next to him is Gage Fabre. His father is the Fabre Noble Family head who reports to Simon and Leana." The gorgeous warrior winked at them, causing Aiden to glare at him. "This is Priest Vi'Aerdan, you've heard a bit about him." Izzy gave him a little wave, which he returned. "Last but certainly not least is Kincaid Bayberry."

Both she and Meryn turned to look at the last warrior who was visibly pale and staring at the end of the table.

Meryn pointed to him. "Why does he look like he's gonna pass out?"

Kendrick coughed into his fist. "I think that may be because of us," he said, indicating to himself and the Ashleigh brothers.

Meryn tilted her head. "Why?"

Law chuckled. "She's really good for the ego."

Kincaid ripped his eyes away from Kendrick to turn to Meryn. "Kendrick is a legend amongst warriors. He managed to smuggle out some of the best offensive and defensive spells from Storm Keep to send out to the warriors, those spells have basically kept us alive." With a trembling hand, he pointed to the brothers. "The Ashleigh brothers are ghosts. They appear whenever they are needed and destroy ferals. How could you not know this?" he asked, still looking wide-eyed.

Meryn shrugged. "Kendrick's my big brother-cousin and Thane is my *athair*, so I don't really get the whole 'being in awe' thing."

Kincaid looked like he was about to swallow his tongue. "What?"

Meryn blinked. "What?"

Kincaid looked over to Ari who shrugged. "I told you this was going to be a high-profile breakfast."

The queen sipped her coffee. "I think I feel slighted."

Instantly the entire Tau Unit stood and bowed over Kincaid's infraction. "Forgive me, Queen Aleksandra, I meant no disrespect. My only excuse is that being in your august presence has scrambled this poor witch's mind," Kincaid said, stumbling over his words.

The queen chuckled at his apology. "You are a dear boy. There's nothing to forgive. Please sit down and enjoy breakfast, I know Cord has been working hard on it." The men sat back down, all four of them looking a bit nervous.

"Y'all are acting like you never come here," Meryn commented.

Ari frowned. "We don't. Brennus usually meets us down at the estate for us to give our reports. We hardly ever come to the palace."

"Why not?" Meryn asked.

Aiden sat back, resting his arm on the back of her chair. "Meryn, honey, you have to remember, before we visited Noctem Falls the Eta Unit hardly met with Magnus either."

"Oh yeah. I guess I forgot," Meryn murmured, staring down into her coffee cup.

Ari leaned forward. "We heard of the virus, but we'd like to verify some of the details we've heard," he glanced at Kincaid, who closed his eyes and cast a soundproofing spell. Ari continued. "I know some things because of what my brothers have told me, but we would like to ask questions of our own."

Aiden nodded. "Of course."

"Is it true that the virus was manufactured?" Gage asked.

Kendrick nodded. "I can confirm that. I saw the magic in the virus myself."

"Magic?" Thane asked.

Kendrick exhaled. "Yes. Whoever did this was able to use magic to engineer on a molecular level. The virus was designed so the only cure was older vampire blood."

"Those damn necklaces!" Priest exclaimed, sitting back in his chair.

"Uh, Kincaid, can you let Micah, Serenity and Zach in the bubble?" Meryn asked, pointing to the doorway where the three looked on, concern on their faces.

"I got it," Justice volunteered. He whispered low, waved the trio in, before casting a new spell.

"I know you weren't having a super-secret meeting without me," Micah said, walking up to the table.

Serenity and Zach sat down, but Micah walked over to Meryn. He leaned over and kissed the top of her head. "You doing okay Dewdrop?"

Meryn looked up at him. "You know?"

He nodded. "When the announcement went out yesterday, I called Aiden and he filled me in." He ruffled her curls before he sat down next to his mate. "I, of course, relayed everything to Adriel during my check-in call. He had already heard most of it from Stefan and Kari's report though." He rubbed the side of his nose slyly. "You didn't hear it from me, but the boys are going all out to get Pip open-air acclimated. They are frantically doing everything they can to come to your side."

Cristo threw his fist in the air. "I knew he'd get Kari to help him report." He eyed Meryn, Aiden and Kendrick. "Y'all owe me."

Meryn's eyes filled and her lower lip began to quiver.

Cristo looked at her a panicked expression on his face. "I was just kidding Meryn."

"I want my brothers," she whispered.

Serenity and Amelia were up in an instant going to her. Amelia all but knocked Aiden out of his chair.

With a disgruntled look on his face, he made room for Amelia to squeeze in between him and his mate.

"Oh Meryn, it's okay," Amelia murmured and she held Meryn close.

Serenity had a glowing hand resting on Meryn's head.

Meryn rubbed her arm over her eyes, looking pissed at her show of emotion. "I'm being stupid," she grumbled.

"No, you're not." Amelia refuted. "You've been through a lot in the past couple days. Of course, you're going to miss the ones who ground you and help to buffer you against the world."

Meryn sniffled. "They better not be rushing Pip."

Micah chuckled and both women helping Meryn glared at him. He held up his hands. "Pip is rushing Pip. He keeps sneaking out the door and hurrying back in. Sebastian threatened to sit on him at one point, of course, he isn't one to talk." He smiled broadly. "A little birdie told me he's working on a care package for you."

Meryn brightened a little. "Meat kebobs?"

"What else? And your Magic Pudding."

Serenity's hand dimmed and she sat back down next to her mate. Amelia dropped a kiss on her little sister-cousin's head and went back to her own seat.

Ari looked around. "What's Magic Pudding?"

Micah threaded his fingers behind his head and tipped his chair back. "Only the best pudding in the world and one of the only things Meryn ate while in Noctem Falls. Evidently, it had fae cinnamon in it, which helped her to eat."

The queen nodded. "Of course it did, she's half fae. Even without her light, her body knew what she needed." Her eyes grew wide. "No wonder you had such a rough time there, you poor thing."

Oron turned to Meryn. "Your light was returned while I was getting confirmed as an Eirlea, wasn't it?"

Izzy nodded. "Yeah, y'all went outside and your mom found Meryn's light in the orb."

Oron's eyes turned sad. "Before Abraxas appeared we saw a second branch form from Eamon's, your mother's branch. It instantly petrified before yours sprouted with a tiny bud," he pointed to her stomach. "No wonder the Elder Guardian appeared."

"The spirits are a sight to behold. I was only ten years old when I was given my father's name of Vi'Aerdan and added to their tree," Priest smiled. "She was one of the most beautiful things I have ever seen."

"Dude, Abraxas was hot!" Meryn said in agreement.

"Meryn," Aiden growled, lifting her into his lap. She giggled as he nipped at her neck.

Priest laughed at her display. "Abraxas, huh? The Hawthorn spirit is Liaylia."

"Pu-ding," Creelee said.

Meryn smiled at him. "I will definitely share with my eating buddy. Can you say meat kebob?"

"Bob!" Creelee repeated excitedly.

Ari and the rest of the Tau Unit looked enchanted by the brownie and sprites who were flittering around the table. Ari turned to the queen. "Are there always little ones here?"

Izzy's new mom shook her head. "Felix looks to Meryn and we gained his brothers when she defended them from their chieftain. Izzy is the one who brought Creelee into our home. We have been very blessed."

Ari was locked in on Creelee. "I've never seen a brownie before. Are they all adorable like him?"

Izzy shrugged. "I have no idea, I only met Creelee when we visited the goblin village in the Dark Forest."

Once again, the men were staring. Gage sat forward. "I'm sorry, I thought you said you went to the Dark Forest."

Meryn nodded. "Yup. They were super cool. Made a killer bar-b-que boar too."

Ari licked his lips. "Bar-b-que boar?"

Meryn's expression became blissful. "So freaking good."

"You know, if you ever need an escort when you go back…" Ari started.

Priest whacked his arm. "I was going to take them."

"Dibs!" Kincaid called out.

Meryn laughed. "He called dibs."

Aiden blinked. "That actually works?"

Meryn nodded. "I told you."

Ari sat back. "I think we should take into consideration Meryn's station. She will probably need a whole unit to keep her safe."

Gage slapped him on the back. "You have learned from your father."

"Don't forget that Ryuu and I accompany them as well," Pierce added.

"You're not leaving me and my one and only behind this time," Micah added.

Serenity was about to speak up when the air around them vibrated. Everyone turned to the doorway where two fae were waiting with exasperated expressions.

"Kendrick, if you would," the queen asked.

Kendrick lowered the soundproof bubble and raised it when the two fae entered. Izzy noticed that although they were male and female, they looked very much alike. The female's eyes locked in on Serenity.

"Ut, oh," Serenity murmured.

"Ut, oh?" The female exclaimed. "You almost die taking Zach with you and all you say is 'ut oh'?"

"Allia, I'm so sorry I worried you," Serenity said, looking contrite.

"*Both* of us were scared to death," the male added.

Serenity sniffled and looked up at them. "Ailain, I wouldn't have done it if it hadn't been absolutely necessary." Zach rubbed her back. "I already throttled her," he advised them.

Allia and Ailain hurried over and pulled both Serenity and Zach into hugs.

The queen dabbed her eyes with her napkin. "I

swear I've cried more in the past two days than I have in the past two thousand years."

Meryn snapped her fingers. "They're Etain's brother and sister, the other set of twins."

Ailain stepped away from the group hug to pull two chairs over so they could sit next to their adopted baby brother and sister.

Allia looked over to Meryn. "It's so wonderful to finally meet you in person. We have read all about you on Facebook. I cannot thank you enough for everything you've done for our brother. He sings your praises every time we speak and has all but ordered us to watch over you," she sniffed. "As if we wouldn't anyway." She looked around until her eyes landed on Creelee. "Is that a brownie?"

Izzy nodded as Oron went around the table with another set of introductions. When he got to Ari and the Tau Unit, Allia giggled. "We know them from sparring lessons."

Ari winced. "Etain has threatened my ability to reproduce if either of you gets hurt during training."

Allia waved a hand at him. "He'd have to come here first. Maybe I should get hurt. He hasn't returned home in centuries."

Ari paled. "Please don't. Your brother scares the hell out of me. He sounded so pleasant when he was describing, in detail, what he'd do to me should you get so much as a splinter. It was eerie."

Allia ignored Ari's plea and turned to Izzy. "Welcome to Éire Danu." She grinned. "I heard about what you did to that tailor." She clapped her hands. "Brava, my dear, brava!"

Izzy smiled back. "The asshole shouldn't have talked about my mate."

Allia nodded. "I back you one-hundred percent. Should the need arise where you must fight again, I will be there."

Meryn pointed to her and looked up at Aiden. "A ride or die bitch."

Allia looked taken aback for a moment, then nodded slowly. "I believe that is the correct term. American slang is so very colorful."

Meryn flashed her the 'live long and prosper' sign. "Word."

It took Allia three attempts, but she finally was able to flash the sign back at Meryn. "Word."

Aiden bopped Meryn's head around. "Quit corrupting the fae court."

Meryn swatted his hand away. "No way. Besides, I heard she was learning how to fight way before I got here, I didn't start that."

"It's true, Commander. I requested fighting lessons at least a decade ago," Allia confirmed. "And learning her colloquialisms will assist us if we were ever to visit the human realm." She turned to Kendrick. "You may want to take that spell down. Molvan was right behind us but got snagged by Portia, he's on his way to update us on how the recall is going."

Kendrick nodded and the spell was lowered.

Izzy tapped her finger on her chin. "Where do I know that name from?"

"Isn't Molvan the name of that douche that tortured Darian?" Meryn asked.

"Prince Darian, please tell me you're not still bandying that old tale about?" A handsome fae asked as he walked through the door.

Darian grinned at him. "My mate was curious about my childhood and it is such a dramatic story."

Molvan rolled his eyes before winking at him. "Had I known you'd make me out to be such a villain, I would have done something more ballad worthy."

Meryn tilted her head. "So…not a douchebag." Izzy watched as her eyes became unfocused. "Shield, no, gate, no…"

"Meryn?" Aiden asked, looking concerned.

Kendrick and Law both stood and immediately went to her side. Each laid a hand on her shoulder.

Kendrick's eyes widened and he turned to Law. "You seeing this?" Law nodded. "It's giving me motion sickness," he said, his other hand going to his midsection.

"What?" Aiden demanded. "What is she doing?"

Kendrick stared down at Meryn. "She's flipping through pictures like spinning through a Rolodex. It's her empathy, but with a boost. Fascinating."

"Wall," she announced.

Law gave one nod, then shook his head. "More than that."

Meryn scrunched up her face. “I don’t know another word for it.”

“The word you’re looking for is battlements. A defensive structure designed to protect whole cities. They usually have openings for shooting through.”

Meryn nodded quickly. “Yeah, battlements.”

Molvan blinked. “I’m sorry, what?”

Law removed his hand when Kendrick did. They looked at each other and Law indicated for him to answer before he went back to his seat.

Kendrick turned to the newcomer. “Meryn has empathy; she is training to use visualizations for impressions she gets from people. For you, she saw battlements, which I believe means that you are one who defends many people.”

“That is an amazing gift,” Molvan said, staring at Meryn. “The queen put me in charge of the recall and relocation efforts to bring everyone home.” He grinned. “My usual position is public works serving the city, so it isn’t far-fetched that I may have stepped on a toe or two.”

Meryn stretched as Kendrick also went back to his seat. “You’re actually nice.”

He bowed. “Thank you.” He turned to his queen. “Your Majesty, I have conferred with Portia and she believes that should we ask our current visitors for assistance. With their aid we could send out a worldwide message to our people calling them home,” his eyes strayed to the Ashleigh brothers.

“Worldwide?” the queen asked.

“Yes, Your Majesty. The entire human realm

all at once. We even have protections built in so that only fae who have not turned hear the message," he confirmed.

"What about half fae?" Meryn asked.

He nodded. "Full and half-blooded fae will receive this recall notice. Any blood that is more diluted is exempt, so we don't run the risk of them not knowing their heritage and possibly raising concerns with human authorities."

"What would you need from us?" Thane asked.

Molvan turned to him. "Simply the extra power needed to get the message to everyone."

Thane looked to his brothers, who were already nodding. "We'll assist," Thane agreed.

"Thank you, Thane," Brennus said.

"I guess we're sort of family now," Thane groused.

Molvan turned to Thane. "How so?"

He pointed to Meryn. "She is my godsdaughter."

The fae brightened. "Congratulations on your discovery."

Meryn blushed. "I think it's pretty cool."

Molvan turned to Oron. "I hear congratulations are in order for you as well. Will you be opening up House Eirson when you move back home? Since its walls butt up against the palace it would be easy to join the houses that way," he suggested, flipping to a blank page on his legal pad.

"Move back home? I thought we were going to live in Lycaonia," Izzy said, looking up at Oron.

Oron rubbed the torc at his neck. "I've never

even thought about opening up those quarters again."

Molvan nodded sympathetically. "I can imagine why, but it would be such a waste of space not to use it, especially with so many returning to the city." He smiled at Izzy. "Especially when Lady Vi'Eirlea begins to add to your family."

"Huh?" she asked.

Oron looked down at her a soft smile on his face. "He's referring to when you get pregnant. As you are human, we don't have to wait a full year for your conception cycle."

"What if I don't want kids right now?"

His face fell. "What do you mean?"

"I mean, I don't want kids right now," she repeated.

Oron's expression tightened. "Why don't you want my child?"

"Danger, Will Robinson, danger," Meryn hissed.

"I never said I didn't want your child," Izzy said, ignoring the little nut.

"Then it shouldn't be an issue," Oron reiterated.

"It is an issue because I'm not ready for kids."

Molvan inched backward. "I'll get with the Ashleighs at a later time," he quickly backed up and practically ran from the room.

"Why not?" Oron demanded, his cheeks flushing.

Izzy stood on shaky legs. "Because I said so!" she yelled. She turned and headed for the door.

"Izzy, get back here!" she heard her mate demand.

She kept walking.

She felt like the entire palace was against her. Everyone here was Oron's family.

"Is otay," Creelee whispered as he patted her cheek, trying to dry her tears.

"Thank you, buddy," she said as she looked around. When she heard Portia's voice, she ducked into an alcove. When the coast was clear, she ran for the gate and down the steps away from the palace.

She made her way toward the Border City until she was standing in front of Dav's tavern. She opened the door and went straight to the bar. She eyed the changes that Meryn had inadvertently caused yesterday and tried hopping up on the stool. Unlike her previous visits, she didn't have Oron or Pierce to help her. It just drove home the fact that she was alone.

She draped herself across the stool so that she was lying on her belly and began to cry softly.

"Here now, what's this?" she heard a familiar voice ask. Warm hands lifted her and propped her up on the stool. It was one of the warriors from yesterday. He looked down at her, worry etched on his face.

"First, the tiny one comes in yesterday saying she needed Sacred Chamomile and today you're in here crying. Whose ass do I have to beat to keep you baby girls smiling?" At his kind words, she felt the dam burst. She clutched at his shirt and began to ugly cry.

"Gods Bryok, what did you do to her?" another voice demanded.

"Nothing, Casek, I swear." She felt a hand smooth her hair. "Do you need us to find your mate?" She shook her head vehemently. "Having a problem with your mate?" he asked. She nodded and looked at him through tear-blurred eyes. "He wants a baby, but I don't know where we live and he thinks I don't want his baby, which is stupid because I love him, which is scary because I've only known him for four days." She felt more tears coming. "I'm not a damn incubator."

Bryok nodded sympathetically. "Of course, you're not." He looked up. "Dav, get your arse in here and draw a pint!" he hollered.

"I'm coming," Dav called then walked through the swinging door. He saw Izzy hiccup crying and immediately pulled out a pint glass and filled it for her. "Here you go, darling."

Sniffling, she picked up the glass and began to gulp its contents. She didn't stop until it was empty. Without saying a word, Dav refilled it. She took a healthy drink of this one, then sat it back on the bar.

Behind her, she heard the door open. "Told ya she'd be here."

Izzy turned to see Meryn with Ryuu and Pierce walk in. "Is he with you?"

Meryn shook her head as Ryuu propped her up on the stool. Meryn made sure that her bracelet was tucked under her hoodie sleeve. "Nope, Aiden and Darian dragged his ass out to do drills. I bet they're explaining to him how dumb he is."

"So it wasn't me being difficult?" Izzy asked.

"Hell, no! Aiden and I basically went through the same thing. I wanted to put on this birth control amulet so we wouldn't have kiddos right away, except we had already had so much sex I was already pregnant; it kinda became a moot point."

Bryok laughed and sat down on the stool on her other side. "Doing drills with the McKenzie is a punishment in of itself."

Meryn snorted. "Please, I bet they're all standing around giving Oron advice on how to kiss ass."

Casek laughed. "That's probably true. Warriors gossip worse than old women."

"Meryn, this is Bryok and Casek," she said, pointing to the two warriors. "They were helping me when I had my meltdown."

The two warriors nodded to Meryn who waved back.

"I just need time, you know?"

Meryn swung her feet. "Yup. I think because you fell in love with Oron and adapted to this world so quickly it surprised all of us when you two were fussing at each other."

"They don't hate me?"

Meryn shook her head. "The queen, of course, is on board for babies, but then again Aiden's mom practically put bad juju on me talking about twins, so that's understandable. Aunt Aleks is probably dying to be a grandma, just like Adelaide." She kicked one foot out, then another. "Oron is like almost five thousand years old and the queen is even older, so I can see why they'd both want a baby right away. But realistically, you haven't known each other that long, so I get why you want to wait."

"At night, when warriors are done imagining their mates, we dream of our children. It's something to hold on to," Bryok said, in a soft voice.

"Now I feel like shit," Izzy said, rotating her glass in her hands.

"We also imagine our mates being happy and ready for a child. Trust me, in no way, shape, or form has Oron ever wished for a child to be born to an unhappy mate. Every male is more than willing to wait until the time is right," Casek said, from his table behind them.

Izzy took another long sip of her beer, thinking about what Bryok said about the warriors dreaming of their children.

"Get an amulet and tell him to wait one year. By that time, you should have your feet under you and my munchkin will need a playmate," Meryn said, pointing at her belly.

Izzy laughed. "They are going to be so much trouble together."

Meryn shrugged. "Probably, but that's half the fun, right?"

Izzy downed the rest of her beer. "I can do a year. Do you think he can?"

Meryn laughed. "I am willing to bet tomorrow's mocha on the fact that by the time we get back, Oron will be willing to agree to just about anything."

Izzy smiled to herself. "I don't want to go back just yet."

"Have another beer and then we can hit some stores. after you left Cord said that a delivery came for you. I bet it's your electronic stuff from Cam."

Izzy took her time with the next drink, and by the time they were leaving, she was relaxed and feeling much better. As they left Dav, Bryok and Casek made her promise to come back and tell them what happens.

Once outside she turned to Meryn. "Casek was right, warriors do gossip worse than women."

Meryn just nodded. "Tell me about it, I live in the Alpha estate. Sometimes I peep out the window expecting to see sweat and muscles in action and they're all just standing around talking."

Izzy laughed then stopped and squinted. In the distance, just past the Border City, she saw that shadow again, only this time a tall figure appeared in the middle of it.

She pointed. "Meryn, what kind of portal is that?"

Meryn turned and the blood drained from her face. "I don't think that's a portal."

A moment later, the breeze carried the smell of rotting cheese, making them gag.

"Ryuu!" Meryn screamed.

Behind them, the door to the tavern opened and Izzy could see the second the smell hit them.

Casek bared his teeth. "Ferals!" he roared.

"Impossible!" Bryok yelled, drawing his sidearm.

Ryuu and Pierce stepped in front of them as Dav turned to the squire. "Get them to the palace!"

Izzy looked down at her wrist. She exhaled as she smiled and pushed the shiny red jewel that had been beckoning to her. They couldn't yell at her for pressing the panic button if everyone was panicking.

"What the hell?" Casek exclaimed.

Izzy looked up in time to see the shadow disappear. She sighed and looked down at her bracelet as bells began to toll everywhere in the city.

"Oops."

CHAPTER FIFTEEN

"RYUU, KEEP THEM HERE. THAT bracelet has a tracking feature, that's what they'll be homing in on," Dav advised when the bells began to go off.

It didn't take the unit warriors five minutes to show up, her mate and Aiden in the lead. Oron went to her and simply wrapped his arms around her, pulling her close. "Gods! I didn't know what to think when the alarms started going off in the palace."

"Why is it always you!" Aiden roared as he scooped up his mate in his arms.

Oron leaned down. "Please tell me there's a real emergency and you didn't just press the button," he whispered.

She felt a moment of irritation before he pulled back and she saw the worry in his eyes. "Because if you did, I think we can still escape to Monroe for a bit."

Her heart melted. He wasn't angry, even believing that she might have pressed the button due to her compulsory nature. "I love you. I want to have children one year from now," she announced.

His eyes widened and he smiled wide. "Really?" he frowned. "You didn't press the button to tell me that, right?"

She shook her head. "No, silly. I saw this shadow thing, then smelled cheese, then Meryn screamed for Ryuu, then the guys came out of the tavern and yelled 'feral' then they started freaking out, *that* was when I pressed the button," she explained.

Oron turned to face Aiden his face ashen. "That's impossible."

Aiden looked from Dav to Ryuu. "How sure are you?"

Dav stared at Aiden flatly. "I may not be a warrior anymore, but I was fighting them before you were born. I know a feral when I smell one."

Aiden winced. "You understand why I asked?"

Dav ran a hand over the back of his neck. "Yeah, we do. Like Prince Oron said, what we saw, should never have been possible."

Meryn snorted. "That seems to be par for the course anymore."

Izzy turned to Priest. "Didn't you say something about having to do follow-up reports on meetings with people who saw shadows? Because that's what I saw twice. One when we were headed back from the Dark Forest and the one just now, only the one today had a person in it."

Oron's hold on her tightened. "What do you mean you saw one the other day?"

She patted his chest. "I thought my eyes were playing tricks on me."

Priest nodded. "That's what a lot of people said in our questioning too. That they never would have reported it, but they'd seen it more than once."

"Where?" Aiden asked.

Priest waved his hand around. "All in the Border City."

Ryuu rubbed Meryn's back. "Let us get these two back to the safety of the palace," he suggested.

Aiden handed Meryn off to Ryuu before leaning down and kissing her forehead. "I'll be along in just a bit. I want to organize the units."

Meryn nodded. "Okay," she turned to Izzy. "Coming?" Izzy shook her head. Ryuu and Pierce left taking Meryn back to the palace.

Oron looked torn. Izzy took his hand. "I'm staying with you, so if you want to help Aiden, don't let me stop you. I honestly feel safer here, surrounded by unit warriors than if I were alone in the palace."

Oron squeezed her hand. "You wouldn't be alone."

"I'm always alone when you're not with me," she explained.

"What am I going to do with you?"

"Just love me, everything else will take care of itself."

Oron nodded then pulled her toward where Aiden was instructing the men. "Dav, do you think you can get help from the Old Guard who reside in Éire Danu?"

Dav gave him a wolfish grin. "Try to keep us from helping," he challenged.

Aiden chuckled. "Father's friends are the same way, itching for fun."

"What do you want us to do?" Ari asked, pointing to the other unit warriors.

Aiden's smiled disappeared. "My mate may be many things, but she is hardly ever wrong. If she says that the impossible is happening, then gentlemen, we need to prepare you to face ferals here in Éire Danu."

He looked over to Micah. "Call Colton, tell him I need Lorcan, Ben, and Graham sent here, A.S.A.P." Micah pulled out his cell phone and walked away to make his call.

Aiden turned to Darian, but he was already nodding. "I'm heading there now to pick them up." He held up his hand with the signet ring. "I'm so glad I don't have to hide this anymore." He closed his eyes and a portal opened three feet in front of them. He gave a short wave, then walked through.

Oron took a step forward. "Aiden, shouldn't you discuss this with the queen?"

Aiden shook his head. "I am in charge of the units, they take their commands from me, not the queen." He gave a wry smile. "Just like with Prince Magnus, the city's ruler can make small, day to day requests, but my orders supersede everything." He pointed to him cheekily.

"Besides, I have you to run interference for me," he said, grinning broadly.

Oron cursed under his breath. "And everyone thinks Meryn is trouble."

Aiden laughed then turned to the assembled warriors. "Starting now, we will be running a two-by-two-by-two schedule. Two units running perimeter patrols, two units training and two units resting."

"Yes, sir!" the men boomed.

Dav had a sly look on his face. "And what about us Old Guard?"

Aiden gave him an innocent expression. "I'm putting you in charge of them. See that they are used to the best of their abilities."

Dav's mouth dropped open. "Sonofabitch," he muttered. Around him, the men laughed.

Aiden shook his head. "You didn't think I was going to try and spearhead everything, did you?"

Dav looked bewildered. "Wouldn't most leaders?"

Aiden shrugged. "I'm in a city I've never been to, amongst men I've never met. It's more prudent to delegate some of the decision making to those with overall more experience and knowledge of the city."

Thane clapped Aiden on the back as he and his brothers walked by. "We need more men like you Aiden McKenzie, you almost make me regret not becoming a unit warrior." Aiden's eyes lit up before Thane looked over his shoulder. "Almost."

"Damn," Aiden said sighing.

Thane chuckled before pointing to the horizon. "Justice, Law, let's go set some D.E.W.s."

Aiden's eyes bugged. "You can create distance early warning lines?"

Thane looked confused. "Of course, can't…" He looked over to the unit witches who seemed equally impressed.

Kendrick nodded at Thane sympathetically. "Trust me, I know exactly how you feel. They haven't been trained in sweeps, either."

Thane scrubbed his hands over his face. "That's old magic," he argued.

Kendrick held up a finger. "Exactly."

"What are sweeps?" Aiden asked.

Kendrick turned to Aiden. "A magical pulse that can take out swaths of the enemy. Originally created when we still had front line battles. The stronger the witch, the more damage the sweep does. The only downfall is that it affects everyone in its path, friend and foe alike."

Aiden grimaced. "We engage in a more guerrilla-style fighting now, sweeps could potentially take down a fellow unit warrior."

Kendrick pointed to the expanse between the Border City and the Dark Forest. "Yes, that's true. But when you have a wide open area to defend, then it can be advantageous."

"Kendrick, could you and Law teach the unit witches here how to do lay D.E.W.s and perform sweeps while Thane and Justice set an outer perimeter?" Aiden asked.

Kendrick exchanged looks with Thane who nodded. "We can do that."

Izzy stepped forward. “Will the warning thing go off when the goblins visit? Telk said something the other day about them coming during the deepest dim. I wouldn’t want them getting hurt.”

Thane shook his head. “They will be set to go off for ferals only. The spell detects creatures without souls, then activates; otherwise, unit warriors running patrols would set them off.” He looked out at the vast landscape. “It won’t be perfect because there will be gaps, but it should help.”

Izzy stared. To their right, the air began to shimmer gold before a portal opened. Darian and three other warriors stepped through. Darian sighed. “Good, you’re all still here. I didn’t know whether to go to the palace or not.”

Aiden clasped forearms with the two of the men and ruffled the blond hair of the third. “Hey, Ben.”

“Where’s my baby sister?” The man asked, ducking his head away. “Mother told me in no uncertain terms that I was to coddle her shamelessly,” the blond warrior announced.

Aiden pinched the bridge of his nose. “Ben…”

The man held up his hands. “Mother’s orders overwrite your jealousy. We all know Meryn loves me best.”

“Thought I might find you here,” a male voice called out.

Aiden looked up, then nodded. “Rex, what are you doing here?”

Rex just stared. “You all arrive, then warning

bells are deafening everyone around the city." He looked around. "Where's Meryn? I would have thought for sure she'd be at the epicenter."

Izzy giggled. "She went back to the palace with Ryuu and Pierce, but she was here," she informed the handsome man. She eyed his arms. "You wouldn't be Elder Rex Lionhart, would you?"

Oron pulled her back toward him as Rex blinked. "Yes, I am. Do I know you?"

Izzy shook her head. "Meryn said that I had to meet the Elder with the amazingly hot arms."

Rex preened. "That woman has impeccable tastes."

Aiden snarled at both Rex and Ben. "She's *my* mate."

Darian led the two other warriors toward the units standing by. "Men, this is Lorcan Ariav, Beta's unit leader, Graham Armstrong, Delta's unit leader and the blond flirt is Ben McKenzie, Aiden's brother, he serves in the Gamma Unit with Oron. They are here, I'm assuming, to get you up to speed on the new drills we created for engaging reapers." He turned back to Aiden to confirm.

Aiden nodded and went to stand next to Darian. "Unlike Noctem Falls and Éire Danu, Lycaonia's perimeters, until very recently had to be constantly defended. Myself, along with Colton Albright and Gavriel Ambrosios have developed training methods to fight this new, invisible enemy." He turned to Graham, Lorcan and Ben. "We're running two-by-two-by two.

Graham, you're assigned to training. Lorcan you're in charge of patrols and Ben you're to float between the two, wherever you're needed."

"Yes, sir." The three answered.

Aiden looked to the units. "Ari, can you assign them quarters amongst the units?"

Ari nodded. "Of course."

"Alright men, you have your orders for now. Ben, you're with me," Aiden commanded. He turned to Kendrick and the Ashleigh brothers. "See you for dinner." He and Ben walked up the street, heading toward the palace.

The men around her exhaled.

"Gods, he's good," Dav said.

Thane watched the unit commander walk away and smiled when Aiden reached up and cuffed Ben soundly. "It would have taken us at least a week to get this organized with the way other leaders posture. Their pride would never have allowed them to hand over major decision making to others. He not only quickly identified what needed to be done, but also asked the right men to do it."

Darian's back straightened. "We follow him for a reason, Thane."

The men all murmured their agreement.

Rex winked at her. "Come along, my dear. These men don't need us around." He placed her hand on his elbow to escort her back to the palace.

"Hey!" Oron exclaimed.

Izzy felt along his bicep. "She wasn't lying, your arms are amazing."

Rex laughed out loud. "I have so missed that little midget."

"Oron we'd better head back to the palace as well. The queen will want our update personally," Darian said from behind them.

"Damn right. Izzy, come back here," Oron ordered.

"No way. I'm getting to know the Elder," she teased.

"Have fun! Don't kill the Elder, Oron," Kendrick called after them, as they walked away.

"No promises," Oron muttered darkly behind them.

They had only made it one street over before Oron pulled her to his side and Darian wrapped an arm around Rex's shoulders in a friendly manner blocking him from reclaiming Izzy's hand.

Rex just shook his head and started going over some of the requests his father had fielded concerning lion-shifters wanting to return to Éire Danu.

When they got closer to the queen's chambers Oron pulled her to a stop, allowing Darian and Rex to enter first. He steered her to the nearest alcove.

"Why are we out here?" she asked.

"Were you serious about having a child a year from now?" he asked, trepidation in his eyes.

"Yes. Meryn said there's an amulet I can wear that will act as birth control. She helped me realize that most of the things that I was concerned about would resolve themselves in a year, like our living arrangements or finding my place in your world."

"Your place is at my side," he said, wrapping his arms around her, resting his cheek on the top of her head. "I will get you an amulet first thing tomorrow. It can come off whenever you're ready, I never want you to feel pressured, this will always be your choice."

"I think I just want more time of it being just us. I've never really been in a serious relationship before, so this is all new to me and throwing a kid in the mix scares the hell outta me," she admitted, then sighed. "But when Meryn said how long you've been waiting for a family, I felt like an asshole."

He stepped back and tucked his fingers under her chin, tilting her head back. "No baby, how you feel is never wrong." He kissed her forehead. "I'm new to this relationship thing too, I should have spoken to you first before I got upset." He looked in her eyes. "It was my own insecurity that made me lash out. Even though I'm a Vi'Eirlea now, it felt like the same type of rejection I've faced my whole life, like you didn't want to have an Eirson child."

Izzy squeezed her arms tight causing him to grunt. "Are you kidding? I'm relying on your fifty percent of the DNA in this kid to keep them alive. If they take after me we'll need a bomb squad." She looked up grinning. "You're the best part of me."

Before she could blink, he captured her lips.

He kept them welded together until they were breathing in sync. Slowly he lifted his face. "If we didn't need to check in…"

She nipped his chin, causing him to laugh. "Later," she promised.

He nodded. "Later."

Smiling they headed back toward the queen's chambers.

Once they joined the others, Izzy remembered why she had left and flushed with embarrassment.

"Thank the gods; she is safe!" Izzy was nearly knocked over when the queen plowed into her for a hug.

"I'm fine," she managed to get out.

"Aleks, dear, let her breathe," Brennus chided gently, pulling her back.

Aleksandra dashed away her tears. "I felt like I couldn't breathe myself when the alarms started going off. Before I knew it, Oron and Aiden had run from the room and I had no idea what was happening. I had to wait for little Meryn to return to update me." She spun around to face her niece. "Meryn, is there something you can do with that computer of yours so I don't have to wait for runners with news?"

Meryn shrugged. "I could get you walkie-talkies and cameras like I did in Noctem Falls."

The queen nodded slowly. "It's a start. I never again want to be trapped here while the fate of my loved ones is unknown."

"Queen Aleksandra, I can personally attest to

the brilliance of this young lady," Rex said as he walked over and dropped a kiss on the top of Meryn's head.

Meryn beamed and peaked around him to look at her. "Did you see his arms?"

Izzy wagged her eyebrows. "He was very charming."

Aleksandra tilted her head. "What's this?"

Rex straightened and blushed when he faced the queen. "Young Meryn admires the shape of my arms," he admitted.

The queen smiled and tapped her lips. "I can see what she is referring to."

Rex's eyes widened as Brennus moved in front of his mate blocking her view. "Seems I need to add another name to the 'not allowed near my mate' list."

The queen stepped around her mate and looped her arm through his. "Stop embarrassing the cub," she admonished.

Brennus chuckled. "You first."

The queen turned to Rex. "I'm sorry dear, I just remember you as the studious little boy you were. So proud to be a Lionhart and such a serious little man."

Rex covered his face with his hand. "Thank you, Your Majesty."

Brennus laughed outright at Rex's chagrin. "Maybe you won't make the list after all."

Micah pretended to be picking up something from the ground and blew on it. "Here Rex, I dusted off your pride for you." He acted like he was handing something over to the Elder.

Rex ignored him and sat down on one of the sofas. “Ferals in Éire Danu?” he asked and everyone quieted.

“It is impossible,” the queen said flatly. She turned to Meryn and Ryuu. “I don’t mean that I think you are lying, but maybe mistaken.”

Meryn looked down at her hands. “Aunt Aleks, I know I’ve only been in your world for six months, but I’ve been personally attacked and fought ferals more than once. This guy reeked of hot ass and Cheetos, he was most definitely a feral.”

Brennus winced at her description but was nodding. “It’s not a smell one forgets.”

The queen walked to the window, turning her back to the room. “There has to be some kind of mistake,” she said sharply.

Oron went to speak, but Brennus shook his head once then pointed to his own chest. Oron nodded. “Mother, Izzy agreed to have a child one year from now,” he announced, effectively changing the subject.

The queen spun from the window, pure joy on her face. “That is wondrous news! I’m so happy for you both. I was hoping that the two of you would work things out. I can’t wait to start buying baby things, they need so much. When I remember how many cloth diapers Darian went through,” she shuddered.

Darian flushed. “Mother!”

She threw her head back and laughed. “Some days, I was seriously worried about what we fed you.”

When Kendrick and the Ashleigh brothers came in Aiden stood and met them at the door. Kendrick nodded and Thane looked worried, but both seemed to agree to whatever Aiden said.

"Are the boys from Lycaonia settling in?" the queen asked.

Thane smiled, but it didn't reach his eyes. "Yes, Ari is showing them around now." He turned to Rex. "He's a damn fine warrior Rex. Your family should be proud."

Rex smiled as he nodded. "Both he and Declan are a true credit to the Lionhart name."

Izzy watched as Aiden looked over to Brennus who gave the barest of nods as he rubbed his mate's back.

Aiden stood, pulling Meryn to her feet. "If you'll excuse us, I promised my brother a tour." He turned to Kendrick and Thane. "Can you join us? I have some questions regarding the material you'll be teaching the warriors."

Both Thane and Kendrick nodded catching on. "I'm glad you have time, there are some finer points to the spell that needs clarifying," Kendrick said, sounding relieved. He held out his hand and Anne went to him. "We'll catch dinner out. I haven't been able to show Anne some of my favorite vendors yet."

Rex sidled up to Meryn. "I've only just sat down to visit. Oh, well. I'll walk with you as far as I can." Meryn laughed and took his hand.

Amelia pouted up at Darian shooting Izzy an urgent glance.

Shit! We're all bailing.

"Darian, we've been here days and I've barely seen outside of the palace. Can't we go shopping?" She smiled at Izzy. "You have to show me where you got your robes."

Izzy nodded quickly. "Of course! It can be sisterly bonding!"

Oh my god, I sound fake!

Brennus began to nuzzle the queen's neck. "We haven't had much time alone," he said, in a sultry voice.

The queen flushed. "I can see that our guests have plans, let us retire early," she offered.

Brennus beamed at them. "You heard her, now shoo, shoo."

"Brennus!" The queen looked at her mate aghast before turning to them with pink cheeks. "Enjoy the city," she said.

They all started filing out discussing their plans. Amelia looped their arms together and they walked with their mates through the palace, out the gates and down the streets.

Somehow she wasn't surprised when literally everyone ended up in Dav's tavern not thirty minutes later.

Aiden stood from his chair after they walked in, looking grim. "Kendrick."

"A please would be nice," the witch said, before casting another ear popping soundproofing spell. Aiden rolled his eyes.

Izzy looked up at her mate and saw that both he and Darian looked pissed.

"They're not betraying your mother," she said loudly and on purpose.

Oron scowled down at her. “What else can all this mean?” he waved his hand around the tavern, pointing to their friends and family.

“It means we are doing everything we can to protect her,” Doran said gently as he stepped from the corner with Celyn and Vivian.

Darian sighed. “Why is she being so stubborn about this? It wasn’t just Meryn, it was also Ryuu, Pierce and a good portion of the Old Guard who saw this shadow.”

Meryn threw a coaster at him. “Why you gotta say it like that? ‘It wasn’t just Meryn’,” she asked holding up her fingers in air quotes. “I don’t lie Darian.”

Amelia crossed her arms over her chest. “Yes, exactly what did you mean?”

Darian backpedaled quickly. “What I meant was, that of everyone who was there she is the youngest and has been in our world the shortest amount of time. Those facts don’t matter to me, but they do matter to my mother.”

Meryn lifted both arms and pointed to Ryuu. “Ryuu saw it. Ryuu!”

Darian looked away. “I know.”

Oron turned to Aiden. “What do we do?”

Aiden walked over and placed both of his hands on Darian’s shoulders. “For now we continue what we started earlier. I will coordinate the warriors and Dav will organize the Old Guard. The warriors will be in charge of patrols and perimeter defenses and the Old Guard will patrol the city where they will be noticed less.”

He dropped his arms, stepped back and looked around.

"I want to make one thing perfectly clear. Technically what we're doing isn't wrong since I am the Unit Commander and all unit warriors report to me." He exhaled. "But the second the queen asks me to stop our efforts or leave, I will do so out of respect for her. At that point, the defense of the city becomes political and every single decision will need to be reviewed. Brennus will do what he can to act as a buffer until we can convince her of the seriousness of this situation, but until then," he looked around. "I suggest frequent meetings here for updates."

"She loves her people like they're her children," Meryn said quietly. "Something else has to be wrong."

Oron stepped so that his shoulder was touching Darian's. "She's right. It will be our job to find out what's really bothering her."

Darian looked around and his eyes held a sheen. "I would rip off my arm to keep her from hurting," he admitted brokenly.

Dav handed him a pint. "Son, do you think there is a person here tonight who wouldn't?" Darian looked around and relaxed a fraction. Nearly every head was nodding. Izzy knew it was because the queen was that beloved.

Izzy moved so that she stood in front of her mate and relaxed against him. He wrapped his arms around her and held her close. She swung her hips and bumped Darian causing him to spill his beer. Oron laughed and she winked at Amelia who was fighting back giggles. “Look at it this way Darian. Your whole family has just gone through some major changes and some serious grief. Maybe she just needs time to make sense of it all. What we’re doing is making sure that the decisions and work don’t pile up on her,” Izzy explained. She thought it was ironic that she was here this afternoon complaining that she needed time.

Darian looked down at her relief in his eyes. “We can do that.”

“Magnus said my flamethrower should be here in the next day or so,” Meryn announced out of the blue, setting her phone down.

Aiden looked apoplectic. “No! No flamethrower! Where in the hell is my phone?” He began patting down his pockets.

Meryn giggled and flashed a cell before dropping it down her shirt, the men around them laughed uproariously.

The tension in the room dropped as Dav began to pass the pints around.

She turned to wrap her arms around her mate’s neck. “How are you?”

“I’d feel better if my mother were acting like herself,” he admitted.

“We’ll figure it out and until then we have her back.”

Oron kissed her nose. “Ride or die.”

“What was that? You want me to ride you later?” she asked, cupping her hand over her ear.

“Lucky bastard!” Bryok yelled.

Oron gave him a shit-eating grin. "Don't I know it."

Izzy knew that she would do anything to keep her mate smiling and that even if Fate threw ferals at them, they would handle it together.

EPILOGUE

ARI WATCHED AS HIS COMMANDER chased his mate around the tavern, trying to retrieve his phone. His older brother, Rex, watched him carefully over the rim of his pint as if he knew something was wrong.

How could he admit to his perfect older brother that, unlike the other warriors who dreamt of their mates to help save them, he was getting dreams of his mate walking away. His dreams were preparing him to lose her.

More than anything, it was the pain in her eyes that sliced at his soul. He feared what she would face would send her away. He could only pray that it wasn't him.

DEAR READER -

Thank you for reading!
I hoped you enjoyed *My Solace*!

For a full listing of all my books please check out my *www. alaneaalder.com*
I love to hear from readers so please feel free to follow me on Facebook , Twitter, Goodreads, AmazonCentral or Pinterest.

Hug me please!!

If you liked this book please let others know. Most people will trust a friend's opinion more than any ad. Also make sure to leave a review. I love to read what y'all have to say and find out what your favorite parts were. I always read your reviews.

IMPORTANT!!
As you know Facebook strictly controls what shows up on your newsfeed. To ensure that you are receiving all my latest news and teasers

you can to sign up for my newsletters so you will receive regular updates concerning release information, promotions, random giveaways and future Live events.

I typically send only 1-2 updates per month and won't flood your inbox, promise! ;)

Alanea

Other Books by Alanea Alder

KINDRED OF ARKADIA SERIES

This series is about a shifter only town coming together as pack, pride, and sloth to defend the ones they love. Each book tells the story of a new couple or triad coming together and the hardships they face not only in their own Fated mating, but also in keeping their town safe against an unknown threat that looms just out of sight.

Book 1- Fate Knows Best
Book 2- Fated to Be Family
Book 3- Fated For Forever
Book 4- Fated Forgiveness
Book 5- Fated Healing
Book 6- Fated Surrender
Book 7- Gifts of Fate
Book 8- Fated Redemption

BEWITCHED AND BEWILDERED SERIES

She's been Bewitched and he's Bewildered...

When the topic of grandchildren comes up during a weekly sewing circle, the matriarchs of the founding families seek out the witch Elder to scry to see if their sons' have mates. They are shocked to discover that many of their sons' mates are out in the world and are human!

Fearing that their future daughters-in-law will end up dead before being claimed and providing them with grandchildren to spoil, they convince their own mates that something must be done. After gathering all of the warriors together in a fake award ceremony, the witch Elder casts a spell to pull the warrior's mates to them, whether they want it or not.

Each book will revolve around a unit warrior member finding his destined mate, and the challenges and dangers they face in trying to uncover the reason why ferals are working together for the first time in their history to kill off members of the paranormal community.

Book 1- My Commander
Book 2- My Protector
Book 3- My Healer
Book 4- My Savior
Book 5- My Brother's Keeper
Book 6- My Guardian
Book 7- My Champion
Book 8- My Defender
Book 9- My Angel
Book 10- My One and Only
Book 11- My Solace
Book 12- My Warrior
Book 12.5- My Gifts at Christmas
Book 13- My Beacon
Book 14- My Salvation
Book 15- My Eternal Light

THE VANGUARD

We Hold the Line.

Book 1- Inception

Printed in Great Britain
by Amazon

56858126R00179